FULL BLOOD

WYRD BLOOD #2

DONNA AUGUSTINE

1
_____

My foot slipped in the mud and my back slammed into the ground, splattering the last few clean parts of me. It oozed through my fingers, finding its way into every nook and cranny I had, which was quite an accomplishment, since I was wearing long pants and sleeves. I dropped my head back onto the ground. Might as well seize the moment to get air back into my lungs, since my hair was covered anyway

Two seconds later, Ryker cleared his throat of some imaginary nothingness. "Are you going to lie there and quit or do you plan on getting up sometime today?" He turned the page of the book he was reading, making a snapping sound.

In my mind, I let out a raging scream that people a country away, maybe even across the Great Ocean, could hear. They all lifted their heads, wondering who had been so wronged they could create a sound of such rage. In reality, I simmered silently.

I raised my head an inch and angled it toward where he

sat, clean and comfy, on a boulder. It was the only dry spot in the field.

He glanced up from his book. He always brought one. Torturing me wasn't enough amusement to keep his attention. A dark, arrogant brow arched, the same color as his raven-black hair and his shriveled heart. He watched me lie there for a few seconds before he sighed, shook his head, and turned his attention back to the book in front of him.

"I have to say, I'd hoped you'd be a faster learner." He cleared some more annoyance from his throat as another page snapped forward. "And perhaps some more stamina."

This was one of those moments that made me wonder how I'd ended up here. At what point had my life taken a jagged turn? When did the boot kick me screaming off the cliff into some crazy existence I could no longer wrap my brain around? Where had I gone so wrong that I was covered in mud, being tormented by someone I considered an ally? Was it when I'd left the Ruin City to find food for a starving crew and gotten caught by Ryker? That had definitely been a wrong turn, but my gut said I'd screwed up before then. Had it been the moment the slavers had caught me way back when? I wasn't sure that had been avoidable, as young and stupid as I'd been.

I should've listened to the worm when it told me to leave here, even if it had made no logical sense to my survival. Ryker had said I'd "juiced" the worms, given them a little hit of magic. Therefore, it was my magic that had answered the question of leaving. How had I not listened to myself?

Not to make excuses, but it had been hard to leave the food they had. Before my crew had come here, we'd been nearing starvation. Hijacking chuggers, the big machines that transported trades from country to country, had turned up nothing for months. The only time we weren't hungry was when we'd been living off hollyhoney, which tasted nothing like bumblebee honey. Hollyhoney came from a nasty, wasplike creature that didn't pollinate flowers but lived off the blood and guts of the dead. That was what hollyhoney tasted like, too. Liquid guts. My gag reflex jerked with the memory of the stuff.

Food had been the first draw but not the biggest. Threats worse than starvation loomed, like losing my very soul. I was the walking dead. Somewhere in my past, I was supposed to have died, but didn't, because two people had agreed to forfeit their lives for mine. Two for one might not sound like a good deal, but when you wanted to cheat fate, it wasn't an eye for an eye. There was interest and penalties on that sort of thing.

Penalties that never got paid, either. One of the two people who'd made the deal didn't sacrifice their life. They'd either died naturally or welshed on their promise. (Who would blame them?) Once that happened, the life was unpaid, and the Debt Collector stepped in.

Ryker was currently the only one that had any knowledge of this man, woman—creature? One could say Ryker was my angel of life, except he acted much more like the devil. I'd always heard the devil you knew was better than the one you didn't. I wasn't so sure about that right now. I might need to roll the dice if things continued.

If the devil *were* here, walking beside us, I imagined he'd look something similar to Ryker. Even as he sat on the stone as clean as could be, he had an earthy ruggedness about him that made me think he wouldn't hesitate to roll around in the dirt a little. He'd probably gotten dirty plenty of times and with plenty of women. I could imagine it now: his muscles bunched, a sheen of sweat coating all that glorious tan skin as he moved above her...

I shook my head, shaking off the thoughts. His magic was getting to me again. It always did something funny to my senses, and it seemed worse every day. I tried to smooth out the hitch in my breathing that came with the tingle of flesh. That was when I noticed I had grit on my tongue. I rolled over onto my side, trying to expel it along with all the thoughts of sweaty flesh rubbing and grinding against each other.

It was time to try and stand again. Not because he wanted me to but because I was becoming comfortable lying in the muck. It wasn't a good sign for future standards. Considering my past of thieving, I couldn't afford to let those standards drop any lower, or who knew where I'd end up—and with whom.

I rolled over, all the way on to my hands and knees, and pushed up, trying to utilize my core—and fell again.

Ryker made a noise that was a cross between a laugh and a huff of exasperation.

"Is this amusing?" Eyes narrowed in his direction, I wished for a nearby rock to lob at his head.

He continued to stare at his book as he answered. "What is amusing is how you made it this many years without learning to use your magic in even the most basic of ways."

He acted as if being one of our kind held no threat. He knew the perils of being a Wyrd Blood in this world. My very existence made me a target. If I'd walked around the Ruins trying to practice magic, flaunting myself, I would've died or ended up chained to a stronger Wyrd Blood. That was what always happened to magic folk. We were commodities, traded and used, unless we eventually became strong enough to be the user. Unfortunately for me, I didn't have a taste for either used or user.

Better to be born a dull, without a lick of magic and an

equal amount of value in the minds of most Wyrd Blood. At least no one gave a shit about you then. You could live your life in peace, kind of, if you found a country run by a Wyrd Blood who wasn't maniacal.

They weren't that easy to find, but they existed. Take this place, the Valley, for example? Sometimes I didn't think Ryker gave two shits what happened here, as long as the wheels kept moving and no one got out of hand. This place was packed full of dulls living gloriously boring lives. As a person cursed with a never-ending tale of close encounters and near-death experiences, boring was heaven. It was what I aspired for. Dinner at sundown and a book by candlelight. I'd filled my quota of excitement by my teens and wasn't looking for more.

"I was too busy *surviving* in the Ruins."

"Surviving" came out like I was chewing on a mouthful of dirt. Actually, there was more dirt on my tongue. I leaned to the side, trying to use my front teeth to scrape it off.

"I told you, stop saying Ruins. Only people from the Ruined City call it that, and the only people who live there are ones hiding. You're broadcasting that you were indeed hiding. If you're going to be a part of my team, you can't be sloppy." Ryker spoke as if it were a foregone conclusion that I wanted to be on *his* team.

"I'm not on your team." I didn't have any problems working on a team, but I didn't work for *him*.

"If Bedlam shows up at our door, you aren't going to be much help in your current state."

Bedlam would only be showing up because he stole their dumb magic stone and killed a bunch of them while he was at it. Ryker didn't mention that little point, though.

Maybe death had been a better choice. His death. I should've killed him. Not that I'd had the chance, but only because I hadn't put my mind to it. If you wanted to kill someone who was stronger than you, it deserved some hard thinking and dedication. After all, he didn't want me to be a quitter, did he?

I maneuvered myself and changed direction, using a different tactic. I'd crawl over toward a patch of grass and get to my feet that way. Once I got up, I'd kill Ryker and take my chances with the Debt Collector.

Ryker made a tsking sound. "That's *not* using your magic. How many days are we going to have to do this?"

He wanted magic? I channeled everything I had and gave it a mental shove in his direction instead. It was strong enough to shift his hand a couple of inches. There'd been a time I'd punched him in the gut with my magic, but he must've seen this one coming.

He shrugged. "Not good enough."

Unfortunately, I agreed. Still, I stared, hoping he could see the rage building in me.

He saw nothing. He wagged a finger in my direction as ice-cold blue eyes remained glued to his book.

I glanced at the title, wondering what was so intriguing that he couldn't pull his nose out of, but I'd only begun mastering my letters. The leather was chipped and the title on the cover was worn away.

I could've asked him but didn't. I ignored him, making my way to the small patch of grass in a sea of mud. My hand landed on a solid clump, and I felt as if I'd just swum across the ocean. I pulled a knee onto soggy blades of grass, happy to have found land.

Ryker's magic wrapped around my other ankle. A tug pulled me back. I landed on my stomach with an *umph*. My fingers dug in, until I was leaving a trail of lines in the mud as he pulled me away from my oasis. He finally stopped after I was back in the worst of the slop, with the added benefit of a mud paddy underneath my shirt.

"You waited until I crawled all the way out?" My teeth clenched together. I would've slammed my hand down, except it would've splashed mud in my face.

"If you'd make a ward around yourself, I wouldn't have been able to do that." Another page snapped.

"My magic doesn't work like yours. It won't cooperate." There was no doubt about it, since I'd been at this for long enough to know. I'd told him repeatedly, but he refused to believe mine might be different than he deemed.

"Yes, it does. This is something the weakest Wyrd Bloods can do, so don't tell me you can't." He was finally looking, but with eyes accusing me of stubbornness or something else he found equally annoying.

There had been some very bad people in my life. People who had abused and stolen from me, lied to me, performed all sorts of trickery and manipulations on me. Still, I hadn't known real hate until this very moment.

"I'm telling you, my magic doesn't work the same way." My words came out punchy, as if I were hitting him in the gut with every syllable.

A suspicious thought niggled my brain. Could it be? Would he do that? "You did something to this mud, didn't you?"

"You shouldn't have to ask. You should know. Use. Your. Magic."

What did that mean? Did he do something or not? Now I was really gritting my teeth, no mud needed.

"If I get out of here, I'm going to kill you. You are *not* a nice person." I still needed him. Maybe I wouldn't kill him, but I'd torture him for a very long time. I gave him my worst stare, because he needed to see how furious I was.

He closed his book and leaned back. "I'm the Cursed King. You're really going to threaten me with death? That's all you could come up with?"

Dammit. He was right. He'd killed more people than I'd probably met. That had been lame, and with this, I definitely could do better. Every battle waged involved a variety of ways to win.

"I think you torture me because you're still mad I stole your supplies and got the better of you." Eyes narrowed, I waited for him to come clean about holding a grudge. There had to be something, because this wasn't the way you treated people you liked.

He stood and walked over as close as he could get before he'd sink into the mud. He crossed his arms and looked down. "Yes, I love watching you toss and turn in the mud. Can't wait to get out of bed to sit here. All. Damn. Day. This has got to be the highlight of my existence." His voice was as dry as the desert.

I'd never been to the desert, but everyone in the Ruins used to say it was worse than the summers we'd have when the wells would run dry and people happily chugged hollyhoney.

"Ryker!"

My eyes snapped to Bobby, a ten-year-old boy who ran messages, as he appeared at the top of the path. The kids loved getting message duty, because it got them out of school and chores for a couple of days a month. They didn't know how lucky they were to have a school in the first place. The kids in the Ruins—Ruined City—would've killed to take their place. Like, literally, they would've killed them and swapped their clothing.

Growing up there gave you a different type of education. I might not have known how to read or write until recently, but I could take care of myself. I guess everyone got some kind of learning, whether it was books or survival. Considering my current situation, mine might be more useful.

Ryker walked over to where Bobby waited. The kid handed him a rolled-up paper with an eager–to-please look on his face. Out of all the messengers, he stuck in my head the most. I wasn't sure if it was the riotous golden cowlicks that refused to lie flat or the way he looked at Ryker as if the man were laying a blessing upon him with each glance.

"Thanks." Ryker took the paper and then did something so un-Ryker-ish, mud must have blurred my vision. He ruffled the top of Bobby's head. The kid's eyes went round, his little jaw falling slack, as if a god had bestowed a miracle upon him.

Ryker gave the kid a nod, sending him off. Bobby floated toward the path, running his fingers over the spot Ryker had touched.

I was gaping myself. Did the devil like children? How could that be? I'd think hating children would be evildoer basics. Must be some sort of long game where he was nice to them so in twenty years they did whatever he wanted, like his guys Burn and Sneak.

Ryker was oblivious, though, as he read the missive. His expression was flat, but even from here, I could feel a tingle of agitated magic seeping over. He shoved the paper in his pocket and walked toward the path.

"Are you leaving?" I sounded shocked, but I had no reason to be. He was the devil. This was what the devil did: leave people in lurches and be nice to children so they could sway them to the dark side later. Nothing surprising.

He walked past my outstretched hand as he said, "Keep practicing."

2

"Damn arrogant, psychopathic lunatic..." The insults fell from my lips as easy as the clumps of mud dropped from my body. Another few inches and my fingers touched grass. I pulled myself up and made my way to the path, leaving a trail in my wake. The stuff that didn't drop off itched. Soggy boots dragged off my heels, threatening to abandon me.

I still wasn't sure if Ryker had done something to that mud or not, and I wasn't staying any longer to figure it out. Damned if I'd be there for him to drag me out come dinner.

Ruck was standing in the middle of the road, staring, as I got to the end of the path. His head tilted sideways as he took in my muddy form. Then he tilted it the other way, as if the problem with my appearance could be solved with a different perspective. His lips shifting to the left side of his face told me it hadn't solved anything.

Bodies weaved around him, as the place bustled with traffic, people walking here and there and generally getting along with their day. Occasionally they'd glance to see what had caught Ruck's attention. They'd follow his stare to me and squint. I'd see them wonder if the rumors were true about how different the people from the Ruined City were. They were probably adding rolling around in the mud to the list of weird proclivities we had.

Ruck made his way toward me. "Where've you been? I saw Ryker come down already."

I continued toward the shower house as he fell into step with me. "Being tortured." The mud on my tongue added more distaste to already bitter words.

"Practice didn't go so hot again?" His voice was soft, as if he only asked out of some unspoken obligation. I didn't need to see his face to envision the cringe. We'd played out this scene enough in the last two weeks to know it by heart.

I stopped walking so I could stare at him. "I told you. He. Tortures. Me."

Ruck shoved one hand in his pocket and raised the other to take a bite out of the cuticle on his thumb. He wanted to disagree with the torture statement but didn't out of fear. He too knew this script by heart.

"Do you see me?" I jerked a thumb toward my chest, daring him to defend Ryker again.

He chewed on another cuticle.

Finally, he shrugged. "Today does look to be worse than normal."

I turned and headed toward the showers again.

He walked beside me for a couple of minutes before speaking. "I'm not defending him, but—"

"That's what people say right before they defend someone." How had I foolishly thought I'd gotten my point across the last fourteen times?

"I think he means well."

"He doesn't mean well. He's just plain mean. He's a sadist. Aren't you supposed to be sleeping right now before your shift?" Ruck worked the late shift on the third watch-tower. We usually had breakfast together, and sometimes lunch when I wasn't being tortured. Most nights he was already on duty during dinner.

I stepped inside the shower house, Ruck still following. Broc, a friendly but odd little fellow who worked the supply stand, handed me a new soap ration and a rag to dry with. He made a checkmark next to my name, refraining from commenting on my appearance, even as he leaned closer to take it all in.

"Ben needed to switch shifts. Wanted to see if you were coming to get dinner?" Ruck said, tucking his hands in his pockets.

"Course I am. I'll meet you over there in a couple minutes."

The corner of Ruck's mouth turned up. He gave me a nod and headed over to the food building.

Ruck and I ate with each other whenever we could, but we didn't get to eat dinner together. It shouldn't have been a big deal, but it was. Life had changed gears a lot faster than either of us had expected. We'd been plodding along, getting by and keeping our heads down. We'd tried to keep a low profile that wouldn't draw too much attention, and somehow we'd still ended up here. Sometimes it seemed like we were skidding out of control, trying to grab on to the only constants we had left, which seemed smaller in number every day as the people around us disappeared.

Tiger was the first of our crew we'd lost. He'd been the easiest, though, since it was his choice. He'd left, but I knew he was out there living life somewhere else, doing his thing. Maybe one day I'd even see him again. Fetch had left last week. He'd said he didn't want to wait around for Bedlam to come kill us all. He said he'd be heading east and would send word when he settled somewhere. Part of me was happy he'd left.

Sinsy was the hard one. Death was never easy, but hers left an ache that swelled so strong I thought my chest would crack open sometimes. I never knew when the pain would hit, either. I'd see a funny scene and want to turn and tell her. I'd have a bad day I'd need to share and I'd be talking into the wind. I'd turn to my side out of habit, expecting to see her before I'd remember she wasn't there and never would be again. Losing her seemed like a wound that would never fully heal.

Then there was Marra... But I wouldn't think about her. It was too much.

ALMOST EVERY SEAT WAS TAKEN IN THE FOOD BUILDING, AND the place buzzed with life and sounds of people sharing their day. I grabbed a plate and got in line, paying little attention to what was being served—some sloppy shredded meat of unknown origin—and scanned the room for one particular table in the corner. That same spot drew my eye every breakfast, lunch, and dinner. No matter how many times I told myself not to look, I'd do it anyway.

Marra was there as usual, sitting with her new friends, her Bugs and Ruck replacements. As always, I kept my eyes moving, taking in the situation and looking elsewhere before she noticed.

This loss had happened suddenly. One morning I'd gotten here late and she'd been sitting at a different table, with different people. She'd been leaning over, listening to what the brunette sitting in front of her was saying, looking serious. I'd carried my plate over to her, thinking she wanted to change up where we sat. When I'd gotten closer, instead of pulling out the empty chair next to her, she'd shoved it in more. I'd stood there, plate in hand, and she'd turned away, silently dismissing me.

I'd stood there for a few minutes, looking like a fool. I'd called her name several times, as if somehow she hadn't realized what she was doing. She never acknowledged it. I'd finally walked back to the usual table and sat down. It soon became clear she wasn't speaking to anyone that had been with Sinsy when she'd died.

For a few days, even a week after, I kept expecting her to snap out of it. I'd stare openly at her, waiting for something. She'd glance over, without a smile or tilt of her head, as if there were nothing but air where I stood, a blank look upon her face.

It had been three and a half weeks since Sinsy, Marra's sister, had died, and three weeks since we'd gotten back from Bedlam. Maybe this was normal. She was grieving. Who wouldn't need their space after finding out your sister had been ripped to pieces by a crazed horde of chewers?

It wasn't like she was blaming us, though. She hadn't *indicated* that she was, and even being mute, she'd always gotten her points across. Even if she did blame us, if that was what she needed, I could handle it. She could hate me if it made it easier. In a few months, or a year, she'd start to miss us and everything would go back to normal.

I grabbed the last biscuit and walked over to the table where Ruck, Burn, and Sneak were already sitting. Ryker happened to be there as well. I'd tolerate his presence because he seemed to think it was his table too, and I was going to eat with my friend. There was always a give-and-take in life.

I put my plate down beside Ruck, ignoring that Ryker was sitting in front of me.

"I don't know why you waste your time with her," Ryker said, indicating Marra.

He spoke as if we were friends and this was open to discussion. As if I didn't want to take my fork and stab him. Right. Now. In the eyeball. Repeatedly.

We weren't friends, not even close, and wouldn't be with the way he'd been acting lately. I chewed on some mystery meat, pretending he wasn't across the table from me speaking.

Ryker lifted his fork and waved it in my general vicinity. "Should I take the silence to mean you're upset with me?"

There was the slightest lift at the corners of his mouth. He tormented me all day and then he thought he could tease me? This was my life now?

"Why would I possibly be upset with you?" I asked. "I understand what you're doing, that you're still bitter that I was able to get one over on you and raid your chuggers. After all, everyone thinks you're the mighty Ryker, and little old Bugs was able to break all your wards." I took a couple bites of meat, telling myself to not address the Marra comment. I quickly lost the fight with myself. "And for the record, Marra needs a little time, is all. She lost her sister."

"She's going to need more than time soon," he said, glancing over at her table.

"What's that mean?" I asked, succumbing to my curiosity.

"Nothing." He turned back to me, and for a second he didn't look like an evil bastard. Then the gleam in his eye returned. He leaned forward, smiling. "Too bad you couldn't break the spell on the mud as well as you break wards. Although you were oh so good at flopping around in it."

If I was gripping my fork like an instrument of violence,

it was completely incidental. I wouldn't really stab him with it. I'd switch to the knife. Much more efficient.

"Don't confuse me with Tatia. Do that to me again and you'll find out the difference." Tatia was the latest girl I'd seen exiting his room in the constant parade that came and went. Word was she used to mud-wrestle for a traveling sideshow.

"I didn't realize you'd been keeping tabs on me." His eyes narrowed but didn't lose the amusement dancing in them.

Damn, it was hot in here. Someone needed to shut down those ovens. It was definitely the ovens, too. It wasn't like I'd gotten caught spying on him. It had been an accident. His place was centrally located. I had to walk by it no matter where I was headed. Still, better to not even admit that much. He'd never believe it with the size of his ego. "Of course I'm not. People talk."

"And you seem to listen very attentively."

"Hard not to when there's so much to talk about. You certainly give them plenty." It was surprising the trail of women in and out of his place hadn't worn the ground down into a crater. In and out. I hadn't realized how many single women lived here, and Ryker certainly liked variety.

I stared, daring him to say different. He stared back, not bothering to deny anything as tingles of magic swirled, making the air thick. Even though there was a table between us and we were in one of the largest buildings in the Valley, it was still too close. His magic had a way of picking me out for its attention and then needling me.

He acted as if he didn't do it on purpose, but no way was it accidental. I knew Burn and Sneak felt it, but they'd side with Ryker if I called them out. The only one at the table that would've been honest was Ruck, and he was a dull.

Dulls didn't feel magic. Craziest thing I'd ever heard, but it was true.

A chair scraped the floor and Sneak cleared his throat.

"When are Knife and his people getting here?" Burn asked, sounding very off.

Wait a second. Why did the name Knife sound familiar?

"Within the next few days," Ryker said, shifting his attention away from me, the magic calming a hair.

"How many people are coming?" Sneak asked.

"As many as he can spare," Ryker answered.

The magic was almost back to pre-argument levels as I focused my attention on Burn.

"Who's Knife and why is he coming here?" I should've asked Ryker, but I'd rather have hazy details from someone I could tolerate than the man who made me crawl around in mud all day.

"Knife Dorley. You must've heard of Dorley? It's not that far from here and even closer to the Ruined City," Burn said. "He's bringing reinforcements in case Bedlam decides to retaliate. Dorley has an ugly past with Bedlam, so they're eager to help."

Dorley. How many chuggers had we hijacked that were headed there? I was glad I'd finished swallowing my food, or I might've been in dire straits as my throat closed. Ruck wasn't so lucky, and choked beside me. Sneak gave him a pound to his back.

I kicked Ruck under the table before he got enough air in his lungs to speak. Didn't matter. His red choking-on-the-truth face already spilled the beans, if there were any beans left in the can.

"Oh, she knows Dorley well." Ryker leaned back in his seat and took the same approach I had. He didn't ask me anything. He narrowed his eyes on Ruck. "How many chuggers did you raid that were filled with Dorley supplies?"

Chuggers, the trucks that had two purposes: haul goods from one country to another, and feed my crew when times were lean. It was unfortunate that there'd been a lot of lean times. When you were starving, you did what you had to. I'd like to see what these well-fed men would do if they were starving.

"None," I answered before Mr. Blow Our Cover could. *Hypothetically*, it might've been ten. It didn't matter, as that couldn't be proven. Plus, it was long past the time worth thinking about. A half a year was an eternity. A lifetime ago. Several lifetimes, even.

The magic flowed again. This time I couldn't tell if it was his, mine, or some strange combination of the two. Cool eyes warmed, and I knew he was feeling it too.

"You do realize some of those chuggers you hijacked originated here?" He slowly tapped his pointer finger on the table.

"Then why'd you ask?"

"To see if you're ever going to stop lying to me," he said.

He watched me as if surprised I wasn't an open book. Why he thought I should trust him might've been written down in someone's book, but not mine. We'd been in a few tough spots together, but the worst of them had been by his doing. That didn't instill great loyalty.

"You have all the answers anyway. Why do you need me to tell you anything? I'm just a thief, right?"

He hadn't called me that in a long while. Even hearing the word was like a thorn sticking in tender flesh. I wasn't sure why I'd said it other than the suspicion he was still angry with me for something. Another reason not to trust him.

Ryker's mouth flattened as if I'd called him the thief. His eyes narrowed, cool blue throwing off so much heat he could've melted an iceberg. He shifted in his seat, leaning slightly to the side but never relenting in his stare. "Don't use that word."

I heard a couple chairs scraping and knew we were about to clear out the table with the magic churning between us. It was like one and one didn't add to two when we were close. We multiplied to ten or something. And times like this? When we fought? It nearly exploded.

I used to think I was the only one who felt it, but lately I'd noticed the effect we had on everyone around us. Burn pulled at the neck of his shirt. Sneak was breaking a sweat. Had it always been this strong, or was it growing? It felt worse, at least to me.

"Why? You use it all the time."

"Used."

I leaned forward, ignoring the wave of magic that made my skin so sensitive I wanted to tear my clothes off. "You basically called me that a minute ago. You implied. I said the word. What's the difference?"

"I was teasing. Big difference."

"Let me make sure my feeble brain understands. You're allowed to insult me but I'm not?" The list of crazy rules Ryker had only grew longer with each day I knew him.

"Yes," he said with utmost confidence.

It was ludicrous, but I was realizing Ryker didn't always do the most predictable things. He was plain crazy sometimes. I guess that was what happened when you were the Cursed King. Maybe all that magic pulsating in your blood drove you nuts after a while?

We stared each other down. Whether I could call myself a thief was a ridiculous fight, but I still wouldn't back down.

It wasn't about that. I was tired of taking shit from him, and if this was the hill I had to die on to assert myself, so be it. Dig me a grave now, because I was going down.

He leaned over a little farther on the arm of his chair, signaling that he wasn't giving up this fight either. It might've looked like a staring contest, but it went deeper than that. It was more about who could handle the building magic between us, the heat it threw off.

"You're about to clear the place out. Even the dulls are starting to feel it," Sneak said. It was a last-ditch effort to break the building tide of magic that was about to smother our table. I knew Burn and Sneak felt it, but the dulls did too?

My gaze flickered off Ryker's for a second, to check out Ruck, who was looking over at Sneak. "What are you talking about? I don't feel anything."

That damn Sneak faked me out. I snapped my gaze back to Ryker's, quick as a rabbit, but I was too late. The magic had ebbed, and he was already gloating.

"Don't you smile. It was less than a second. Less than half a second. That wasn't a win. I was tricked."

"Oh, that was most definitely a win."

Ruck looked up from his now-empty plate. "What was a win? Sometimes I have no idea what you two are talking about."

I would've explained, but the whole thing was too embarrassing to repeat.

3

I dug my hand into the dirt moistened by the morning dew and then stopped myself before I made a significant hole. I wasn't worming it. I didn't need any more conflict, even internal. I couldn't leave this place, and so what was the point in asking the worm if I should go? It was official. My worming days were over until I had a better question to ask.

I didn't know why it had told me to leave anyway. Bottom line was that I couldn't, not until Ryker negotiated with the Debt Collector. He said he'd help me even if I left, but it wasn't like I could trust him. It was like my entire life was wallowing in that soul-sucking mud from practice.

I stood, eyes not leaving the dirt. I squatted back down. I hadn't wormed for two whole days. Even worms deserved the right to redemption, didn't they? Wasn't two days enough protest for them to get the message and give me a logical answer that made sense?

I dug into the ground with commitment and found a plump little sucker. The plump ones were good. They'd have the extra nutrients they'd need to steer toward the right answer.

I cupped my hands, whispering my question. "Should I stay or go?"

I laid it down gently, not wanting to jar its body into confusion that could cause an error. It wiggled its way a finger's length toward the wrong answer. I picked it up before it could make a gigantic mistake.

"I see what you're about to do, and you better think long and hard before you do it. Knee-jerk reactions lead to epic regrets, you little sucker. You might not think there are repercussions for worms, but I can smush you like the bug you are."

I gave it a second to absorb the warning and then placed it down again. As soon as it hit the dirt, it wiggled its plump self in the wrong direction, again, as if it knew I was all bluster. I was full of it and it was safe. That wasn't the surprise. How the worm knew too was a bit of a thinker.

"You're lucky I'm too tired or I'd really do it."

I kept watching, thinking it would take a turn at the last second. It didn't. I stood, a ragged sigh dragging from my chest as I slumped.

"Why do I ask? You know nothing." I leaned over. "I can't leave. I'll be dead. Not to mention I lost a challenge I'm still bound by. Did you forget that when you were crawling your way to the wrong answer?"

The worm disappeared into the dirt, giving me a final wiggle of its backside.

Ruck walked over and stood beside me. I wasn't surprised he was up this early. One, his schedule was all out of whack from the late shift, and two, neither of us had slept very well since Sinsy.

For some reason, my sleeping problem was worse when

everyone was in bed. It was the only time the Valley quieted down and you were left with only your thoughts for company.

When I looked at Ruck beside me, his eyes were a little flatter than they used to be, the shadows a little darker underneath. It wasn't the barely rising sun. I knew mine looked the same.

He pointed to the worm, which was nearly out of sight. "Why do you keep asking it? It's been telling you to leave every day since we got back."

I kept looking at the dirt, at nothing. "I keep thinking it'll say something different."

"Bugs." Ryker's deep voice cut across the distance. He was standing down the lane, feet shoulder width apart, which was quite wide. His dark hair rustled with the breeze. In the soft light of morning, he almost looked like he could climb up on a white horse. But he wasn't a knight and never would be. He was the Cursed King, capable of mass murder simply by walking through a crowd.

It was the one thing I didn't mind about him at the moment. I'd never been fond of the color white anyway. White was only good for snowflakes. Snowflakes couldn't withstand what was coming for me. I'd need people beside me that wouldn't melt under some heat and wouldn't blanch at a little dirt on their hands.

Ryker tilted his head and then started back in the direction of his place. He clearly wanted something, since we didn't practice until after breakfast.

"He wants me to meet him at his place," I said, stating the obvious.

"So?" Ruck asked.

He didn't get it, just as he hadn't understood how uncomfortable dinner had been. A talk at Ryker's place seemed innocent enough, but it was actually hell. Didn't matter if we were discussing the weather or war. Our magic mixed in a funny way when we were in his house. Sitting in his place, enclosed in a normal-sized room, was like waiting for magic to hit me, over and over again.

I'd never followed anyone into hell, but I couldn't let him walk off. I wouldn't know what he wanted, and I wasn't that kind of person. I needed to know things. I *liked* knowing, and Ryker knew all sorts of stuff.

I took a last glance at the dirt where the worm had disappeared before I gave Ruck an I'm-going-in look.

He nodded back.

I took off at a jog and caught up to Ryker, hoping I could get my answers without going inside with him. That magic, the potent stuff he lugged around that could kill people, would get so much worse in his place. It was like combining a thunderstorm and some metal rods. It shot straight for me and lit me up.

Sometimes, once in a while, I kind of liked it. That almost made it worse.

"What's up?" I asked him a few feet from his door.

"We need to talk," he said, getting closer and closer to his place.

"About what? Did you find a new stone to steal?"

"No. We've got other priorities at the moment."

I watched his back until it disappeared into his place, the last apartment in a row of homes. Two more doors lined the building, one leading to Burn's place and the other to Sneak's. It was another redeeming quality of Ryker's. Lots of other Wyrd Blood erected castles. He didn't give a shit. I liked that.

But I still didn't want to go inside.

"Bugs," he called.

Shit. I walked in. I left the door open as I headed to his couch, one of the few pieces of furniture in the place. It was well worn, like most of his furniture, and he didn't care.

He walked over and shut the door. "Stop jittering."

"I'm not." I pressed my hand over my knee. If I had been, it wasn't my fault. We weren't even arguing, and his magic was already revved up. "Is there a problem?"

His magic was stronger than mine, and he also had more control. If he didn't get his pulled in, I had no shot at dimming mine, and we'd continue this ping-pong match until one of us had a magical black eye.

Ryker leaned both hands on the chair in front of him. His knuckles were white where they gripped it. "There might be. The Debt Collector is willing to meet."

The Debt Collector, also known as the magical creature that held my life in his hands. That wasn't an exaggeration, either. Ryker had bought me some time by having a witch do some mojo, but I was an hourglass that had been flipped. My life was pouring out.

Ryker had sent messages out to anyone who might know where he was, but I hadn't really believed we'd get a reply. Now the Debt Collector had replied, fast. Too fast. That didn't bode well. Only someone with the upper hand didn't need time. The desperate clung to every minute, hoping the next second would give them an alternative. I knew firsthand.

Ryker's magic flared up and hit home like a bolt of lightning, flashing on the horizon and showing the dark terrain. My palms grew clammy and my crossed ankles swung to the beat of my pounding heart.

"Watch your magic, Bugs."

Watch your magic. Your magic is out of control. Do something with your magic. I was sick of hearing over and over

again about how *my* magic was out of control when his was
kicking the hell out of me like a bucking bronco.

He should try and control *his* magic for a change. No one
seemed to want to tell him he was on a downward spiral. I'd
tell him, not that it would get me anywhere, but I'd wait
until I got the rest of the details of the Debt Collector first.
Ryker could be a real bastard with withholding. Information
should be shared generously, but he thought it should be
hoarded for a rainy day.

I'd get what I needed and then I'd tell him he needed to
get his magic under control. A little introspection wouldn't
hurt him instead of pointing that finger all over the place.
He'd get another couple of minutes to point while I got my
answers.

"You only sent word out a couple weeks ago, correct?"

He nodded once, sparing me any trivial words that
might've lifted the heaviness off that single movement. Okay,
so we both thought it was fast. Maybe fast wasn't really bad.
I didn't know the full content of the message yet. Needed all
the facts if I was going to make a determination. The Debt
Collector might be very efficient for all I knew. Creepy didn't
mean you were a slacker. There were plenty of sick and
crazy individuals who were highly productive.

"Did Old Bones write anything else?"

His chin dropped. "Old Bones?"

I forced tense muscles to slouch against the back of the
couch. "I envisioned him being gaunt and wearing a large,
ratty black robe. Seemed fitting."

His eyes crinkled a bit, as if he were doubtful, but he let
it go. "Time and place. That's all."

White knuckles spread to bunched forearms. The shoulders rounded into a neck you could've strummed a tune on.
The eyes were intense, but that was pretty much status quo.

"Where?" I asked, realizing I was going to have to drag every detail out of him.

He walked to the edge of the couch and leaned a forearm on the wall. "Three days from now at the ancient temple outside the Ruined City."

"Right outside the Ruins?"

"Yes. And stop calling it the Ruins."

I ignored his Ruins comment. I was too freaked out about where we were meeting.

Before magic had burst into existence, there had been temples everywhere. People would go pray, talking to unseen gods, asking for this and that. I'd explored the temple he was talking about many times. I'd even stashed hauls in it. I could've thrown a stone at it from the window of my old pad.

"This has to be a recent move."

"I'm sure. I think we were going to have this meeting whether we called for it or not. He knows we want something, but I think he wants something as well. If he was ready to kill you now, he wouldn't bother meeting."

I stood. If he told me to get my magic under control again, it might burst out of me. I was clinging to calm by the skin of my teeth.

Now what? Was I going to march in there and say, *Hey, don't take my soul because I'm such a great girl. I only steal for good reasons*?

"Will your magic work on him?" I was getting very good at breaking wards, but I'd stalled out on making them. My magic was useless for protection, but I was standing in front of the Cursed King. That should mean something.

He rubbed his shadowed jaw as if he'd been thinking this over more times than I had. "I don't know. He's not a dull, and I'm not sure he's a Wyrd Blood either. Using magic on something magical always comes with a risk. It might be our only option, but it could blow up in ways we can't imagine."

That wasn't good. After I'd learned Ryker was the Cursed King, I'd felt a little securer. It hadn't been a thought-out type of security, where I checked off a box, but a gut reaction. It had popped up when I realized I'd hooked up with a person who could wipe the world clean. Some people might've run scared after they found out who Ryker really was. Me? I'd slept a little sounder.

I paced the area. "We have to go—or I do, anyway."

"I agree. I think we go early."

I shot him a look over my shoulder that said, *Of course you'd have to make it worse.*

"It's the only thing he might not expect if he is planning something."

I took a few more steps. The logic was sound, but that didn't make the stone sit any easier in my gut. This one was going to be giving me heartburn tonight as I lay in bed and dreamt of sleeping.

There was only one way I could make this palatable enough to keep down. "We go alone. I don't want to risk anyone else."

The only person I had left was Ruck, and I couldn't lose him. The idea of Burn or Sneak dying didn't sit too well either. I wouldn't have any more blood on my hands. I was still trying to get rid of the stain Sinsy's had left, and that was a doozy. Sometimes it felt like her blood was still dripping from my fingertips.

"Agreed."

He couldn't have said anything that would've rattled my nerves more. I might've appeared calm—calmish...at least something shy of having a total meltdown, but I was *oh shit-*

ting like a maniac on the inside. Ryker wasn't an over-reac-tor. If he was worried about his people, that meant I should definitely be in an all-out panic.

"We leave at first light tomorrow."

I nodded and headed for the door, needing to be alone so I could think straight. "I'll see you after breakfast," I said, figuring he'd still want to practice today.

"No. Skip it today."

I froze at the door. Within a few seconds, my heart jump-started my feet enough to get me outside. Ryker didn't want to torture me anymore, because there was no fun in torturing a dead woman.

4

The walk from Ryker's place to mine was dulled by exhaustion and a skeletal creature that wouldn't get out of my head. I didn't know if Old Bones would actually look like a skeleton, but that was how I envisioned him. He dealt in lives. Only fitting he'd look like the Reaper. I was so dedicated to my illusions that I didn't notice the girl waiting by my place until there was no feigning a new direction.

She was probably around my chronological age by years. But the innocence in her eyes said she was shy of my life experience by a couple decades of hard knocks and at least fifty kicks in the gut.

There were a lot of people like her walking around this place Ryker ran. I tried not to hold their pampered lives against them, but it didn't make me want to hang out with them, either. I didn't have the time to swap pie recipes or talk about dying cloth.

I thought of making a quick right, but she had the look of a person who'd follow, and I wasn't in the mood to do laps to see who could run the fastest.

"Hi," she said, raising her hand and following it with a

peppy little wave, as if the giddy but slightly desperado tone hadn't been enough to send me running. I needed to get away from her rainbow before I was lured in by the mirage of pretty colors.

"Hi." I'd heard in polite society you were supposed to reply to greetings even if you didn't want to. Since I didn't know how long I'd be living here, I'd made a decision to get on the "good people" list. You never knew when that social shit might come in handy. A soft-skinned, dull people might not seem very useful, but you never knew when one would block a bullet.

Only issue was, what did I do with her now? She was standing in front of my door, looking like her feet had grown roots. I could try and climb in through my window, but that might undo the effort I'd put into the greeting. I slowed to stop, since it was that or walk into her.

She wrung her hands. "I heard you know things?"

"Know what things?" No. Not a good line of questioning to open up. Of course I knew things, everyone did, but there were probably very few of those things I'd want to share.

Her chest inflated enough to blow out a lung. I launched into damage control before the air headed back out with a tide of more questions.

"I don't know what you heard, but I know nothing. And the stuff I do know is usually wrong." I took a step to the left, trying to get around her and in my door. She swayed with me. I broke right, and she wobbled that way.

I swished a hand, motioning for her to get out of my way. I smiled while I did it to take the bite out of the dismissal.

She didn't move. "But you read worms, right?"

Read worms. It sounded like a dirty version of reading tea leaves or tarot cards.

"Nope. I can barely read books." Although I'd made

some progress of late, I was far from tackling anything that didn't give me a few picture hints. A lot of people from the Ruined City couldn't read. Ruck could, but he'd learned before I'd met him, back when he had a family.

"But I heard—"

"I'm very tired. Had a rough sleep. Maybe we can do this some other time?"

A glimmer of Ruck's head bounced in the distance. He was heading for me, and then he caught sight of the chick standing next to me and turned around. *Thanks, buddy.*

She took a step closer. "I just need you to ask them one question, please. I've tried to read worms, but they lie there in a pile no matter how many I try."

"How many worms did you dig up?" What was wrong with this woman? Worming wasn't for everyone. I couldn't have random people yanking worms from the ground like they knew what they were doing and piling them up. What would happen when I needed them?

I headed toward the tree line and had to stop to go back and grab her arm as she stared at me in confusion.

"I'm going to do this for you, but only this once. In exchange, you need to leave the worming to the professionals from now on. And you need to spread the word that you can't dig worms up and think you'll get answers. It doesn't work like that."

"Okay. Yes, definitely. I'll do whatever you want."

That I believed. For now, anyway.

I stopped in one of my favorite worming spots, behind a nice Pluckabessy bush, and knelt on the ground. I grabbed a stick and drew out a circle, making a Y on one side and a N across from it, remembering how I used to not know either of those letters.

"What's your name?" I didn't really want to know, but I

didn't want the worm to be confused whose question this was.

"Kallie."

"What's your question? Make it simple, because I only do yes or nos."

She nodded vigorously before asking, "Will I get pregnant?"

I knew from her tone she was hoping for a yes. I looked at the sky, but stopped short of shaking my head and sighing.

"How old are you? Don't you want to do anything else before you have kids? Isn't this a little early?" *More importantly, do you have any idea the hell is headed our way?* Ryker had stolen a magical stone from Bedlam, and the Debt Collector might be showing up at our doorstep any second.

Of course, I couldn't ask her that. I had a feeling it might cause an avalanche of panic, followed by a stampede out of here. And where would they go? There wasn't anywhere better. I'd been enough places to attest to it.

"I want a family," she said, her voice small and her eyes big.

At least that I could understand. I stared down at the dirt, running my fingers through it and wondering if there was anything I could say to stop her. Probably not. She looked to be the stubborn type. Still, I'd give it a try.

"Look, things are calm now, but you know this world." No, I didn't think she did know this world at all. She'd been living in a cocoon. She knew nothing but her biological drive. She probably wouldn't really learn until she was running for her life trying to save her child. "It's turbulent and rocky, and there's been wars breaking out for years. Maybe you should wait a while."

"That's what Bakely says, but I'm done waiting to live my

life. I'll never regret having a child and a family, no matter what anyone says."

She had a point, and maybe a little more spine than I'd given her credit for. Who was I to dictate what she should do? Hell, she'd managed better for herself living here than I had. Maybe I should be listening to her?

I dug through the dirt and grabbed a slimy little bugger. I cupped it in my hands. "Will Kallie have a baby?"

I placed it down, and it shot over to Y quicker than I'd ever seen.

I stood. "Yep. You're going to have one."

She brought her hands together and did a little jump. "When?"

I opened my mouth to tell her that I'd held up my end, but then she grabbed my arm.

"Please! Just one last question."

I sighed, loud enough to make sure she knew she was pushing it. Then I relented and squatted back down with an irritated grunt. "This is it, though."

I dug up another worm. I could've sworn I caught some attitude in its wiggle, as if it wanted to leap from my palm. I moved it toward Kallie a smidge, and the wiggling picked up steam. If this thing had a middle finger, it would've been waving it at us right now.

I moved it away a bit and told it, "Look, I understand, but you're going to have to take one for the team, or your brethren are going to be baking in the sun after a"—I glanced to see how closely she was listening—"dull digs your asses up," I finished with a whisper.

The worm slowed and then stopped squirming altogether.

"Appreciate that." I spoke louder as I asked, "Will Kallie have a baby soon?"

I placed it down, and it wasted no time heading to Y again.

"Thank you!" Kallie looked as if she wanted to hug me.

I stepped out of her reach quickly. "Sure. Remember, don't tell anyone about this."

She nodded. I hoped she'd keep her mouth shut for more than the hour or two I figured her for. Even that might be an overestimation.

Kallie walked away. That was when I saw Marra. She stared at the fresh dirt by my feet, her eyes fixated on the spot for a few minutes until they switched back to meet mine. It was the first time she'd looked at me in weeks.

Now that she acknowledged me again, I wished she hadn't. Her eyes were haunted with an emptiness I feared would suck the soul from my body if I looked too long. But this was Marra, the girl I'd hunted beside, raided beside, and killed beside. We'd cried together when her dog died and laughed when one of us had fallen in the mud. We'd nearly starved together, and we'd survived because of each other. I wouldn't turn from her as she tried to find her way out of the darkness.

She knew everything that had happened when we'd left. Between myself, Ruck, and Burn, we'd filled the picture in pretty well. Even after we'd told her every minutia, she'd always waved her hand, asking us in her silent way for more. The night before she'd cut me off, I'd spent the entire day going over every detail again. That time had been different. When she'd lifted her hand, instead of waving for more information, she waved toward the door, asking me to leave. That was the last time she'd acknowledged me, until now.

She walked over slowly, and every muscle I had tensed. I didn't know if she'd hug me or hit me. She stopped a foot away and pointed at the freshly turned dirt.

She waited until I nodded, confirming what she'd already seen.

She pointed at the dirt and shook her head, eyes glued to me. The message was clear. She didn't want me to worm again. She blamed the worm for Sinsy's death, and that was when I knew for sure she blamed me. I did.

Sinsy's death would forever stain my soul. I went to sleep seeing her smile, and then would dream of her cries. How she'd died. People say dying in battle is a good way to go. I wished one of them would say that to me now. Bottom line was that there was no good way to go. Every way sucked. And if being torn apart by magical wolves was battle, it certainly wasn't my choice of deaths.

If Marra didn't want me to worm anymore, I wouldn't. If that was all I could offer, then it was hers.

"I won't do it again."

She took my hand and placed it on my chest, over my heart. If she was a Wyrd Blood, she would've asked me to bind my promise with magic.

"I won't," I repeated.

She squeezed my fingers. It wasn't comforting. It was desperate. The ghost that haunted her enveloped me in its chill.

"I swear it." I would've sworn to anything at that moment to have her stare trained somewhere else. The person in front of me wasn't the Marra I'd known. Maybe Sinsy hadn't died alone. We all had our limits, that final wind that toppled us. She might right herself in a while, or perhaps this was it, but I'd do anything to help her right herself.

She dropped my hand. She walked away, and I could breathe again.

Ruck stepped forward, probably having watched the

whole thing from a distance. "Did you agree to what I think you agreed to?"

"Don't give me that tone when you abandoned me to that other one."

He nodded. "She looked way too needy. I could spot it all the way over there. Have to be careful, because that shit can spread. I need to save my strength for real battles." He shoved his hands in his pockets and gave me his signature sigh. "So I'll take your non-answer about Marra to mean my assumption is correct."

"Want to get breakfast?" I asked, ignoring the topic of Marra completely.

I knew him so well that I could have this argument without him. I'd say I agreed to not worm. Ruck would disagree. I'd tell him it was the right choice and we'd end up in the same place anyway. No point in hashing it out. That was the beauty of our relationship. Some arguments didn't even need to be had.

"Sure." He turned, and we fell in with the rest of the people heading toward the food building. He waited until we were almost there before he said, "What did Ryker want before?"

Of course Ruck would expect me to tell him. I told him everything, or I used to. But not this. "I've got to go check out a lead with Ryker, but I can't talk about it."

He stopped a few feet short of the food building door, forcing the rest of the diners to swerve around us. "You're coming back, right?"

"I'll always come back." If I could help it.

And if I couldn't, I wasn't taking him down with me.

5

"Come on. Get up."

It was still dark out. The light wasn't even filtering in through my eyelids yet. Why was Ryker in my room? Why did he sound like he was beside me?

"You said first light." If the sun wasn't getting up then why was I? I stuck my face in the center of the pillow.

I could feel him standing there, unmoving, his magic pouring over me. Fuck. How was I supposed to get another ten minutes of sleep like this?

"It'll be first light soon." He grabbed my blanket and pulled it off in one quick tug.

"What the—" I scrambled up, grabbing for it.

"You don't sleep with bottoms?" he asked calmly.

Thankfully, my shirt covered most of me as I scrambled to grab the blanket back. "No. Not when they aren't dry."

How many sleep clothes did he think I owned? I'd hung them over the chair last night to dry from their recent washing, where they hung right now.

The blanket back up to my waist, I looked up at him. He was still staring at my lower half, as if he could see what was beneath the blanket. Not to mention his magic was tingling across my skin. If he didn't cut it out, my magic was going to reciprocate, and then we'd be a big magical inferno in another minute. One of us was going to have to do something about this control issue. If he wasn't going to have any, I might need to really sort this out. We couldn't both be a mess.

It was about to get unbearable when his gaze jerked up and he said, "Meet me by tower one in five."

I gave him a nod and watched him leave, wondering what had set him off this time.

The sun still hadn't risen as we walked toward a field right outside the border of the Valley. In the center, a monster of a machine waited. Wheels taller than my head with a body of mottled green and tan. It wasn't running yet, but I knew the sound it would make. I used to listen for its mighty roar. It made my fingers itch for a bow and arrow and the thrill of the hunt.

I'd spent so many years trying to survive, scraping by one meal at a time, that I never thought I'd miss any part of my old life. The adrenaline that would churn in my blood, cranking me up to a hundred, buzzing in me hours after a successful hijack. I ran my hand along the hard, cool metal, caressing an old friend, my heart beating so loud it pounded in my ears.

Ryker stopped beside me. "Don't get too excited. It's not loaded with supplies."

"We're taking this? We aren't walking?" I'd robbed plenty of them, but I'd never gotten to actually *ride* one. Would it be as exciting?

Ryker walked past me to the door and threw a bag in the cab. "Part of the way. I want to get there quickly."

He popped the trunk and then climbed up, holding a small black box in his hand made of dragon scales. It was the only thing you could keep a fire stone in that wouldn't melt or transfer heat, and the only way to keep a fire stone good until use.

Chuggers ran on fire stones, mined from the Eternal Volcano. You could only get them when the volcano was dormant, which, despite its name, did happen occasionally. It hadn't stopped flowing in about fifty years, though, and no one knew when it would stop erupting again. Until that day came, there were no more fire stones.

He popped the hood and dropped it in. Steam was already rising as he shut the hood and jumped down.

I walked around to the other side, about to climb the ladder that led to the door. Ryker reached over my head and pulled the door open. His hands found my waist and hoisted me up, the little sizzle that always happened flaring again.

I needed to suffocate the life from it. He was the Cursed King. I couldn't want the Cursed King to touch me. It was a trick anyway, his magic messing with my head. He tortured me on a daily basis. What kind of masochist would I be to want him? That *proved* it was only his magic at work.

The excitement of riding in the cab was choked to death as soon as Ryker climbed in and reality hit. I was going to have his magic smothering me the whole way.

"You sure we shouldn't walk?"

His hands on the wheel of the chugger, he turned toward me. "Yes. What happened to the excitement of two minutes ago?"

It crossed my mind to feign fear of machines. There were lots of people that were scared of any kind of machine. That wasn't my problem. It was the man driving the machine. But I couldn't fake being that weak, even to get me out of this cabin.

"I'm fine."

6

_____

We were a few hours into the ride and I was in a cold sweat. It had nothing to do with Ryker's magic and everything to do with where we were going. The goal was walking out with my soul intact, but I didn't know the price. I could only imagine souls were quite expensive, and I wasn't planning on killing anyone else to save mine. There was a difference between killing someone because you had to and murder.

The chugger slowed about ten miles shy of the temple ruins, and Ryker drove it into a hollow between several large trees. It was the best place to stash the chugger.

Instead of hopping out, Ryker turned to me. "No matter what happens, don't show him anything he can use. Hold on to me the entire time we're there in case things turn."

In case things turn. Why was it that whenever someone had said that to me, it was always a bad turn and never good?

"Okay," I said, mouth dry, and not from lack of water. "Are you going to get all, you know, Cursed King-ish?"

"We're making it out, one way or another, even if we're the only ones." His face could've been carved from stone.

My face, on the other hand, popped an "Oh" as I watched him climb out of the chugger. Yep, the Cursed King was preparing for mass murder, and I wasn't altogether unhappy about it.

I opened my door and slid down, landing hard on my feet. As unsettling as this was, I had the best possible person by my side. When Ryker said we'd make it out one way or another, I believed him. He was a survivor, and considering how long he'd lived, which was a lot longer than me, he was damn good at it. Considering that I was relying on him to keep me alive too, I wouldn't cast aspersions on how he did it.

We covered the rest of the ground quickly and in silence, not slowing until the temple loomed ahead. The sun sat right behind the point of the temple's pyramid. Smaller buildings were scattered around it. Even a hundred yards back, I could feel the foul magic that clung to the place.

I'd come and used the temple as a stash house when needed, but I'd never liked it. After magic had come into existence, word was that things had gotten pretty crazy. There were stories of all sorts of blood sacrifices that had happened here. Even dulls avoided this place.

Well, if this was it, so be it. I took a step ahead.

Ryker grabbed my hand. "Don't forget what I said."

"I got it. No death wish here."

We walked forward together as the temple loomed. It was made of solid stone with a single entrance and two men standing right inside.

They were dressed in black robes, but it wasn't their clothing that threw me. It was their companions. One guard had a snake wrapped around his neck, its fangs planted into the man's flesh. The other had a snake wrapped around his arm, and that snake had its fangs sunk into the crease of his arm. Both guards' eyes were heavy-lidded, the way people who chewed dope sticks often were.

"What is that?" I whispered. "Why don't they knock them off? Are they too high to realize they've got snakes feeding on them?"

"They don't want to. It's the snakes that are making them high. The snakes will eventually kill them, but they don't care. They pay the price willingly for the short-term peace they feel. Plus, they can't shake them off anyway. Once the snake bites in, if you pull it off, it releases venom and kills you instantly."

Ryker stepped forward to enter first. For once, we were in complete agreement.

As we walked into the dark entrance, it was even worse. I could see the bruising and shadowed skin around where the snakes held on. I could see the long fangs partially sunk into the flesh, the drops of blood that dripped down from the wound, a slow leak of life.

Ryker's hand dwarfed mine, feeling like iron around my fingers as he moved past the guards down the hall. I wasn't sure why he bothered to tell me to stay close when the only way I'd be able to leave his side was if I parted ways with my hand.

I felt power surging from up ahead and leaned around Ryker to see a man sitting in a chair in the middle of the main temple room. A ray of light, from an opening in the tip of the pyramid, streamed down dramatically, as if he'd planned it. The sun glinted off thick white hair. There wasn't a hint of color to him anywhere; even his eyes were solid white. The skin was unnaturally smooth, and his white robe blended right into the color of his skin. His magic didn't feel like anything I'd encountered before. Whatever this creature was, he wasn't human.

He watched as we moved forward, and snakes slithered along the ground, swarming and hissing as they headed toward us. They'd veer away at the last moment. I wanted to leap onto Ryker's back, but my feet stayed on the ground —for now.

We walked into the room and were swarmed. Before I could react, Ryker was swinging me up in his arms. He made a jerking motion, and a snake flew off his leg, tearing at the fabric of his pants. The other snakes around us went deadly still. Like, real dead. Not playing. But there were more farther away.

"Back them off unless you want to lose them," Ryker said.

"Don't take offense. They wanted to greet the Cursed King." The Debt Collector's voice was eerily high, and as strange as his appearance. What bothered me most was I couldn't tell where he was looking with the solid white eyes.

"They should know better, and so should you." Ryker let my legs swing down and took my hand again.

"That's all right. No harm done. Come here, my little lovelies."

The snakes that lay dead by our feet twitched, and then were slithering toward the Debt Collector. He reached to the ground, and I watched as the snakes slithered right into his palms. I watched as they appeared to slither underneath his skin before disappearing. They were part of him. If Ryker couldn't kill the snakes, could he kill Bones? Could anyone? It was a display with a purpose. He'd wanted to provoke Ryker into killing them.

The Debt Collector sat back. I didn't glance at Ryker— not that I thought he'd show his emotions openly, but maybe I'd pick up a hint. That had to have freaked him out as badly as me, or what else had he seen in this world?

The Debt Collector arranged his sleeves as if nothing odd had happened. "I appreciate you bringing her to me. Simplifies matters."

I couldn't see Bones' eyes, but I knew they were on me now.

Everything had a price, even my soul. Time to see what the price was. "What did you want?" I asked. "I'm sure there is some way we—"

"You. Can't. Have. Her." Ryker edged forward, his hand on mine nearly cutting off the circulation to my fingers, and I didn't mind even a little.

Well, if I hadn't already known Ryker had the biggest pair of balls in all the kingdoms, I did now. Bones *absorbed* snakes, I wasn't sure if he could die, and Ryker was ready to throw down anyway.

Bones smiled. "Technically, she's already mine."

The Debt Collector nodded, and one of his men entered the room. He had a snake coiled around his neck so tight that I wanted to pull at my shirt. He stepped forward with two pieces of paper.

Bones waved his hand toward the papers. "I have a binding contract."

With a flick of his wrist, the papers flew into the air, turning into sparkling dust until they formed an image of two people. I knew they weren't real, but it didn't stop me from staring transfixed. My memories might've faded, but I knew them. I hadn't seen them since I was a small child, but I'd never forget their faces. I watched as they each signed a piece of paper in front of them with red ink and elaborate pens.

It hadn't been the slavers who'd bargained to keep me

alive in hopes of selling me for more. It had been my parents. So much for keeping my expression locked down. A cry escaped my lips, and I would've run forward if Ryker's hand hadn't gripped mine, tugging me back.

The image was gone. The papers back, floating in the air until they drifted to lie upon Bones' outstretched hand.

"You bastard!" I screamed, pulling forward, but tethered to my spot by Ryker, who refused to let go.

"Two signed contracts. That's the price. Two souls to save one. Your life wasn't paid for in full." He held up the contracts. "The male didn't kill himself. He died naturally. I was to be paid two souls and I only received one." His words reverberated through the room, causing an ache in my ears.

With every word, my magic was growing, exploding around me. There was no controlling it. I didn't want to control it. I wanted Ryker to let go of me, and then I was going to tear Bones apart, piece by piece. I didn't know how I'd do it, but the rage in me said I could. It urged me on, telling me I could destroy him.

Ryker pulled me closer, forcing me to him when I would've lunged. His arms wrapped around me, and I could feel his magic surrounding me, smothering.

"You're not getting her, so what do you want in exchange?" Ryker asked. I was glued to him, an iron arm around my waist, his magic caging me further.

"I'm going to kill you." My words came out slow and calm. I'd see him dead.

The Collector leaned forward, "Mighty words from someone so small." He tilted his head, a smile revealing white fangs. "But maybe not so weak?"

The Debt Collector leaned back, as if he'd just learned a secret that amused him.

"What's your price?" Ryker asked.

I struggled to breathe as my rage demanded more from my heart than I was used to giving. I could feel Bones' attention on me. I felt a wave of magic trying to push at me, Ryker's magic firming around and pressing it back.

Even through all the revelations of today, there was one that was slamming into me. Ryker, the Cursed King, the man who had his arms wrapped around me like steel and his magic like iron, had just pushed back at a creature that was terrifying. They were at a stalemate. If I hadn't wanted to run from Ryker before, I should definitely be thinking of it now. Except running from Ryker meant I might be running to Bones. At least one of the monsters in this room wanted me alive.

"Fine. You want a trade? I want the stone you collected from Bedlam."

"That's not on the table," Ryker said.

Seriously? He wouldn't hand over a stone for me?

"Then her life still is." The Debt Collector shrugged bony shoulders, and white fingers waved in the air, as if it were no difference to him. "I'll give you three months to reconsider."

I strained against Ryker's hold. Trying to zap him. If he felt it, it didn't show.

"We're done," Ryker said, turning, with me in tow.

We walked past the guards, down the hall, and out of the pyramid. My fingers were still curved into fists. I wanted to kill Bones. Neither of us said a word. If I spoke, I'd explode. Ryker's magic was still cranked up, but it wasn't smothering me anymore. Mine was way worse.

I couldn't speak. Not until I got away from him. I couldn't even think clearly after what had happened.

I pulled away from him for the fiftieth time, and he

finally released me once we were a hundred or so feet from the temple.

"Why did you do that?" he asked, voice low, but there was no mistaking the fury.

He'd beaten me to the punch. That was *my* line. "Me? You mean why did *you* do that? You had no right to hold me back. That was my call, my decision."

"Did you not hear me when I told you to keep calm and not give him anything? And what did you do?" he asked, pointing at me. "You lost your shit." He turned away and walked a few paces farther away.

Because he told me? When did he think he took ownership of what I did? Oh no, I'd about had it with Ryker and his orders. I'd let it go too far, and now he thought he could dictate my life.

"You didn't have the right to hold me back. It's my choice. Not yours."

"If you'd gone after him, you'd be dead," he said, as if I were an idiot to think otherwise.

"You don't know that."

"You think you would've been able to kill him? You can't even control your magic."

"At least I would've given it a good fight."

"No, you wouldn't have. That's the problem. You aren't capable of giving it a good fight. All you did was show your hand."

If he didn't shut up and soon, he was going to see how much of a fight I was capable of as I was the one stalking towards him now. "I'm sorry my blood doesn't run as cold and calculating as yours."

"You should be thanking me that you're alive." He dragged fingers through his hair. "Although you certainly have made that more difficult. He knows how much magic you're carrying. He's not going to let go. Any hope of negotiating is useless now that he knows your worth." He took a few more steps away, shaking his head as if he were on the verge of strangling me.

Suddenly the smothering cocoon of Ryker's magic made sense. He wasn't trying to confine mine. He was trying to conceal it. It would've eased the anger I was feeling, except for one major problem. And this was a doozy, the kind you choked on.

"He would've let me live if you gave him the stupid stone, but I guess that's too important." The fucking stone. That was all Ryker cared about. It was the only reason he helped me, because I could help him get more stones, and it didn't matter if I lived or died.

"You're right. I wouldn't. And I won't."

He turned back to me, walking steadily in my direction until I was afraid he'd trample me. I held my ground, too much anger brewing to even consider backing down. He'd stopped me from killing Bones, but he was welcome to take his place.

He didn't stop until his toes brushed mine. His head angled down, eyes boring through me and magic riling my senses. I didn't let it intimidate me. He might be able to pull off that move with the snowflakes who lived in the Valley, but I'd cut my teeth in the Ruined City. I was forged in fire, not grown in soft afternoon sunlight.

"That stone might be the only thing that can kill him. If I were to give it to him, and he reneged, there'd be nothing I could do." He leaned his head ever so slightly closer. "Do. You. Get. It. Now?"

I wanted to rail at him, sink my nails into his flesh and tear his arrogance apart. Only one issue: I sort of did get it now. Damn it. Still, didn't let him off the hook for being an ass.

"That stone could really kill him?" I asked, all the heat and anger turning lukewarm.

"I'm not sure how many I'll need, but yes. It might be the only thing that will."

I hummed. Definitely couldn't hand that over, then. I hated when he was right. "I might be seeing your point."

He backed up, removing himself from my space, and continued to walk. Was he going to leave me here? No. He still needed me.

But he was still walking away. I wouldn't put it past him to leave me for a little while just to screw with me, because that was how he rolled. I let him continue for another few minutes before I broke into a jog and followed.

Didn't take long to catch up with him, since the big bluffer had slowed his pace. Staring at his back and trying to avoid getting whacked by the branches swinging behind him, I said, "You should've told me."

"I said, 'Don't show him anything.' Excuse me if I didn't break it down for you. I didn't think I had to." His voice was just shy of a yell; he clearly wanted to make sure he was heard.

"You need to tell me more," I said to his back.

"Or maybe you need to trust me more." He continued without even glancing over his shoulder.

"Well, no wonder you fucked up, because that's not going to happen anytime soon." See? It was all his fault.

7

The walk back to the chugger wore away whatever anger I had left for Ryker. He was right: I might've died if I'd had my way. His brisk pace in front of me showed he might've been hanging on to his aggravation, but I didn't care. He wasn't completely in the right and I had more disturbing issues to worry about.

What had happened in my past? I'd thought I'd been discarded by my parents, but you didn't sacrifice your life for someone you didn't want. I didn't remember much of my time with them. I'd never tried to hold on to those memories. I'd shoved them away, and hadn't thought of what could've been. Thinking back to that time now was like meandering around in a fog as thick as pea soup.

There were a couple of things that I'd never forget, though. Waking up on the dead pile. Back where I was born, a small country called the Court, that was what they'd called the place where the deceased were dumped before they were incinerated. I hadn't been sick. That much I knew, because I'd never forget the shock of waking up on the dead pile. I'd gone to sleep in my bed the night before, the way I always had.

Before I could escape the pile on my own, the slavers had come and collected me, as if they'd known I was going to be there. Had my parents orchestrated all of that to then sell me to the slavers? But then why sacrifice your life? It didn't add up. Although only one person did sacrifice themselves, if Bones could be trusted. Had my father had different plans for what would happen to me?

I spent the rest of the walk to the chugger riffling through what memories I could dredge up out of the swamp I'd sunk them in. It wasn't until I ran out threads that I noticed Ryker had been silent as well. Fine by me if he didn't want to talk. Silence was better.

I climbed up into the cab without help, wondering how I was going to get out of this. I'd figure something out. I always did. Damn if I'd let Bones suck the life from me. Wasn't it bad enough that he took my mother's life?

An hour into the ride and Ryker still wasn't speaking, but I knew he was watching. His magic was poking the hell out of me. He was reaching epic proportions of out of control. It was a good thing we didn't have a bad mix, or he would've killed me already.

"Can you keep to your side of the cab?" I asked.

"I'm not..." His brow furrowed. "Minor slip."

I could tell that admission had been rough coming out, and yet I couldn't stop myself from digging in a little more. "Minor? I'm lucky I'm alive." I leaned farther away from him and perched a heel on the seat, using my knee as an armrest.

He glanced over at me. "No thanks to your efforts."

I rolled my eyes, and they snagged on his pant leg, the

one the snake had went after. Its fangs had left a hole where it had tried to sink its teeth in. Tried or had? That was dried blood on his skin. Hadn't he said that if they bit into you and you tried to pull them off, they released venom?

I dropped my foot back down and leaned closer, getting a better look. "You were bitten."

He wasn't flushed or sweating, and I didn't see any redness around the wound, either.

"No, I wasn't."

"I can see the blood."

"It was a scratch from walking through the bushes."

A scratch that left two perfect spots? Right where the snake would've bitten? Perfectly sized for the spacing of fangs? Bull.

He didn't bother looking at his leg, and if he was worried about being called out on it, it didn't change the slope of his shoulders or his grip on the wheel.

I moved back to the other side of the cab, my back to the door. "Why can you pull the snakes off when you say no one else can?"

"After I answer all your questions in depth to your satisfaction, shall we discuss what you remember from your childhood?"

Bastard. I looked ahead, pulling my knee back up and hugging it. "Fine. Keep your secrets."

Whatever. He had his skeletons and so did I. We all had a vault we kept locked. If you didn't, you were a weirdo with no life experiences behind you. No experiences meant you were useless to me. He could keep his secrets as long as he was still going to help me, because I definitely needed it. My time was running out.

I chewed around a hangnail as I asked, "Why three

months? He knows you're not going to give him the stone. Why the pretense?"

"I'm not sure," he said, as he turned his head slightly toward his window.

In other words, he wasn't ready to tell me what he was guessing at yet. Didn't matter; I knew what mattered now. I needed those magical stones Ryker was so intent on gathering more than he did.

My knee-jerk reaction had been to go in all fists and fury on Old Bones, but the cold, wet mist of the walk back to the chugger had dulled the fire and sharpened a couple of things up. If I was going to get out of this mess, I needed allies, and strong ones. Ryker still wanted his stones, so he needed me. But I needed him more than ever because I wanted them too. He had one from Bedlam. Did he have any more? If he didn't, he still had a better idea of where to get them.

"What exactly are these stones?"

"Just magical rocks," he answered.

And he wondered why I didn't trust him? He didn't trust me either. Still, Ryker acted as if he was going to help me, and that was what mattered most right now. But things changed. What if Bones made me too much of a liability? Lots of people agreed to help with all sorts of things. Then they realized what they'd agreed to and went running, possibly screaming, for the hills. Bones definitely appeared to be the type of favor that would send someone screaming. Ryker didn't strike me as a screaming type, or a runner for that matter, but there was always a first.

Look at me, for example. I wasn't a community type, but I was communing all over the place lately. I broke bread with people and said hello, or at least nodded, once a week.

I really needed to know where I stood with Ryker and

how much I was going to be able to depend upon him. What I needed even more than that was leverage in case I found out I was standing in a ditch. With mud. If there was a ditch involving Ryker, there'd be mud too.

I did a gentle poking around at his magic to gauge his mood as best I could. I'd avoided other Wyrd Bloods for so long that it wasn't an exact science for me. I didn't know how much I could poke before he'd sense me. That wouldn't do at all, since I needed him unguarded for my next topic.

I reached out with the lightest feel, barely skimming. His magic was calmer than it had been. The waters would surely churn up again in the future, considering our history. The timing was as good as it was going to get.

I relaxed back, my arm outstretched, resting on my knee. I tried to hit my most casual tone ever, while hoping my magic didn't give away my anxiety. I needed to exude I-don't-give-a-shit.

"Let's lay our cards out on the table, shall we?"

He shifted the stick on the chugger, picking up speed, before he glanced over. "Sure. Let's lay them out. I'd love to see what's on your table."

As soon as he agreed, I realized I needed the big spiel, the type I definitely didn't do. That kind of thing included a hard sell on what I brought to the table. I'd been hiding my magic for years, and now I needed to make big, sweeping declarations on how great it was. Yes, Ryker was a Wyrd Blood, and already had an idea of what I was holding, but that didn't mean this came naturally. Boasting about my magic made me feel like a slug about to jump off a cliff and fly. This probably would work out as well and I'd end up a slimy mess, a blob against the rocks.

"You've been helping me so far because you know I can get you through any magical ward out there. There's also my ability to 'juice things,' as you say. If I could turn Burn into a flamethrower, who knows what else I might be capable of? And according to you, my magic hasn't fully matured yet."

I left out the worming, even if there was some asset there. It didn't matter. It wasn't reliable, and worse, Marra asked me not to do it. Worming was off the table, but Ryker didn't need to know that yet. Even with that, maybe not a slimy mess after all. I sounded like a catch. I'd want to help me and then drain me for everything I had, too. He definitely should. It was the smart move.

I angled slightly, better to watch his profile while disguising it as a comfortable position. He continued to watch the road ahead of us without speaking. Didn't he hear me? What was wrong with this man? Plus, it was his turn to sell himself.

The silence continued to roll on.

"Would you like help?" I asked in my least helpful voice.

"That would be wonderful."

I shrugged off the taste of sarcasm. "You have established resources in place and you're very good at killing people. Best I've ever seen." Some people might not think that was a plus, but those people didn't live my life. When every stronger Wyrd Blood you met saw you as a possible asset to acquire, you'd want a grade-A killer on your team, too. I must've done something right somewhere, because life had handed me the best killer known to man.

He tilted his head, giving me a slight nod. "Nice. I'm a wealthy killer."

He could kid, but that wasn't a joke. "That's no small feat in this world."

"Do I have any other cards?" he asked, eyebrows rising.

"None that I'm aware of, but I think that's a decent hand

as is." And that was as much flattering as he'd get. Didn't want him to rethink the balances here.

"That's all right. I'm fine with your assessment."

Time for the kill. "So, then you see the obvious? You need me as much as I need you."

He shrugged. It made me want to reach over and shake him. Why did he insist on making everything so difficult? If I wasn't playing it cool, I'd stick my head out the window and scream.

He leaned back, his wrist resting on the steering wheel. "Well, are you going for it, or you going to sit there and pretend you're not staring at me for another hour?"

I shifted my gaze to the front window. "I'm not staring at you." Anymore. And he acted as if he didn't do the same.

"Don't tell me you don't have the balls to ask."

Oh, I had balls. I had bigger balls than anyone I knew. If I were a guy, I wouldn't even be able to pull my pants up. I'd have to wear skirts, they'd be so gigantic.

"I want in on the magic stones deal, fifty-fifty, down the center."

"No," he said quickly, as if he couldn't be bothered to ponder it for a second.

"They can kill Bones. I need them more than you, and if you don't agree, I'll quit." Who was I kidding? I couldn't quit. He was the best asset I had. Plus, there was another little problem that hadn't been mentioned but was still looming. I'd challenged him to a fight and lost. I'd basically shackled myself to him, and that hadn't been undone.

"You can't quit. Did you forget you lost that challenge?"

Of course he'd bring it up. I couldn't even quit with dignity.

"Which you said you were going to get undone and I could go whenever I wanted."

"I haven't figured out how yet." He gave a half-smile that said he wouldn't figure it out until he got what he needed.

"I'm not going to help you go after all these stones and then sit back and wait for you to decide what to do with them. I'll rot away in my room first." This was not going down this way. It was too important, and I wasn't as helpless as he'd like to think. I either got what I needed out of those stones or he was getting cut off.

"You'll sit back and do nothing? That doesn't strike me as who you are."

"If you knew who I was, you'd know I'm telling the truth." There was no bluff here. I wasn't helping him collect the only known weapon against my enemy and then not let me use it the way I saw fit. That was my line in the sand—or mud, in this case.

"Fifty-fifty is off the table, but you can have full access to use them to kill Bones."

"Deal." The word was out of my mouth before I thought about it. He'd tricked me. He wanted more stones, so of course he'd use them to kill Bones. I'd said yes as if he'd done me a favor. That was what you got for negotiating when you were still running high on adrenaline and emotions. I should've sat here silently like him.

"You were going to use them to kill him anyway. I should've gotten more out of this deal."

"Too bad you already agreed." He smiled. "We both still get what we want. Does it matter?"

"Maybe." Mostly to my ego, though. I sucked at negotiations. How was I even alive right now?

I didn't bother arguing or threatening to back out. It really didn't matter, as what I wanted now, more than anything, was to kill Bones. It wasn't only because he was trying to kill me. It was because he'd had a hand in my mother's death, if not my father's. The details of why she'd done it and how I'd ended up on the dead pile were still unclear, but it wasn't something I could let go unanswered.

I wasn't going to roll into a ball and cry. I'd accepted the loss of my parents a long time ago. Did I feel emptier? A little colder? Like another piece of me had been stolen? Yes. That was why Bones was going to die the worst death I could deliver.

The Chugger pulled to a stop as the sun dipped behind the trees. I climbed out of my side of the cabin and immediately felt the tingle of Burn's magic approaching. Ryker turned toward the same direction and was heading toward Burn before he broke the trees.

"What's wrong?" Ryker asked.

"We've got three dead."

"Where and how?"

"In the South Bend, and we don't know. They were found in their house. We can't find any cause. Neighbor discovered them a couple hours ago. They hadn't seen them all day and got nervous."

Ryker was on the move, and I was right behind him.

"Did you contain the area?" Ryker asked Burn.

"I've got a couple people keeping everyone back just in case."

"In case of what?" I asked, following. I didn't wait for an invitation or ask permission. With all the threats looming large, if there was a suspicious death, I wanted to see what happened firsthand, and no one would tell me otherwise.

Burn glanced back at me. "It's something contagious."

I hadn't been in the South Bend. I hadn't known there *was* a South Bend. We quickly made our way through the heart of the Valley and up a small, well-worn path I'd disregarded in the past. It led to a cliff edge where a simple cable system was set up and ran across a deep gorge. The cables on this side were wound around a large pulley, with an equally large wheel attached, which would put the cables in motion once turned. Hanging from those cables was a bench. An ordinary, everyday, old wooden bench. These people were crazy.

A giant of a man, sitting on a stump and smoking some type of cigarette, stood as we got nearer. "You crossing?"

"Yes."

At Ryker's response, he flicked the smoking stub of his cigarette into a barrel filled with sand and lumbered toward the wheel. I watched as he took a firm grip on the spokes then eyed the distance across the divide.

Ryker took a seat, and so did Burn. I took another glance at the gorge we'd be crossing.

"Either get on or get out of the way," Ryker said.

I hopped on in between them, closed my eyes, and curled my fingers around the edge of the seat in a death grip.

"Jimmy," the man yelled. "Incoming."

I kept my eyes shut the whole time. Each jerk of the bench as it creeped forward along the cables had my fingers squeezing the wood tighter. It wasn't until the thing slowed to a stop and I felt Ryker and Burn stand that I popped my eyes open.

As soon as my feet hit the ground on the South Bend, the difference was immediate. If I lived in the heart of the Valley, this was the suburbs where the families lived. The buildings here were spread out, some with small fences around them and yards out front.

I knew right where we were heading as I saw a small cluster of people milling around outside of the house. No one got very close, and I didn't think it was because there was a man and woman standing in front to keep them out.

Ryker nodded motion to the right, and the two guards both looked at me before moving to the other side of the street. They were Wyrd Blood. I knew it because they hadn't only glanced at me, they'd scanned me for markings. That was what Wyrd Blood did. That was what I was doing to them—not that I could see anything on them either.

How many Wyrd Blood lived in the Valley that I didn't know of? Were they all ordered to stay away from me? Well, hell, this was a little embarrassing. I kept my head high, pretending nothing was amiss, other than the dead bodies we were about to visit.

The crowd parted as we approached, and I eased in behind Ryker, like I had every right to be there. Burn fell in behind me, and I couldn't help but think it was to keep a buffer between me and any more Wyrd Blood that might stray over accidentally.

All thoughts of that issue vanished as I walked inside and saw the woman, man, and baby, all lying still on the ground. Several lanterns had been set up around the room. It made it easy to see there wasn't a drop of blood, a bruise, anything that might indicate how this had happened.

"Has anything been touched?" Ryker asked, walking around the room.

"I don't think so. As soon as I was called, I put the guards out front." Burn was looking over the scene, but it was clear this was his second or third go at it.

"When was the last time they were seen alive?" Ryker asked, kneeling near the man.

"Last night."

I stared at the sweet face of the baby. I didn't know kids well, but this one didn't look old enough to walk yet.

"Don't touch. Whatever happened, it might be contagious," Ryker said.

I picked my way around the living space of their house, making sure my boots didn't come within an inch of grazing them. Burn and Ryker were doing the same.

The family's clothes were perfect, and even up close, there were no signs of a struggle or injury. It was as if they were fine and then simply fell dead. Their expressions were slack. I didn't know if they'd been in pain or not.

I circled back around, drawn to the baby lying next to its mother. Hadn't even had a chance to live yet. The mother's face was angled toward him, her arms still wrapped around his chubby body.

I leaned in slightly closer. "There's a drop of blood coming out of the woman's ear."

Burn and Ryker both crossed to where I was.

Ryker squatted down beside me, taking the nearest lantern and bringing it close. "She's right."

"Do you think it's..." Burn took a step back, shaking his head. "I don't even want to say it."

I stopped looking at the bodies and devoted my attention to Burn. "Don't want to say what?"

His lips were pressed together, the line of his shoulders tense. "It could be the Boom."

"They were new, only been here a few days. They might've had something already." Ryker straightened and turned to Burn. "Get the buriers out here, but make sure they know to take precautions. We need you to find who they've been around. Who they sat with at dinner. Anyone they've been near needs to be quarantined immediately…"

Ryker continued to talk over a plan with Burn as memories of children skipping in a circle, all holding hands and singing as they played, ran through my mind. How many times had I seen and heard them do this in the Ruins?

Down goes one and circle wide.

One of the children would drop to the ground. They'd laugh and skip around and continue singing.

Down goes two, better run and hide.

Another child dropped to the ground.

Down goes three, prepare for doom.

I could hear the laughter as another dropped to the ground.

Down goes more, we all go boom.

The remaining children fell to the grass, giggling. People nearby would tell them not to tempt fate, that the Boom might come for them.

"I thought that was gone?" I got to my feet and stepped back a few paces.

Ryker turned to me, looking just shy of grim. "Survival instinct isn't exclusive to humans. The longer you're alive, the more you realize that everything wants to live, including viruses."

9

Burn had stayed behind to wrap up a couple more details, and I climbed onto the seat beside Ryker for the bumpy trip back over the gorge. We were several feet away from the edge when I realized I still couldn't keep my eyes open.

"If it's the Boom, how long will it take to know if it's going to spread?" I hoped he wouldn't notice my eyes were closed tight.

"It won't take long. A day or so."

"We could be dead tomorrow." My life span might've gone from a few months to a few days. That seriously sucked.

"Wyrd Blood are immune to the Boom." The chair rocked as he moved.

I gripped the side.

"We've got more Wyrd Blood coming with Knife tomorrow night. Until you get control of your magic, I'm going to need you to be careful avoiding them once they get here."

It was a well-known phenomenon that two Wyrd Blood

interacting could cause an accidental death. I hadn't realized until recently that it was avoidable. I'd thought you toughed it out and the strongest Wyrd Blood lived. A few Wyrd Blood wasn't our biggest issue right now.

It was alarming enough that I turned and opened my eyes. "How can they come? What about the Boom?"

He shifted, making the seat swing again, oblivious to the height we could drop from. "They won't get here until late tomorrow. If more die before then, I'll turn them around. If no one else dies between then and now, it's safe.

"If they do come, I need you to avoid them so it's not awkward."

The chair slowed, and we both climbed off and headed down the small path toward the center of the Valley.

I ducked a branch. "Awkward how? You mean if they accidentally kill me and you have to find someone else good at breaking wards?"

"They won't accidentally kill you. You're too strong. You'll kill them, and then that'll be a pain in my ass." He said it the way you'd talk about having to wait in line for something.

"Because *you'll* have to kill me?" I asked. I didn't know where that question had popped out from, but now that it was *out*, I was holding my breath, waiting for his answer.

He shot me a look over his shoulder, as if to say he didn't have time for my stupid shit. "No. It'll be a pain in the ass to go kill more of their people if they whine about it. Not a headache I'm looking for."

I nearly tripped as I stared at his back. "You'd do that for me?"

"You're one of my people."

"But I'm not your people."

He turned, raised a brow, and then huffed as if he'd

heard something slightly amusing but not worth discussing. "Fine. You're not."

He said it like a man who didn't believe words meant anything. In a world full of magic, words could bring down empires. Then again, people lied all the time and words often did nothing. Tough thing to debate when you didn't know which side of the argument you fell on. I'd let that one go until I decided myself.

"Would you really kill them?"

"I just said that I would. Consider it a courtesy kill, if you prefer. Point is, that's what will happen, and I'd like to avoid it."

I was still in a bit of a daze when I made a right, heading toward the third tower, where Ruck would be working right now. I needed to tell him to lie low. Then I'd go to Marra and tell her, even if I had to scream it through her door. Then I'd digest the fact that Ryker was willing to not only kill his enemies for me, but allies, too. After I thought it over, maybe I'd be able to decide if that made him a monster or the best person I could've aligned with. Maybe both?

"Where you going?"

"I have to—"

"Whatever it is, do it later. We've got more to discuss." His hand found my lower back and he steered me toward his place.

It was late. Ruck would be on the tower for a while, isolated, and Marra would be settled in for bed. I could scream through her door later.

He didn't say anything else until we got to his place, and I found myself not wanting to run the way I often did at being stuck in a room with him. I settled on his couch as he remained standing.

"Even if your magic doesn't kill them, other problems

could arise from the side effects. Burn and Sneak don't seem to be affected; that doesn't mean others won't be."

"Other side effects?"

"Not every Wyrd Blood is going to be controlled."

Oh damn, he felt it too? I'd wondered if he did, but it wasn't something I'd been ready to admit to. Was he feeling it right now? I was.

I shot up off of the couch. "I need to use your bathroom." I stumbled awkwardly out of the room and down his hall until I had the door shut behind me.

It was too much in one night. There was Bones, then the Boom, and now this Ryker revelation that my magic affected him the way it did me. And I couldn't forget that he was willing to kill for me. How was I supposed to think clearly?

Did that mean he wanted me? I mean, I couldn't deny I'd thought of it. I was a woman with feelings, after all. It wasn't my fault, either. It was the magic. Maybe he'd wanted me to come back here because he wanted me and not just for the stones? He'd basically said as much, hadn't he?

I could be dead in three months. Did I really want to die a virgin?

I splashed some water on my face, telling myself to calm down and act cool.

By the time I walked back into the living room, we already had company. Burn was on the couch and Sneak was leaning against the wall.

Ryker was perched on the edge of the table, arms crossed as he seemed to be catching them up on the meeting with Bones. "I want every reading person we trust to be scanning the scrolls and books. If they can't read, they need to be out collecting more books for people who can. I want them to buy everything that might have any connection to the stones, or the Debt Collector, no matter how questionable or how high the price. The Debt Collector knows something that we don't. We need to find out what it is." Ryker turned around and grabbed a sheet of paper on the table. "Sneak, come here."

Ryker stood and laid a map out on the surface, with Sneak beside him.

Ryker tapped on a spot. "Send some of our people here. Have them work their way around to the rest of the spots and trade with the locals for info. We don't know how many stones are out there, but all of these spots are rumored to possibly have one. We don't have the luxury of time, so send everyone you can."

I sat on the couch, and Burn held his bottle up. "Care for a sip? You look like you could use it."

I went to reach for it, and he held it back. "Hang on." He lit a fire underneath the bottle as he swished the liquid around for a second. He handed it over. "It's better warm."

I sipped. The sourness made my taste buds rebel as the spiciness burned my throat.

"What is that?" I asked, handing it back.

"It's my own special blend. Good, right?" He smiled and took another sip.

I nodded as I saw Ryker ducking out to talk to more people who'd just shown up outside. Had to be more Wyrd Blood, since they were keeping their distance.

"Did he tell all the other Wyrd Blood to steer clear of me?" I asked, taking the bottle back when he offered. I walked over to the open door, where I could see Ryker talking to a couple of women and a guy. I vaguely recalled seeing all of them before, but never up close.

One in particular I'd seen recently. She was a stunning redhead, and she'd been leaving Ryker's place around three in the morning. I hadn't been spying. I'd had trouble sleeping and happened to notice her when I'd visited Ruck on the tower.

"He's being careful, is all," Burn said, coming to stand beside me.

I took another swig from the bottle, liking the way the drink warmed the chill in my chest that had settled in after the events of the day.

The redhead laid a hand on Ryker's arm and tossed her shiny hair over her shoulder. I took yet another swig. What the hell? Did he want me or her? If this were a race, looked like she was in the lead.

Sneak walked to the door. "I'm heading out."

"Yeah, me too," Burn said, making his way to the door as well. "Bad day. Can't wait to go to sleep and hope tomorrow's a better one."

"Watch how much you drink. That stuff is strong," Sneak said as they both gave me a wave goodbye.

I held up Burn's bottle. "I'm good. See you guys tomorrow."

I watched as Burn and Sneak said a few words to Ryker before heading home. By the time they left him, only the redhead was left by his side. I saw her glance toward me.

Ryker said something to her, and she nodded, a small smile on her lips before she turned away. Was he telling her he'd meet her later? Was she going to be the flavor of the night? Would she crawl into his bed as soon as I left here?

And why did that make me want to rip them both limb from limb? I had no claim on him. No one did; that was obvious. He spread himself out liberally, but not to me. Why not me?

What was wrong with me? I was a woman like anyone else. I wanted to feel, know what it was all about. I wanted to walk out of his place the way all those other women did, their faces glowing with bittersweet memories. They knew they couldn't have him all to themselves, but they obviously still thought it was worth it.

He walked back in. He stopped a few feet inside, looking at the bottle in my hand and then my face. "How much of that did you drink?"

"Just a few sips." And another for good measure, because the only courage I had right now seemed to be coming from the bottle in my hand.

I took a couple of steps and placed the bottle down on the table near the couch, as if to prove I hadn't had that much.

He tilted his head slightly. "Something wrong?"

"Not at all."

I was either going to do this or not, but I couldn't simply stand here. If I left, that redhead would be back. I knew it in my bones. For once, I wanted to be the woman that walked out with the flushed skin and glow.

I swallowed so loudly that I thought he could hear it from across the room. As he stared, I kicked off one boot and then the other.

His eyes went to them and narrowed. Then they slowly traveled back up my body to settle on my face. I could see him wondering what I was about, but he wasn't sure. I could still pretend it was something else, like my feet hurt. But I didn't want to. I wanted one night. I wanted to be the woman he was with, just once. He'd said he felt the magic sizzling between us. He wanted this too.

My chest heaved as I took in a deep breath. It was do or die. It wasn't like he was stingy with his nights, either. I was a cute girl, wasn't I?

I dropped my eyes to the floor, losing some of my nerve as I unbuttoned my pants and shimmied them off my hips.

"I just want to tell you before we do anything, I'm not expecting anything from you."

My pants discarded on the floor, I pulled at the hem of my shirt. "We have business between us, so it'll be a one-night thing."

By the time my shirt cleared my head, I'd started to sense that something was wrong. Why wasn't he saying anything?

I didn't want to look at him, but I did anyway.

His eyes squinted. His lips parted. And still, he said nothing. He wasn't moving toward me, either. I'd been hoping for a change in temperature, but I'd expected him to heat up, not freeze.

Oh no. He didn't want me. Maybe I'd misunderstood what he meant about the magic. Maybe it made him want to kill me or something?

Where did I throw those pants? "Sorry. I see all these girls come and go. I didn't think it was a big...deal..."

Why had I done that? I shot toward my shirt, lying on the couch. I kept my face down so he wouldn't know you could've roasted a steak on it.

Not a big deal. Nope. Definitely not. I'd made my first overture toward someone and they'd turned me down. Not the worst thing ever. No one got things right on the first try.

I got my pants off the floor.

"Bugs..."

I didn't need to look up. That was all he said, but the way he'd said it told me everything. When I'd thought do or die, I hadn't thought I'd die of shame.

I jerked my pants up so quickly that I lost my balance and fell on my ass. It was okay. I landed right next to my boots. It was a small blessing, but I'd take it.

He stepped closer. I hadn't looked at his face again, but his legs entered my vision, and they were way too close.

"Bugs, it's not—"

I jumped to my feet. "It's not a big deal. Just wanted to see what all the fuss was about. No need to discuss it."

Boots on, I scrambled back a couple of feet so I could clear him easily and make my way to the door. He didn't say anything more as I left. I was grateful for the silence as I scrambled out of there.

10

For the first time ever, I'd beaten everyone to the dining hall. Unless no one was coming to eat today? Had word spread about the Boom already? Maybe they'd rather go hungry than risk contamination? No, these people wouldn't think that way. They'd assume that the unfortunate newcomers had brought something in with them and had died, keeping their little illness confined because life was rosy that way.

I glanced at the clock I could now read thanks to one of my learning books. It wasn't even seven yet. That was what happened when you were awake nice and early. I'd like to say my only problem sleeping was the usual worries over the Debt Collector, sadness over the deaths, or the fear of the Boom killing everyone. I wasn't that selfless. Humiliation had creeped in and taken up a nice chunk of my wakefulness. The memory of stripping for Ryker pounded in my head the way my boots had pounded on the floor as I'd practically run out of there.

I was pushing eggs around my plate when the rest of the world began to straggle in. Ruck was among the first wave.

He did a cursory glance at the table and headed toward the food line. His eyes swung back to me as if he'd had a delayed reaction to my sorry state. I hadn't gone to the watchtower last night as I'd planned, figuring I'd see him early this morning.

I shrugged.

He kept staring. I shrugged again, adding a wide-eyed *keep it moving*. The last thing I needed was for everyone to follow in after him and wonder what he was staring at and why.

He studied me for a few seconds more before he went and got a plate of food. I prepared myself for the onslaught of questions about to head my way. I also took the time to wrap up whatever traitorous emotions were leaking out of my eyes before more people showed. When had I become a broadcaster?

Marra walked in with her Bugs and Ruck upgrades by her side. I'd walked past her place last night, but no one had answered the door. If she'd heard my warning, I couldn't say.

A month ago, she would've been the first person I spilled my night of many humiliations to. I used to tell her everything. Now, I watched in silence as she walked across the room, letting her friends get in front of her in line, probably to have a larger buffer between her and the original Ruck. I caught her looking up ahead at him but not once at me. I stared back at my eggs. Today was already going shitty enough without wallowing about Marra.

Ruck slid into the chair next to me. Instead of digging into his steaming pile of food, he turned. "Why do you look like shit?"

I opened my mouth but then shook my head, inserting food in my mouth instead of giving him answers. I had plenty of words, but embarrassment hammered them back down my throat and shame nailed them there. I'd thrown myself at Ryker, the man who fucked everything that walked, and he'd turned me down. I'd rolled myself out like a rug, waved the flag in front of him, and he'd wanted no part.

Sleep had stuck its tongue out at me as I'd made a mental list of my various shortcomings. Was I too short? Too skinny? A lot of the women I'd seen hanging round him were voluptuous. My breasts were barely a handful, even after gaining some weight. It could very well be my hair. It was full but almost to a fault, sticking up here and there and generally misbehaving. It also couldn't decide what color it wanted to be. Some strands wanted to be brown, others gold.

Why did I care? I'd been looking to use him. I wasn't in love with him. None of it mattered.

Except he'd slept with so many women and he didn't even want a one-night stand with me. I wanted to drop my head face first into my eggs. Was it my markings? Did he think they were ugly?

I dropped my fork on the table just in case I decided on the face-full-of-egg route. I didn't need to lengthen the list of problems with an eye patch.

"Do you want me to try and guess?" Ruck asked, his voice softer than I'd ever heard. He was staring at me like I was going to tell him I was about to die again. I *wished* it were that easy.

I shook my head. This was not the time for a guessing game. My luck, he'd guess Ryker had shot me down right out of the gate, and then he'd want to move on to level two, where he tried to guess why. I'd been stuck on level two since last night. I didn't need anyone showing me up with all new disgusting things about me that escaped my notice. My list had been comprehensive enough to ruin my night, possibly day, maybe week.

"You gotta tell me. You can't leave me hanging this way," Ruck said.

I debated doing exactly that as I watched Ryker walk in. He didn't look over. He went straight to filling his plate.

"Oh shit. Something happened with you two." Shock raised Ruck's voice above a whisper.

I elbowed him. "Shut up."

People kept piling in as Ryker made his way down the line getting his breakfast.

"By the way, did you hear about the deaths?" I asked Ruck, shamelessly using the deaths to get him on to a new topic.

"Yeah. Ben told me when he relieved me this morning. Said there's a chance it's the Boom, but no one believes that." If he was concerned, it was hard to tell with the way he was shoveling bacon and biscuits in his mouth.

We'd been here less than three months and he was already getting warped by the snowflakes. I needed to set him straight, and would, as soon as I could speak again.

That time was not now. Ryker was done getting his food and heading our way. He stopped in front of us, plate in hand, but didn't sit. He always sat at this table. This was *the* table. And if it was filled, we overflowed onto the next table. But it wasn't. Me and Ruck were the only ones sitting at it. There were four empty chairs.

Ryker didn't want to sit here anymore. He didn't want to be near me. He thought I'd carry on. I'd become a stalker, follow him around and grovel, begging for his attention. I'd thought it couldn't get worse.

I squared slumped shoulders, tipped my chin up, and

refused to look away. I had nothing to be ashamed of—other than the very long list of things I'd come up with last night, but no one knew about those.

His gaze locked with mine, and he didn't have his normal I-don't-give-a-fuck look on lockdown.

Holy magic. He felt bad for me. He pitied me. I might struggle with words, but I was an ace at reading faces.

Shoulders slumped, chin went down. My hasty resolution went out the window, and I looked everywhere but him. He kept staring. I could feel it.

I glanced over to the side of the room, trying to act casual when it was nothing of the sort. It was tense and horrible. Why had I done that last night? I grabbed my fork again, pretending I was busy eating while I rearranged my plate of food.

"You've got a shift tonight?" Ryker asked, turning his attention to Ruck.

"Yeah," Ruck replied, sounding as awkward as I felt. It was like a contagion. If it kept spreading, he would be turning red and not sleeping soon.

"A large group from Dorley are heading in tonight. Wanted to make sure you knew," Ryker said.

"Sure."

There was a pause, and I knew Ryker's attention was back on me. I could feel it burning, chafing my senses. I should look at him, act as if it were nothing to me, but I was a coward who looked at the clock instead.

Still he didn't budge. I counted the seconds, tracking his non-movements. Tick, tick, tick. An agonizing minute later, when I realized this wouldn't end until I ended it, I looked up.

When our eyes met again, I wasn't sure what was there. They were so packed full of emotions I'd have to be a speed reader to catch them all. I wanted to think I saw regret mixed in, but I couldn't be sure. Was he sad he hadn't taken me up on my offer, or did he regret he hadn't stopped me before I'd stripped?

"I've got a busy day. No practice today."

"Yeah. Sure." The fork slipped out of my hand, banged on the table, and dropped to the ground. I reached down to retrieve it, giving it immediate priority and hoping Ryker would be gone before I sat back up.

He wasn't. His eyes stayed on me, searching for something I couldn't quite dredge up from the dinged ego I was sporting. I tried to force a smile on, a *we're just friends and ain't that great* gesture, but it must've been as pathetic as I feared. He stared for another second.

I didn't know if he was hoping for another attempt, but he'd gotten the best I had, both last night and today.

Finally, he gave up. With a half nod, he turned and left.

Ruck groaned as soon as Ryker was out of the building. "What the hell happened between you two?"

My elbows hit the table and I dropped my face into my hands.

"You want to know what happened? If humiliation could kill, I'd be dead and buried."

11

M y legs hung over the edge of the landing of the watchtower as the Valley got ready to retire for the night. A stray kick from my heels hit Ruck's shin—again. He didn't complain, only shifted over, giving me more room. Since Ruck's leg was most likely mottled with bruises at this point, it was the safest move.

I'd retreated to my room and books after breakfast, despite Ruck stalking behind me. Hours later, I'd finally climbed up here and spilled all, as Ruck squinted and nodded.

"Are you going to say something?" I asked. I'd been waiting for a response for a good five minutes.

He cleared his throat, took a deep breath, and then gave me the best he had. "It's not *that* big of a deal."

It was the first thing Ruck managed to say and completely conflicted with the faces he'd made as I'd relayed every embarrassing detail.

"How many people have you stripped in front of before getting sent packing?" The words alone made my face go supernova.

"I mean...I can't say that I've had that exact experience, but I'm sure I will at some point." He waved the straw he'd been chewing on as if to enforce how sure he was.

I doubted it. Ruck never got turned down. He didn't know how bad it had been. Even now I was getting aftershocks. A vision of Ryker's face as he realized what I was doing in his living room flashed in my mind, and a groan escaped.

"Hey, at least no one died today," Ruck said.

"That's good. That's definitely good." Except right now I almost wished I'd died at breakfast. It would've been less painful. Still, no one dropping from the Boom by now was a good sign. According to Ryker's timeline, it meant we were probably safe.

I watched as the people walked home for the evening, wondering how their days had gone, had they worried about the Boom or assumed life was good, when a taller head caught my eye.

Ruck whacked my arm. "*Stop* looking at him. You don't want to appear like a stalker. The next few days are going to be very important to how this plays out."

I turned my full attention to Ruck. "And you wonder why I didn't tell you right away."

"I'm trying to help you out," he said.

"I wasn't looking at him. He showed up where I was looking." This was Ryker's country. If he was walking around down there, it would be impossible to avoid seeing him. That had nothing to do with *trying* to see him. I'd happily go anywhere else right now that I'd be guaranteed not to see him, but I was stuck in this place.

"You just stripped for him and I'm supposed to believe that?" Ruck chuckled.

"You're lucky you're the only person I have left here, or I

swear I'd push you off this tower." I punched him in the arm.

He ignored the punch and used the same arm to point in the distance.

"Holy magic, is that them?" he asked, looking far ahead in the distance.

"If it isn't, we've got a big problem." I could see a large group beginning to make their way across the field, some miles before the border to the Valley.

"Where are we going to fit them? There looks to be a couple hundred heading here."

"I hope they don't mess the place up. I feel like we only just got here."

Ruck looked over his shoulder, toward where Ryker had been. "Can you go down and tell Ryker they're here?"

Oh no. Tomorrow morning would be soon enough to see him again. "I'll stay here. You go."

"I can't leave my post, and I don't want to sound the alarm."

I stood, dreading what I'd have to go do. I scanned the people walking around the village and saw Ryker already heading toward the border. He was easy to spot. "It's fine. He's heading out and he doesn't look tense."

I sat back down, and Ruck and I watched as the horde of new people arrived. As they poured in, it felt like a swarm invading.

12

It was suffocating. They were like a virus spreading. How was this ever going to work? Even as I walked to breakfast, one of them bumped into my shoulder. Worst thing was, he kept going. No "sorry about that" or anything. I turned to call him out on his offense, and perhaps a little bit more if he was thickheaded.

Ruck grabbed my arm. "We don't want to pick the first fight. Looks bad."

He was right. Plus, the dick who'd bumped me was walking away as if nothing were amiss. Stupid idiot probably didn't know good manners. I was from the Ruins, and even I'd learned how to behave like a civilized person. You couldn't act like that with all these snowflakes around and expect to get along.

I turned back around. "They're animals."

"Yeah, I don't like this one bit," he said. His tone was raspy, the way it got when he had a splinter he couldn't dig out.

I swung the food hall door open and was nearly trampled by more newcomers pouring out. By the time we weaved our way in, you only had a few inches of buffer before you walked into another body. Keeping my arms pinned to my side was causing a yell to build up in my chest. If that hadn't been bad enough, every person who walked past me had food piled a foot high on their plate.

"So good," I heard one guy say as he passed.

"I know. I'm on my third serving," the guy next to him replied.

My mouth dropped open as I turned to Ruck. "Did you hear that? They're eating *everything*. Haven't they ever been fed before?"

I could tell from Ruck's sneer he had taken note as well.

I threw my hands up, not caring if I accidentally nailed someone in the face. "I gotta go. I'm going to grab a biscuit and get out of here before I do something really bad." I hadn't intentionally zapped someone in a while, but I felt a charge coming on.

I cut the line and grabbed a few biscuits, daring the row of newcomers with an evil glare to say something. No one did, and I darted out of there before my fist met someone's face.

One annoyance behind me, I made my way to the path. Practice with Ryker was never something I looked forward to, but even less now. I hadn't seen him since the infamous meeting at yesterday's breakfast, and I'd done a lot of thinking in that time. Bottom line was that I had bigger problems than a little embarrassment and rejection. He didn't want me sexually. So what? He still needed me, and I needed him. My time was ticking away. I couldn't get all girly and weird.

The field was empty, which was nice, since I could finish my biscuits in peace. I sat on the stone Ryker normally hogged and made myself comfortable, knowing I was the early one for a change.

MY BISCUITS WERE LONG GONE AND HE STILL WASN'T THERE. I hadn't wanted to see him today and he didn't bother showing? At least yesterday he'd told me. This time I didn't even get a message delivered. Did he not realize my life was slipping away? The higher the sun got in the sky, the more my blood boiled. By the time I decided to leave, I was stomping my way down the path to his house.

Fine, I'd tried to sleep with him and he wasn't interested. It shouldn't have been a big deal, but our entire dynamic had gone to shit in that moment. Ruck thought dying a virgin was the worst possible end, but living with Ryker post-offer was clearly purgatory.

If he thought he could walk all over me now, he was going to see what the bottom of my boot felt like as I kicked his ass. And I would. It was all about determination.

I marched toward his place, each step getting a little stompier.

To make matters worse, I was waylaid on my way there. The optimistic face of the girl running toward me made me want to stomp back up the hill.

"You're Bugs, right?"

"Let me guess, you're a friend of Kallie's?" I knew that chick who'd wanted me to ask the worm if she would have a baby wasn't going to keep her mouth shut.

The girl nodded vigorously.

I threw up a hand before she could speak. "I've retired. I don't worm any more under any conditions. No exceptions."

"But—"

"No. Exceptions."

Her face fell. I ignored the drop. I continued my way to Ryker's, leaving a melting snowflake in my wake.

When I got there, the door was locked, but I could hear the voices inside, and then it struck me. What if more people had died? Just because Ruck and I hadn't heard meant nothing. Maybe that was why Ryker had stood me up?

I lifted my fist, ready to bang on the door, when Ryker opened it.

"Is everything okay? Did anyone—"

"No. Nothing new." He squinted. "The runner didn't get you the message?"

"What message?" I asked, my hands on my hips. No one was dead? He left me sitting there and everyone was still living?

"Needed to cancel."

He was canceling on me again. Seriously? I was the one that didn't want to practice, so why was he the one that kept standing me up? I was never stripping for another man— ever. I'd die a virgin and it would be a blessing.

I was about to tell him that when I heard a cough from somewhere inside.

"For a small package, she does pack a punch," a deep male voice said.

I poked my head in the door because I was still on the stoop, having not been invited in. Ryker was probably afraid I'd spontaneously shed my clothes if I came in.

My attention shifted from Ryker to the company in the room. The new guy was standing over by the table, his arms crossed. His hair almost appeared black, except for the auburn highlights, and his eyes were nearly as dark. He had thighs the size of logs, and the rest of his body matched.

For all the muscles, that wasn't what was imposing about

him. It was his magic. I could feel the ebb and flow of it, even as it was so nicely contained. He was polite, keeping it in check, but it was strong. Not quite as strong as Ryker's, but easily in the top five I'd encountered.

This had to be Knife, the leader of Dorley. I stepped inside to get a better grasp on the new Wyrd Blood that would be on my turf.

It was clear why he was a leader. He was too strong to follow someone else, and no one was caging this man with the feral look he had about him. It also made sense why Ryker and Knife played nice with each other. If these two went at it, they'd scorch half this world.

Knife was appraising me in return. "You need to get that under control a bit, no?"

Great. Another asshole who thought my magic was chaotic and was going to tell me daily. Just what I needed.

"My—"

"Keep your Wyrd Blood away from her and there won't be a problem," Ryker said from a few feet behind me, having shut the door and followed behind.

Was this the same man who constantly told me I was out of control? Did he really tell this guy, who had to be the one and only Knife that it was his people's problem? Maybe I wouldn't mind the invasion.

"Bugs, if you haven't guessed, this is Knife."

"Knife? As in the guy who brought all the people who are eating our food stock bare? That Knife? Nice to meet you." I nodded, smiling.

He nodded in return, as if I'd left out all the words before "nice to meet you."

"And you're Bugs, the girl who raided our chuggers, robbing the food that you now begrudge us? Equally nice to meet you."

I walked over to lean on the chair, mirroring his position. "By my estimates, your people are going to be eating us out of more food than whatever I took by the end of today."

"Would you care for an accounting?" Knife asked. "I can supply one for you."

"Let's call it even," Ryker interjected. "Because we are. Remember?"

He was talking to Knife. I had no idea what he meant. As far as I knew, I was in the hole for as many chuggers full of food as I'd stolen. The ones they could prove I stole, at least, which might be none.

Knife glanced over at Ryker and tilted his head. I glanced as well, trying to tell him with my eyes that I didn't need anyone to defend me. I could handle Knife on my own and still make it to lunch with a few minutes to spare.

My attention was jerked back to Knife. His eyes ran over every inch of exposed skin I had, as if he'd find my markings there. He knew I'd have them. Every Wyrd Blood, or person of magic, did. If they were on my arms, I surely wouldn't have worn short sleeves.

"Where are they?" Knife asked, as if he had every right to interrogate me.

He didn't, which I'd clear up fast. You didn't vomit out a question like that. I'd spent most of my life in the Ruins and I still knew you didn't do that. First his men eat all the food and now this crap? Between his people and him, it wasn't painting a very civilized picture of Dorley.

"Where are yours?" It wasn't a question so much as an attack.

He put a hand up. "No offense." Then he shrugged, but he didn't stop looking.

Too late. I was offended. I'd have to nail down this guy's schedule so I could avoid him. It was that or I'd end up killing him, and I had too many people in line to squeeze him into the schedule.

I straightened and took a step toward the door. I'd seen more than enough. Burn and Sneak had been dead-on. He was insufferable, maybe worse than Ryker.

"I'll show you mine if you show me yours."

I stopped mid-stride. I'd get to see his? That changed *everything*. The guy was packing some serious heat, and I'd gotten to see so few markings, or hardcore ones, like the kind Ryker and I had. Ryker wasn't exactly whipping his shirt off and letting me examine them. Then again, neither was I. And due to lack of mirrors, I hadn't seen mine in forever. How could I turn an opportunity like this down if he wasn't bullshitting me?

I turned, keeping my excitement buried. He'd be the type to look first and then screw me. "You show first."

Knife grabbed the hem of his shirt, and Ryker's magic flowed up. If Knife noticed, he didn't care. He finished pulling it off, displaying a nicely formed chest and killer abs. Too bad Ruck wasn't here to appreciate them.

I was more interested in the hard, jagged lines criss-crossing his torso. Markings on the torso were a big deal. The only thing that trumped them was markings on your back. The stronger the magic, the closer to the heart. But for some reason, nothing trumped the back. Other than Ryker and I, these were the best markings I'd ever seen.

I stared for as long as I thought I could, without getting weird. The light seemed to reflect off his markings as if they were slivers of metal weaved into his skin. I could've looked for days.

"What can you do?" I asked, forcing myself to keep my distance and not touch them.

Knife looked around the room.

"Don't," Ryker said. "An explanation will suffice."

Knife let out a laugh before turning his attention back to me with a gleam in his eyes. "I'm like a live razor, spinning lightning fast in every direction." He swung his hand in the air with a dramatic flair. "I hit something and I can slice it. Someone hits me, they lose a hand, and I've got great range."

That sounded downright nasty, but now I was positive about Ryker and Knife's relationship. In this world, if you couldn't beat them, you'd better make friends with them. Although I wasn't completely sure Ryker couldn't beat Knife. You'd see Knife's magic coming for you in a wave of bloodied bodies and screams. Ryker's snuck its way in. You were dead before you knew what hit. I still remembered walking out of Bedlam among the bodies. I'd been stuck on the top of that tower and had no idea of the bloodshed happening below.

"Now you," Knife said.

I turned to give him my back as Ryker came closer, his magic heating my skin. Knife drew my attention back to him.

"Seriously?" Knife asked, his voice soft, as if he didn't quite believe they'd be there.

"Seriously." I pulled my shirt up until the hem rested on my shoulders, while keeping the front tucked close to my chest.

"Holy fucking magic," Knife said breathlessly.

I heard steps getting closer and a hand grazed my back, but it was Ryker's touch.

"They've grown," he said. His hands went to my shoulders and angled me toward the door.

I looked over my shoulder at Ryker. "Really? How much?"

"Enough." His hand trailed down my back. "This is where they used to end." His hand moved down another inch or so. "This is where they are now. The rest are more intense, as if the vines have grown."

I hoped he blamed the chill for the goosebumps breaking out on my skin.

"I've never seen them in direct sunlight before. Did they always shimmer like this?" Ryker's hands traced the marks.

For someone who didn't want me, he was getting awfully touchy. "I don't know."

"No way that's only wards," Knife said from by the table.

Only? Wasn't that enough? I shoved my shirt down, looking for an excuse to cover my flesh. "I'd put my wards up against your weed whacking any day."

"No offense. They just don't look like wards." Knife's brows dropped. "If the markings are increasing, her range will too. She needs to get her—"

"And I told you, you need to keep your people away," Ryker said.

Knife flashed an annoyed look but didn't say anything more. If anyone was paying attention to me, they would've seen pure confusion. Who was this person that kept defending my lack of control?

Although they both had a point, even if Knife didn't realize Ryker agreed with him. Accidentally killing another Wyrd Blood didn't seem like fun. Eating breakfast and taking out another life as I made my way back to my room. Strolling to the showers and racking up another murder. I'd end up stuck sitting in my room for however long they stayed.

I'd heard enough. I was going to have to do something, and soon. Now I needed to figure out how.

13

Dinner was better than breakfast. Still busier, but at least you could walk a straight path in the food building. Knife had brought so many people with him that they'd split dinner service into two shifts. You couldn't tell by our table, though, with only Burn and I. No one tried to sit with us, either. I wasn't sure whose expression was scaring them off, as neither of us looked very jolly. And for as much interaction as we were having, I might as well have been sitting by myself.

I cleared my throat, gearing up to make some sort of social effort, but didn't bother. Burn's gaze was stuck on Marra like a fly caught in a vat of hollyhoney.

Maybe the silence in the midst of the overwhelming chitchat wasn't a horrible thing. It sort of reminded me of my brain at the moment. I couldn't quite form any logical thoughts or plans, but I had lots of chaos running around inside. Although I'd prefer the silence to be of the content variety, and that definitely was not the case for Burn.

I glanced across the room, to Marra's table. How could she sit there and eat with her Bugs and Ruck imposters, pretending that Burn wasn't staring at her like a dog looking for a scrap? I'd never discussed the Marra situation with Burn, but I'd secretly hoped she talked to him. She was making it really hard to excuse her behavior. When she ignored me, at least I could handle it. With Burn, it was akin to kicking a puppy.

"When was the last time you two spoke?"

His head whipped back toward me, color tinging his cheeks. Man, he had it so bad that he hadn't realized he'd been staring.

"I don't remember." He looked up as if it were a struggle. "Few days after we got back?"

My guess was he knew down to the minute. He probably remembered everything he'd said to her, too. And whatever she'd signaled to him, or the toss of her hair, the way she smelled.

I bit into a dry biscuit. Who baked these things? Did the good cooks get put on the second shift? One day of the intruders and the food was going way downhill.

But back to the Burn problem—seemed she'd cut us all off at the same time. I'd learned she blamed me. Now I was thinking she blamed us all. I saw the gaping wound in Burn's heart, the one that was bleeding out through his eyes, and I wished I'd taken all the blame.

Burn was the type of guy to leave you cookies and not tell you they were from him. He'd shadow you home if he thought you were having problems. You'd never have to ask for his help, and he'd never mention it. He was *that* guy. He deserved the best, and what he was getting from Marra was the stuff you tried to wipe off the bottom of your shoes.

"How's that teacher doing? You talk to her lately?" *Because there's other fish in the sea, buddy. You only need to look around and you'll find a nice girl.*

"She's fine."

He wasn't looking over his shoulder at Marra anymore, but he wanted to. I could tell. I'd done the same thing with Ryker. Not that I wanted him either. Not sure where that comparison even came from. Why was I thinking of him? Burn needed me.

"I got the sense you liked her?" *Remember that? The other woman?*

"I guess." He shrugged.

If Marra wanted to ignore me, it was one thing, but watching her ignore everyone else was quickly eating through my patience. We'd all lost Sinsy. Yes, Sinsy hadn't been my blood sister, but she'd been like a sister.

Sinsy had been there for my first period, when I thought I was going to bleed out and die. We'd kept each other up at night with stories of the places we'd go one day and the lives we'd have. Mostly, it was the life she'd have. I'd always known mine was destined for turmoil, since I was a Wyrd Blood. But her dreams had helped to keep me going.

There wasn't a morning I woke that part of me didn't expect to see her for breakfast, or a night I didn't miss telling stories with her. Marra wasn't the only one who'd experienced a loss.

Forget it. If Burn wanted to stare at her and dwell, there was nothing to be done for it—at the moment. I'd figure something out, though, even if I had to talk to some of the newcomers and threaten them into flirting with him.

I scanned the intruders, looking for someone that Burn might like. He needed a girl who smiled a lot. That was a big one. No sardonic expressions or arrogant eyebrows. That was bad news. Definitely no Wyrd Bloods with sudden control issues who were constantly bossy and then defended you for no sane reason.

I took a bite of dried turkey, realizing there was a trend with this new cook, and decided to take advantage of the moment with a little prying.

"Have you noticed something off with Ryker's magic lately?"

Burn's chin jerked up. "Not at all. What do you mean? Why do you ask?"

"It's overwhelming lately. You haven't noticed?" Was this the same guy who was breaking a sweat the other day when there'd been a chill in the room? Was he going to flat-out lie? And badly?

He lifted his hand and made a pinching gesture with his fingers. "Maybe a little bit. Probably tension. He's got a lot on his plate."

Ryker's plate was definitely full, I'd give him that. Except Ryker wasn't the type to buckle. If he could stroll into Bedlam like it was a Sunday stroll, and stand against Bones, why would he start losing it now? "When I first met him, his control of magic was super tight. I could feel the individual threads of it moving exactly as he wanted them to. It's crazy that he'd lose that much control in such a short time. Do you think he's sick?"

Burn's lips turned down and he waved his hand. "Nah, not at all. He'll be fine. Probably a hiccup."

I slumped back. Hiccup? That was what Burn called Ryker's complete downslide? Did he not want to tell me Ryker was sick? No. He couldn't be sick. He looked like the healthiest person I knew.

"How's the reading coming along?" Burn asked.

"Fine." Just like that, he changed the subject. It was as clear as the sun shone that I wouldn't get any answers from him. That was fine. If Ruck started losing it, I wouldn't rat him out either. My only hope was that Ryker kept it together for a little while longer until I got out of my current mess.

"I've a got a book on magical theory that might interest you," he said in between trying to swallow a piece of dried meat.

"Thanks for the offer, but if the words are bigger than 'dog' or 'cat,' it might be a bit premature."

"I'll drop it to you anyway. It's worth the struggle."

"Sure. Thanks."

We both fell back into silence, but at least he wasn't staring at Marra anymore.

I WAS LYING IN MY BED, FLIPPING THROUGH A BOOK WITH THE prettiest pictures, while trying to pull all my magic close to me. The place had gone quiet hours ago, with only the occasional candle glowing in a window to show life. It was the perfect time to practice trying to get my magic under control without distractions.

How much progress I was making was debatable, but something was happening. It was brutally uncomfortable every time I tried, like I'd stepped inside an inferno.

If I was doing this right, I couldn't imagine ever having complete control. I was drenched in sweat when Ryker appeared at my door. I'd left it open, hoping the night breeze would help.

I dropped the book to the bed and sat up. At least things seemed to be getting back to normal with us.

"I can't control it. Every time I do, I'm boiling up after a few seconds."

"Your magic doesn't want to be confined. It'll get better." He leaned a shoulder on the doorjamb.

He'd come here for something, and I knew he'd tell me what it was without having to chase him down. In situations like this, my patience was infinite.

As he watched me, something about the intensity around his eyes made me want to fidget.

"What's up?" I asked. Patience was overrated. It only made things take too long.

"There's something we're not seeing." It was late. The sun was down. There was plenty we couldn't see, but I was certain this was a lot deeper than what Ruck and my neighbors were up to.

Always with the mysterious stuff. He knew I wasn't the patient sort. Did he do it to screw with me? No. It was simply him, the Cursed King, in all his dark and shady glory.

"Could you elaborate on that?"

He walked farther in the room. "I can't figure out what the Debt Collector is waiting for. I don't know if he's using us to collect more stones and then he's going to attack here, or if he's waiting for you to age."

"Why would he wait for me to age?"

"Souls are like fine wines. Some age better. He might've decided to let you age a bit more before he takes you."

"You think he wants my soul to age out?" I shouldn't have asked questions, at least until the morning. That was some creepy shit to have to sleep on. Some things shouldn't be said at night, only in the early light of the morning to help dull them.

He shook his head, as impatient as I was for once. "Not your soul. Your magic."

"I thought he got my soul." Which was plenty, in my book.

"I'm wondering if he gets both."

Fuck. Shit. He had to be kidding.

I watched him. He didn't look like he was kidding.

No, he definitely wasn't kidding.

"Huh," I said, rocking back a bit. "Well, that's interesting." And creepy and disgusting.

He nodded, as if agreeing with all my unsaid thoughts. He turned and left. I was smart this time. I didn't ask him to elaborate on anything else.

14

B urn came running up to me as I left my room. "We need to talk."

Instead of talking, he grabbed my hand and dragged me behind him.

"About what? I've got practice." Not that I should care if I left Ryker waiting for me. He didn't care if he wasted my time yesterday, as I'd sat on the boulder eating dry biscuits. Still, I did need some work. I had all sorts of issues and wasn't too proud to admit to it.

"Ryker is waiting at his place for us." He continued to tug on my arm, dragging me after him.

I nearly tripped in a rut in the road but caught myself. "Burn, what's going on? You're going to yank my arm off my body."

He stopped suddenly, looked down, and dropped my hand, as if he hadn't realized he'd been dragging me. "Sorry. Got excited." He leaned forward, grabbing my shoulders. "I might've found something for your problem."

"Really?" He didn't look like he was messing with me. Burn wasn't the type to screw with you anyway.

"Yes," he said, eyes wide as he stared back.

"What?"

His lips parted, then his face crinkled. "I'd rather explain it all at Ryker's. Easier that way."

Ryker's wasn't too far away. I could make it there and not burst. I started off in that direction, ignoring the fact that I already sensed a big old *but* about to hit in Burn's fix.

Burn and I were walking at a brisk pace when Ruck jogged up and joined us.

"Where you guys heading?"

"Burn thinks he has something to fix me," I told him, not slowing down. "Why aren't you sleeping?"

Ruck tilted his head back toward the direction of the tower. "Ben was late to shift, so he's making up the hours today. I've got some time to kill."

"Great, you can come with us." I looped an arm around Ruck's, not giving him a choice. He'd probably want to be there anyway. He'd already complained about having to hear everything important second hand. Plus, I might need moral support for the *but* that would follow.

Two minutes later, we were at Ryker's, the door wide open.

Ryker was standing in his living room, along with Sneak and Knife. Ryker's gaze landed on me, before shifting to my entourage.

Burn walked in and went to the center of the room, pulling all of the attention in his direction.

Ryker leaned against the wall, crossing his arms and making himself comfortable. "Well? What did you find?"

My attention darted to Knife and back to Burn. "Should we do this now?"

"It's fine," Ryker said. "He won't repeat it."

Ryker didn't say *or else*, but it was definitely heard.

"You know the book we got from the Cave Dweller?" Burn asked, looking to Ryker.

Ryker nodded. At least he knew. Considering I was the one whose life was on the line, maybe I should be kept up to date as well. But that was a fight for later. Now I needed to know what Burn found out, and if it came from the Cave Dweller, it might be something legitimate.

"The Cave Dweller is helping?" Knife asked, surprise in his voice.

"We've got a deal with her," Ryker said, not mentioning the part where Ryker had promised her protection and the Cave Dweller had given her eye to seal the deal.

I could still remember the bitter taste as it squished in my mouth. I couldn't help glancing at Burn. He'd lost a touch of his coloring—probably reliving the taste too.

He got himself back together pretty quickly and pulled a book out of the back of his pants, placing it on the table. It was small and covered in black leather that was worn on the edges. "If I'm understanding correctly, there is a spell that merges magic together."

The pieces immediately clicked into place. Ryker had said it was suspected that your magic was tied to your soul. If my magic was tied to someone else, did that mean...

"Would the spell lock my soul down with whoever I tied my magic to?" I asked.

Burn smiled widely, happy I was seeing the link. "In theory, I think so. It would block the Debt Collector."

"Or he'd take both lives," Sneak said. He wasn't a big talker, but when he spoke, it was typically worth listening.

Burn was shaking his head. "No, I don't think so. He'd have to have a signed contract to take two. I'm not saying that there aren't some downsides, but nothing that I believe would cause a huge problem."

And here came the big *but*. I waited for Burn to continue.

"You can't kill the other person. Hopefully whoever you did this with wouldn't care if they couldn't kill you. Another issue is, there's nothing written about how to reverse it."

Burn was watching me for a reaction as I walked over and took a seat on the couch. "That doesn't sound too bad so far," I said. As far as a *but*, it could be a lot worse.

"There's one other thing," Burn said. "The combined magic could shift to whoever pulled on it. One person could conceivably take all the magic and leave the other with next to nothing if they were so inclined. I'm guessing the stronger Wyrd Blood would have a considerable edge in determining that balance."

I nodded. That wasn't a total deal breaker. I'd have to find someone who was weaker than me. That ruled out Ryker. I could never do this with him and leave myself that vulnerable. He'd be able to take all my magic.

Ryker stepped forward, picking up the book and flipping it to the spot that Burn had bookmarked.

"I'll do it," Knife said.

He was the last person I expected the offer from. I'd thought Sneak or Burn would offer first, maybe Ryker. Not Knife.

"Why?" I asked.

Knife leaned on the table. "That's the most obvious thing in the world. You're strong. You'll be an asset. You're worth the risk."

Now I got it. There was an old adage: *There's more than one way to cage a Wyrd Blood*. It was especially true for females. I'd heard plenty of stories about Wyrd Bloods marrying to shore up an alliance. This was, in essence, marrying our magic. It wasn't the life I wanted, but you couldn't always be picky if you wanted a life. At least with Knife, I'd have the upper hand. My magic wasn't fully matured yet, and chaotic, but it was stronger than his. There wouldn't be as much of a risk.

Knife must've seen the wheels turning or noticed I hadn't outright rejected it, because he added, "Dorley is a good place to live. You'd be happy there. I'd make sure of it."

A swell of magic filled the room, enough to make all of us break out into a sweat soon if it didn't stop. Ryker's magic was ricocheting off the walls and bouncing all over the damn place, making the air nearly unbreathable. Except Ruck seemed perfectly comfortable. Damn how I envied him sometimes.

Burn slumped to sit on the table and ran an arm across his brow. Ryker pulled it back in, as if he hadn't noticed. He was lucky he hadn't killed any of us.

Ryker turned to Knife. "She's not going to Dorley. You're not taking her anywhere."

I was afraid that even if his magic was under control, his fists wouldn't be soon. Figured he'd have a problem with this. Who was going to help him get more stones if I didn't need him anymore?

"She's got a problem. This is a good fix," Knife said, straightening to his full height, which was still shy of Ryker's by an inch or so.

Ryker looked at me and then back to Knife. "Even if she wanted to, and it doesn't look like she's jumping up and down with excitement at your offer, you aren't strong enough. You join your magic with hers and you'll be dead in a day."

I'd thought Ryker was going to beat him black and blue from his expression, but it wasn't Knife's flesh he was looking to bruise. Ryker had given Knife's ego a kick to the gut, the kind that knocked the wind out of you.

"I'll be fine. No worries," Knife said.

Was that true? If I killed the guy, what would be the point in any of it? If he died, I'd be hanging out there with no ties to stop Bones from getting me anyway. Unless Ryker was wrong. How did he know how it worked? None of us had heard of it until a few minutes ago.

I stepped forward. "Why do you think my magic would kill him?"

Knife smiled so widely I thought he was going to break out into laughter. Ryker had the exact opposite reaction. His full attention turned to me. "You're considering this?"

"I have to." Why did he make me feel like the worst of traitors right now? My life was on the line. Of course I was thinking about it. Anybody would've.

The room fell silent. Magic sizzled just above what was tolerable as the tension escalated and stayed there for a few minutes.

"You aren't doing it," Ryker said, as if he had the right to make that call.

"It's my life on the line. My decision."

Ryker didn't respond, and it was almost worse than having a drag-out brawl. He kept staring at me like I'd betrayed him as his magic swirled around me like a cyclone. His jaw was so tense that I feared it was going to break in two.

I got it. He'd lose his ward breaker. Considering what he was hunting, I wouldn't want to lose me either. Did I want to leave here? Not even a little. This was the best home I'd ever had, and I didn't want to get stuck with Knife forever. But maybe I wouldn't be. Burn said he wasn't sure if it was final, but I knew death was.

Knife tilted his head toward me. "What do you say, Bugs? Wanna get magically hitched? I don't think I'm a bad catch, and considering it's me or death, I'm looking pretty good right now." He buffed his nails on his shirt.

Ruck leaned in and whispered, "He's not bad looking. You could do worse." Ruck cleared his throat to get Knife's attention and then waved a finger back and forth between the two of us. "If she goes to Dorley, you know we're a package deal, right? She goes, I go."

Knife looked Ruck over briefly. "You'll be welcome and made very comfortable."

Knife was staring at me, and so was Ryker. Except I couldn't meet Ryker's eyes anymore because of that weird guilt I was feeling. What was wrong with me? And him? Did he expect me to continue hunting stones until I suddenly ran out of time and died?

Either way, I wasn't answering anyone now. Life had never gone in the usual pattern for me. I was used to some crazy twists and turns, but I still wanted time to think over something as drastic as this. Bones had given me months. I wasn't jumping into anything until I had to.

Thinking clearly about anything was nearly impossible right now with my head clouded by Ryker's overwhelming magic. It was going to bring me to my knees soon. I'd have to leave so I didn't explode.

"Ryker, you gotta pull back—"

"I'll do it," Ryker said, staring at Knife, who was breaking a sweat, along with the rest of the room.

Wait a second. What was he going to do?

"Do what?" I asked. He couldn't mean merge. He didn't even get stuck with the same girl more than one night a week.

"We're going to merge our magic." Ryker's magic had

suddenly calmed. It didn't matter anymore because my head was reeling without it.

"You will?" Burn asked. His surprise was so canned that I wondered if it came with a side of potatoes. In that second, I knew he'd wanted this from the very start. That little manipulator. What was he playing at?

Ruck covered his mouth to cough, but it sounded more like a laugh.

"Huh?" I said. It echoed through the room.

"You're only offering so I don't get her," Knife said, his words as sharp as his magic supposedly was.

"It doesn't matter when I offered. First off, she's mine. Second, you're lucky because I'm saving you from yourself," Ryker said.

"Hang on a second here," I said. "I haven't agreed to anything."

"Exactly," Knife said. "Tell 'em, Bugs."

Ryker ignored me, pointing at Knife. "There's no choice. You're not capable. Even the smallest amount of her magic attached to you will shred your soul like a rag doll. I have to do it."

"I'm willing to take the chance. Let her decide," Knife said.

"Fine, you want to hear her tell you she won't kill you? Fine." Ryker turned to me, fully expecting me to do just that.

What the hell was wrong with him? He'd rejected me not even a week ago. Now he assumed I was going to choose him to lock magic and souls with? Risk him taking all my magic for himself so he could leave me weak and abandoned as he collected stones? I didn't know if I'd be stronger than him one day, but today I knew I wasn't.

"Bugs, tell him," Ryker said as if it was a done deal. As if the idea of being joined to him was a foregone conclusion because he said so.

He acted as if there was some grand mountain of trust between us. There wasn't. Why would there be? We only shared the confidences that we had to. He couldn't even stand to sit at the same table with me lately, and I was supposed to trust him not to use me for all I had, especially since he'd been trying to do that since I'd gotten here? Knife wanted to use my magic too, but at least with him, I'd have some control of my life.

"I need a minute."

"What do you mean, you need a minute?" Ryker stared as if he didn't know my name anymore.

And then it clicked. He thought I would do whatever he wanted because I'd tried to sleep with him. He was so used to the women giving him whatever, falling all over themselves to do it, that he couldn't fathom me saying no. What an arrogant, egotistical bastard.

"Yes. I need a minute."

He put a hand on my waist, steering me to the far end of the room. "Are you really going to chance this because of your pride?" he asked softly.

I saw Ruck, the closest to us, slap a palm to his forehead as soon as Ryker said the words.

"This has nothing to do with *my* ego." Yes, maybe my pride wanted to stick its tongue out at him, but my decision had nothing to do with it. I'd wanted to sleep with him; I'd never wanted to hand him complete control of my magic.

I stepped away from Ryker, putting a few feet of buffer in between us, and turned to Knife. "I appreciate your offer, but this doesn't need to be worked out this second. There's no reason to make a choice when other options might come to light. I've still got almost three months left."

Knife nodded, taking the answer in stride with a shrug. "You know I'm the better choice for you, Bugs."

Ryker's lower jaw was back to clenched. "There is no choice. She made a magical challenge and lost. Her forfeiture was to stay here. She's stuck."

"You said you'd try to get that undone," I said.

"I might know someone who can undo it," Knife added.

"Sure you do," Ryker scoffed.

No one spoke. No one moved. The magic had gone back to steam levels, and it seemed like it was going to grow, if the standoff was any indication.

Ruck slapped his hand on his forehead again, this time making a grand gesture of it. "Oh shit, I forgot I told Mary Jane we were going to stop by."

He slung an arm around my shoulders. I watched a rainbow of emotions play out in the room, from cool blues to red hot, as I let Ruck save me and take the fall for an awkward exit.

We walked like we were expecting Bones himself to grab our collars and drag us back through the door. We didn't run, though. That would've been way too obvious.

15

I was stretching my legs. A person was allowed to walk. A lot of people were doing the exact same thing, since the double full moon made it more like dusk than night. Was I supposed to stay inside in case Ryker was out and about as well? And there was less congestion in this part of the Valley. It had nothing at all to do with him or where he lived. I could walk where I wanted, even if it was right by his place.

Ryker was standing outside his door, talking to some girl I'd seen arrive with Knife's group. The way the woman was smiling, it wasn't a business meeting. I leaned a shoulder on a nearby building, keeping most of my body behind a nice, fat bush. Not on purpose. It happened to be where I wanted to take a break.

The moonlight hitting her skin gave her an ethereal quality that she didn't have the first time I'd seen her. I hope Ryker noticed that as well and wasn't duped into thinking she was prettier than she was.

His back was to me as she stared and listened to him. She threw her head back, laughing and flipping long black hair. He was probably saying something dripping with arrogance and tinged with humor. She was dumb enough to giggle. Even when I thought he was funny, I didn't giggle. Although most of his jokes were at my expense. He called it teasing. I called it being an asshole.

There she went, laughing again. I could see the air practically flowing in and out of her ears with each exhale. She looked utterly vapid. If they went inside his place, I was going to have to rethink my alliances. I couldn't work with a man who had such low standards, let alone tie my magic to his.

Knife's magic tingled up my spine, and I shoved off the wall before he could get a peek at what I'd been watching. The last thing I needed was for people to think I was obsessed with Ryker when I was perfectly fine having a business-only relationship. I turned to walk in the opposite direction. He stood there, staring at me, plain as day.

I gave him a nod and continued to walk. If he was here to get answers from me about his offer to merge magic, I wasn't ready to give them. Considering he wasn't doing it to save my ass, but to gain some power, I didn't feel overly indebted to him for the grand gesture of selfishness.

He followed. "Staring from afar isn't the way to get him," he said, shoving his hands in his pockets and looking as if he were getting comfortable for a nice, long chat.

He was guessing at what I'd been staring at, but he couldn't know. Still, it felt like someone directed all the sun's rays right at my face and then notched them up a thousand degrees, and it wasn't even daytime.

"Get him? I don't know what you're talking about. I don't want to get anyone."

"You mean you *weren't* spying on him from behind a bush?"

"No. The cackling caught my ear and I wanted to make sure a rabid animal hadn't broken in to town."

I didn't have to see his face. I could hear his eyes grinding in their sockets as they rolled around.

"Kid, you don't only have your heart on your sleeve, you plucked it out of your chest and dropped kicked it to his feet. Right now it's getting squashed into the mud by the women trampling over it to get to him. It's no wonder you're looking so pathetic."

I resisted the urge to crawl under a rock and made a show of tapping my finger to my chin. "Wait, weren't you there when I turned down his offer of being linked? I could've sworn you were in the room."

He laughed. Loudly. "I'm not saying you don't have pride. I would've turned him down too. First, he clearly thought you'd jump to do his bidding as soon as he offered. Second, he didn't offer until he realized you might take me up on mine. You made the right choice. That's not up for debate. But neither is the fact that you have it for him, and bad. I was there when you nearly melted into him because he touched your markings."

Figured Knife would've noticed that.

"Was there something you wanted, other than this conversation we aren't going to have? If there is, please get to it." I picked up my pace, and his longer legs matched it easily. How ridiculous would I look if I broke into a run? Did I care?

He held up his hands. "Hey, I'm trying to help you, is all."

"I don't think you help anyone but yourself."

He smiled a little too widely, as if he'd received a compliment. "Not completely true. I make the occasional exception if the situation is interesting enough."

"Again, did you have something else you wanted to discuss?" I stopped walking, hoping to end the conversation. The idea of talking about this all the way back to my room was as appetizing as chewing on the Cave Dweller's other eyeball.

He stopped as well. "He knew you were watching him back there."

My jaw dropped, and I snapped it shut. "No, he didn't."

"He definitely did. I would've." He watched me, letting that little tidbit sink in like a splinter under a nail. "We're older and more in control of our magic. We've got a larger radius. He knew you were watching him, and he was screwing with you because you turned him down."

My lips parted but nothing came out as the other ramifications unfolded in my head. How much had Ryker sensed? Had he felt my irritation?

"And yes, he knew he was getting to you, too." Knife nodded, adding a little shrug that shoved that splinter a bit farther in.

I turned and walked. Knife walked beside me, like a sticker bush I couldn't escape.

"Sitting around and waiting for him to want you isn't the way to handle this."

"I'm not waiting. I'm stuck," I said, but my words had gone from having the gusto of a hurricane to a toddler with a slight cough.

"There might be a way to undo that. Strange that you haven't bothered to ask me how or broach the subject first. I'd think that you would've sought me out as soon as you'd heard me utter the possibility."

I'd thought he was bluffing. Why bother asking someone you didn't trust? It wasn't worth discussing now either, so I continued on in silence.

"You know, there are other men that would be interested in you. You've got a lot to offer."

"That's right. I've got a lot *to use.*" This was all calculation and maneuvering. I might be reeling in humiliation, but it hadn't emptied out my head and stolen all common sense. Did he think if he threw a little mud on Ryker I'd jump at his offer?

"How old are you? Haven't you figured it out yet? Everybody uses everybody; it's the way the world works. You're not one of these cupcakes. You didn't grow up here. You know better." His voice finally lost that blasé tone I'd wanted to shake from him. At least I was finally talking to the real Knife and not the too-cool-to-touch version he liked to spread wide and far. I'd seen the grit hinting under his casual surface. I'd preferred it. At least it was really him.

"That's not the world I want to live in."

"The world you want doesn't exist and never will. Those ideals didn't fill your bellies during the cold, long winter. The food you stole in the real world did. You're a survivor, Bugs. Don't go changing and getting stupid because you've got a crush. That's not how people make it. And definitely not Wyrd Blood. We don't have the luxury of being invisible like a dull. Although, for the love of magic, I don't know why anyone would want to live that life. You're special. Embrace it. Rise up and use it. Stop being a doormat."

He walked off, leaving me with those words. As harsh as they were, he did me a favor. It had taken a while for it to set in, but it finally was, and deeply. Ryker would do anything to protect me, but it was only because I could break wards. It was never really about me, only what I could do for him. That was the real world.

I could keep kidding myself that I didn't really want him either, but I did, or at least some part of me did. Why, I wouldn't delve into, but I was going to have to kill that part off and quick. When I did finally end up with someone, it wasn't going to be for my magic.

16

A brown leather-bound book sat on my bed when I got back from breakfast. It had too many pages to be like the books I normally read. I flipped it open and was proven correct when I saw all the small—but very long words—filling the pages. I flipped through it quickly and could only find a handful of pictures that were small and sketched. I closed it again to look at the front.

The author's name was so long that I didn't bother trying. The title looked a little more manageable.

"Ma-G-Al? T-E-Y." Oh. "Magical Theory."

Burn must've left this. It was the book he'd spoken of. How the hell was I supposed to read this? I was barely reading "dog" and "cat." Was he crazy?

I flipped through again, looking for bookmarks. You'd think he'd at least indicate the good stuff, but there wasn't a dog-eared page or a leaf anywhere.

I tossed it on the bed for later, when I had a few hours to sound out a page or two, and headed out.

The path was only a few feet away when a messenger

ran over to me. She was all limbs and lanky, as if she'd gotten hit with a growth spurt recently but her appetite hadn't kept up. She stopped beside me and bent forward as she sucked in air.

"Ryker says"—she dragged in a couple more breaths—"to go to his place today."

"Thanks."

She smiled, proud of her delivery, and ran off again without catching her breath.

I trudged over to his place, slowly. Hopefully he was canceling today and I wasn't going to get stuck in a small room with him.

The door was open, so I let myself in. There were footsteps in the bedroom as I made myself comfortable on the couch. The steps got closer, and he walked past me, his scent drifting over, along with a good whiff of magic. I didn't think he'd intended the magic part. This was the first time I'd seen him since he'd made the offer to merge magic with me. Or should I say, block someone else's offer? Use, use, use. It was becoming a tune in my head that would play over and over.

It was true that I was using him too. I'd given that a lot of thought last night. Who was using whom more? I still needed him for protection, and I needed those stones. He needed me to get the stones. These were all situations that would end eventually, one way or another. If I was still alive, I could walk away and decide to take my chances alone. He could decide to do the same. If we merged magic? All bets were off. I might be walking away a dull in a Wyrd Blood's body.

He stopped in the middle of the living room, staring my way with a curious look. "What are you thinking?"

It was unnerving how much he could pick up on from my magical energy. That was one skill I needed to learn, like yesterday.

I crossed my arms. "That instead of dawdling around here, we need to be out getting more stones." Stones meant I wouldn't need to merge with anyone.

"I'm working on a location. Have you thought about merging magic?"

I should've known he'd go there. Was he going to stall with the stones so he could get his mitts on my magic?

"Yes. I think it's the solution of last resort. I don't see any need to do that when we might figure something else out, like getting more stones."

Magic swirled so hard and fast that strands of my hair lifted. He stood there, arms crossed, nailing me with his stare. The very first time I'd met him, I'd worried he'd kill me with his magic. I didn't fear that anymore. It wouldn't kill me. I'd felt it wrap around me too intimately, like a shawl or a warm hug. I'd felt other magic I'd clashed with, and I was beginning to know the difference. Even at full blast, his magic wouldn't harm me. There was something weird going on there that I hadn't quite figured out, but I sensed in some place I didn't understand.

"Are you considering binding with Knife?"

I'd told him I wanted stones and his brain went to Knife. The idea someone else would steal one of his toys drove him nuts. That was all I was to him, too: a toy, a pawn, a tool. A girl pumped full of more magic than she knew what to do with, or how to use, that he bossed around. The idea someone else would steal his fun was burning him up, and I liked it.

"Maybe," I said, shrugging. "I stay here; I go to Dorley

with Knife. What's the difference? It's all the same in the end to me."

He didn't move. He didn't speak.

I'd pushed it too far, in his opinion. Had it been that I put Knife on the same level with him? Could his ego not handle that? Maybe that wasn't so bad. My ego had a hard time with a lot of the things he'd done lately. Ryker could use a kick to the ego too, from my perspective.

He was a stone except for the magic near boiling around me. I dragged a breath in and realized it wasn't altogether uncomfortable this time. His magic did strange things to mine. Maybe this wasn't such a good idea. There was tingling going on in places that shouldn't have been feeling anything and had nothing to do with rage.

"Make no mistake about it, you will kill him. His magic isn't strong enough," Ryker said.

"I understood the first time you told me, but you don't really know that for sure." I stood and took a step toward the door. "Are we going to practice today, or should I leave?"

He stared for a second as I wondered if he'd throw me out. Then he tilted his toward the couch. "Sit. We're practicing here."

Shit.

His magic swelled around me.

I hated it.

I loved it, which made me hate it even more. It was like being surrounded by lightning, every fiber alive and sizzling, as if before him I'd been slumbering in a coma for years.

I hated him. If I could leave this place right now, I would.

That was why the worm kept telling me to go. It knew Ryker couldn't help me anyway, and I'd be tortured until I eventually died.

"You're doing it again. Concentrate," he said as he walked in front of the couch, where I sat a sweaty mess.

"What am I doing?" We'd been at this magical tug of war for hours.

"You're pulling my magic to you. You can't control your own. Pulling mine isn't going to help."

We'd been having a battle of wills for hours. I knew what he was looking for. He wanted me to quit, say it was too much and I needed a break. Prove that he was stronger than me. I wouldn't. I'd keep going until he dropped beside me.

"I'm. Not. Pulling." I'd never try to pull anything from him—not his magic, for sure.

I glanced at Burn where he sat at the table, slumped over and sweating with his head propped up on his palm. He was collateral damage, and I didn't feel one lick about it. He deserved a little pain after his manipulation.

Burn had stopped by to grab a book from Ryker, and neither of us had let him leave. I'd said I thought practicing might work better with more Wyrd Bloods around, and Ryker couldn't have jumped on my excuse any faster than if it had been his idea. That was how I knew he was miserable too. We'd see who cracked first.

"Burn, do you feel like I'm pulling?" I asked.

His lower lip jutted out slightly and he shook his head. "No. You're not pulling." His voice came out as if we were torturing him. I guessed we kind of were.

"Burn, you can't afford to be nice," Ryker said.

Burn made a jerking movement that might've been shrug on a better day. "I'm not being nice. I'm not feeling it."

He was so beaten down that he couldn't even lie anymore.

"Maybe it's you?" I crossed my arms and raised a brow, trying to mimic the condescending gesture he'd given me countless times today. I wasn't sure I could pull it off. I wasn't a big enough ass.

"It's not me."

I stood, needing to stretch my legs and catch a little air near the door.

"And I think it is." As I stood, wishing the wind would pick up, I caught sight of a woman heading straight for here. It was one of Knife's people.

Her hips thumped back and forth so much she could've kept beat for a band with them. Her hair swished with every step, swinging luscious black tresses. She dressed like she knew exactly what she had to work with, leathers that barely clung on her hips and fit like they'd been made for her. Her shirt hung open low enough that I could see the ample cleavage, and it was tied high enough to show a flat belly. I watched her approach in my over-sized shirt and baggy leathers that needed a good cleaning.

I stepped away from the door as she neared, trying to avoid a side-by-side comparison that wouldn't fare well for me.

She knocked a second later, poking her head in.

"Ryker?" she asked, fake timidity seeping into her words, a complete opposite to the way she strutted. Sure, like she didn't already know it was him.

"Yes?" he answered, stepping closer.

"I'm Violet. Knife sent me over. Said I might be able to help you with some of the books? I'm a real fast reader." The way she said it made me think that she wasn't only fast at reading and the insinuation was intended for him to pick up on.

Knife. That bastard knew I was here and was screwing with me. It worked. If this were a contest, he'd get first.

For some reason, Ryker glanced back at me, his magic making me warm again.

It shut off suddenly as he turned back to her. "Yeah. Come in."

She did, giving him a look like he was already hers.

Violet wasn't a Wyrd Blood. Actually, the majority of the women I'd seen trailing in and out of his place weren't. Was that the problem with me? He didn't like Wyrd Bloods who had too much magic? He was only into dulls or low levels?

Ryker glanced at me and said, "Let's call it a…" All of his attention was outside.

I walked over to the door to see Sneak running toward us. No one seemed to notice or think it was odd. He was cloaking himself so people didn't know there was a problem.

"Violet, you need to leave," Ryker said, opening the door as Sneak approached.

"What?" she asked. Clearly, this wasn't the way things worked for her.

"Now. I'll call you when I need you."

She stood stunned for a second but finally walked out the door with the help of Ryker's hand on her back.

Sneak rushed in, and no one had to ask him anything. He burst the second he stepped inside. "We've got six dead in the West Corner."

I moved closer, not wanting to miss a word. His tone was hushed, as if he thought someone passing by might hear. He didn't need to bother. The news wouldn't stay quiet for long. This time, even the snowflakes would get rattled.

Ryker's attention was zeroed in on Sneak. "Any signs of the cause of death?"

Sneak's eyes dropped to the ground. He shook his head as he explained, "They were all from the same building but different units. No obvious cause other than a couple of them had the trickle of blood in their ear, but it's been too long for the Boom."

Six? No one had died for days, and now another wave. I agreed with Sneak. It didn't match up to the Boom, or not *only* the Boom. But I'd seen this happen in the Ruined City.

This was some sort of foul play, maybe by the Debt Collector or maybe from Bedlam. Who could tell at this point, and I was sure Ryker had other enemies I hadn't heard of yet.

Ryker, Sneak, and Burn were out the door, and I was right behind them. I'd only made it a block when I saw Ruck running over to catch up with me. I could tell from his face that word had already spread.

"Why aren't you on the tower?"

"I'm on break and just heard. You're going to go check it out?"

I glanced at the guys disappearing from sight and stepped in between Ruck and them. "You can't go. Go back to the tower."

"Why?" He looked up ahead toward where Ryker and the guys were getting farther away. "It's not the Boom. It's been days."

I grabbed both his shoulders. "Do you remember the time the raiding crews came into the Ruins and we tried to fight back?"

His lips parted. "You think…"

"Yes." I gave him a shake in my desperation. "I can't let it kill you." I couldn't lose Ruck and not lose what was left of me with him.

I'd had the misfortune of standing in front of a dull as she'd died. If that was ever Ruck, I wasn't sure I could hang on. "You know how bad it got. Please, stay here and keep your distance from everyone else."

Each word sank in as he remembered with me. A shudder ran through him before he met my eyes, nodding.

He took a step back and said, "Go."

"Thanks." He didn't want to stay behind, but he would do it for me.

I took off running, weaving through people. The guys had moved pretty fast, so they were almost at the barracks by the time I caught up to them. I ran up and then past Ryker, putting a hand to his chest.

His attention immediately turned to me, his eyes landing on my hand. I never touched Ryker intentionally— if you didn't count the times I'd tried to hurt him.

"What?" he asked.

"Clear the area of dulls."

His eyes narrowed. "You sure?"

"No. But knowing what I've seen, it's what I'd do."

He stared for a second more. He lifted his head in the slightest nod before yelling, "I need this area completely cleared, now. I want everyone back at least fifty feet."

Every head swiveled toward Ryker, and then people couldn't scramble away fast enough.

Burn moved closer, knowing something had changed. "What's going on?"

"Everyone here is getting relocated and we're warding off this section." Ryker turned to me, his eyes sending a message that he followed up with a nod away from the area. "I need more Wyrd Blood to handle this."

What he didn't say was that if I stayed, the Wyrd Blood he needed couldn't come too close. I nodded, feeling as if I'd lost a foot of height and my spine had slumped forward.

"Sure." I bit the corner of my lip and turned. I picked up my pace, getting away from the area so that the people who could help, were able to.

17

I scrubbed the soap into my hair, rubbing my scalp and skin raw as I thought of all those people helping while I was showering. I pulled my magic tight to me and felt the heat of it burning and then slammed the soap down. This place had been peaceful for so long. It was hard not to think I had a dark cloud trailing me that was about to wreak havoc on a bunch of dulls who wouldn't know how to handle the chaos while I was rendered useless.

Would there be more dead? Would this be the same as the Ruins, when people started dropping all over the place with no rhyme or reason? Was it retaliation from Bedlam? That at least made sense. The Debt Collector didn't make sense, but that didn't mean it wasn't him.

Someone tripped outside my stall, and I jerked, running suds into my eyes. A second later, I heard Ruck yell my name from somewhere farther down.

I jerked toward the sound, water rushing even more suds straight for my eyeballs. By the time I darted my head out of the curtain, my eyes stung and my vision blurred. The burn in my eyes was nothing compared to the acid burning in my gut.

"What? What's wrong?" I yelled, not sure how far away he was.

I heard his steps and saw his blurry form approach. I held the curtain around my top, not that I had anything Ruck wanted.

He stopped a few feet from me. "Ryker asked me to come and get you."

"So you scream for me like the place is on fire, knowing what's going on?" I rubbed a hand over my eyes, only making matters worse, like I was sudsing them up.

"I can't very well go stall to stall looking for you. What a colossal waste of time."

There weren't that many stalls, and only a few of them were being used. I didn't care enough to argue. Ryker was calling, which meant maybe there was something I could do.

"Give me a second." I ducked back in and toweled off as best I could, struggling to pull leather pants up over damp legs. My hair dripped everywhere and still had soap in it, but I didn't care.

Maybe Ryker had gotten some answers. Maybe the deaths weren't suspicious at all. Maybe all the people who'd died were all newcomers too. They could've been friends who got back from a trip together and had eaten the same poison berries. It could happen.

"What's going on? Any news?" I asked as we headed out of the shower house and I followed Ruck toward Ryker's.

"He's hoping you have answers." Ruck smiled, realizing how screwed that made us.

"Ah, shit."

"Yep." His arms swung as we walked, making a snapping-clapping combo he only did when his nerves were frayed. "I already told him everything I remembered. He wants to quiz you now."

Oh joy. This was going to be a fun night to top off a shit day. Ryker's door was open as we approached. I could hear Knife's voice as we got within a few feet. "My people are here. I deserved to know what we were walking into and what's going on. You should've told me about the other deaths."

"I didn't think it was a problem or I would've told you. Right now, I. Don't. Know. Anymore," Ryker replied.

Ruck put a hand on my arm, halting me. He threw a thumb in the direction of Ryker's, then tilted his head in the other way.

It was a good idea to let them finish before we walked in, but I took a step forward anyway. Ruck didn't realize that there was no buying a few minutes of time. They already knew I was close, if Knife had been telling the truth the other night. They sensed my magic already.

"Bugs, you coming in anytime soon?" Ryker asked, even though he couldn't see me.

Yep, it was true. He knew when I was around, even if it was twenty feet away. Ruck was staring toward Ryker's place, squinting as if he wasn't sure he'd heard him right.

I gave him a tap to his arm and an I'll-fill-you-in-later look. Then I walked the rest of the distance.

I stepped inside, with a reluctant Ruck behind me. Ryker was on one side of the room, with Sneak and Burn. Knife was on the other, a tall blonde beside him. She had hair hanging to her waist and legs for days. She was also packing some magic, but it seemed well controlled.

Still, I hesitated to walk any farther. Knife tilted his head to the blonde. "This is Dezz. She's solid. You should be good."

Dezz? How was I supposed to figure out what she could do with a name like that? And why did he want to tie himself to me when he had a woman like *that*? Was she a total asshole or something? Yeah, I might have more magic, but she was stunning.

"Hey, it's really nice to meet you," Dezz said, and then smiled so easily it was as if her teeth were greased and she actually enjoyed meeting people. No, not an asshole either. Man, people really were magic-hungry.

"You too." I smiled back, my lips moving like they were rubbing over sandpaper. Whatever. I'd tried.

I side-eyed Ryker. Was he staring at Dezz? I wasn't even into women, and I wanted to stare. You couldn't *not* stare if you had eyeballs. Burn and Sneak were, but Ryker was staring at me. Interesting. He'd probably already stared at her for a good while before I'd gotten here. Or he was as magic-hungry as Knife.

"What do you know? Tell me everything you've seen," Ryker said.

I walked farther into the room, taking a deep breath. "Not a lot. I think it's some sort of Boom that's been messed with. If it's like what I've seen, it kills like the Boom, but not as predictable." I shoved the wet hair from my face. "I'm guessing you already know about the raids in the Ruined City looking for Wyrd Blood?"

I'd be shocked if anyone in the room didn't know. The practice of sending out raiding crews to mine for Wyrd Blood in the Ruined City to see if there were any fresh magic to snatch up had been going on for decades. In the dozens of times I'd seen them come, they'd never left the place the way they found it. What little we did have would be looted and stolen. The women raped, and some of the men, too. You were considered lucky if you made it through a raid unscathed.

"Of course," Ryker said, with what sounded like a clean conscience. The other side of the room was quiet. The silence was damning, and I stared at Knife.

He flipped his hand out as he said, "I might've sent a few people, once or twice. It wasn't unusual. Everybody did it but Ryker."

How many times had I been run out of my home? How often had I come back to nothing left, whatever food stores I'd built up gone, or smashed and ruined? He was one of the reasons my crew had gone hungry. I had a bone the size of a dragon's leg to pick with him, and my glare in his direction made it clear we'd be doing just that after this emergency was handled.

"I'll help you kill him later, but right now I need the rest of this story," Ryker said.

Ryker was probably happy I was pissed off. Anything that kept me from merging with Knife was another step in his direction, so *he* could use me. Still, I put it all aside, since we had people dropping dead right now. I'd add to the body count once I knew that the innocent would be okay.

I crossed my arms over my chest, thinking back to the details that were still fresh. "Most of the time, we didn't get much notice. But this one time, a scout spotted a raiding group heading toward us days out. All of the different crews, all the people who lived in the Ruins, bonded together. Didn't matter if you stabbed someone's brother the week before, screwed their sister, and stole their goat—for that small span of time, we were in it together.

"We laid a trap a few miles outside the city, right where the road narrows and the forest edges you in. We ambushed them with everything we had: arrows, swords, knives. They were better armed, but we were hungry for vengeance and had the numbers. They lost so many soldiers that they turned and ran. It was payback for years of torment and loss."

I walked to the table and perched on the corner as I thought of what had come next. "Like idiots, we celebrated for two days straight. The Ruins had never been so joyous. We shared food and drink with each other as if we had an endless supply. We talked of how we'd scared them off. We stupidly thought that word would spread and no one would mess with us again." I slid back and perched a heel on the edge, bringing my knee up to my chest. "We daydreamed about building our own country, purely democratic. We'd all vote to see who would run it. We'd be the first seed in a new world."

If Ryker or Knife were bothered by what I was saying, they didn't let on as I told the story. I was so lost in my memories that maybe I didn't notice. "We were young and stupid and never saw it coming. Five days later, the sickness struck. At first it was only a few, and then there was a lag of time. We thought we were safe. But then it came back, over and over again. I never knew how many had died. It was impossible to count, since so many fled."

I pointed to Ruck where he'd gotten comfortable on the couch. "We used to talk about how the Boom had found a way to not only kill a body, but kill a soul. Back then, I'd thought maybe we were crazy and paranoid, that it hadn't been them." I looked about the room, knowing everyone understood but feeling the need to make sure I hammered it home. "Seeing what's happening here, I think it's the same and it's being organized."

Ryker stepped a few paces closer. "We don't know that

it's not a mutated strand of the Boom, but it needs to be looked into. Do you know where that particular raiding party came from?"

"They didn't exactly fly banners or write their names across their chests." I looked to Knife. "Did you now?"

He straightened. "Did I send a few people out from time to time to see if I could recruit a couple Wyrd Blood? Yes. I'm guilty. Did some of my people get out of hand sometimes? They might've, but it wasn't on my orders. But I don't mess with biological warfare."

My gut said to believe him. I tilted my head slightly in Knife's direction, giving him a silent *we'll see*. He'd better be telling the truth, or I'd use that dragon bone to stab him in the chest.

He nodded toward me, as if to reassure me of his honesty.

"How long ago did it happen?" Ryker asked.

"Two winters ago," I replied.

"Burn, have someone go over our ledgers. I remember word reaching us about a bad outbreak of the Boom in the Ruined City around then. See what details we might have on the comings and goings of nearby countries at that time." Ryker's attention switched back to me. "I want you to worm it. See what that comes up with. We need whatever answers we can get."

Right then, I felt like I had a dozen worms all squirming around my stomach. There would be no worming anything. It was only a matter of telling him now or later. I'd like to think he'd lose interest, but he wouldn't. He was a leave-no-stone-unturned type, give it everything you have or don't bother. Normally, I liked that about him.

Knife asked, "What's 'worm it'?"

Ryker's brow dropped slightly as he watched me, and I

knew he was already questioning my lack of reply. "She juices worms with magic and uses that as a divination tool. It's unreliable but better than nothing."

I turned to Knife. "He's right. It's not a reliable source of information."

Ryker leaned a shoulder against the wall, seemingly relaxed to the unobservant. "It's not *reliable*, but we should do it anyway."

Knife and Dezz moved toward the back of the room, farther away from Ryker. So did Burn and Sneak. I saw Dezz begin to fan her face, and then Burn leaned over to Sneak and say something too low for me to hear. They were talking about the magic that was starting to bounce off the walls. I swear, it was happening more and more often with Ryker. Or maybe it was something that was happening when our magic commingled? Either way, everyone noticed it but Ryker.

"I don't think it's a good idea after Sinsy," I said, hopping down from the table in case I needed to exit the room quick.

"You used to worm it every day, sometimes twice. Now you won't do it when we need it?" he asked, stepping closer to the door.

"It's not reliable." I crossed my arms and walked around the table. "Hasn't worked out in the past. It's not a good idea." I wasn't telling Ryker about the promise I'd made to Marra. He'd tell me it was stupid. I wasn't sure why he'd call it that, but I was sure of it.

Ruck let out a loud groan that sounded like it would last for days. "Oh, for magic's sake, tell him already."

I shot him a look. I would've jumped over the table and planted a palm over his mouth, but I was pretty sure he'd already screwed me.

"What are you talking about?" Ryker's attention snapped

to Ruck, as if it were a race to stare him down. Our stare-downs were greatly different. Mine was more of a delivery. *Shut the hell up.* I didn't need to glance at Ryker to know his was more of a *fess up before I make you.*

I groaned, much less dramatically than Ruck, but definitely as aggravated. I rested my arms on the back of a chair as I watched my friend blow my game skyward.

"Are you going to tell him?" Ruck asked, giving me a last chance.

"I wouldn't want to steal your thunder," I said.

Ruck ignored the tone and turned to Ryker. "Marra made her promise not to worm anymore."

18

"Everyone out but Bugs," Ryker said.

I turned my head to the side, letting out a slow sigh. While I was still trying to figure out why they should stay, they were all scrambling out the door.

"Real nice," I said to Ruck as he walked past me. Big snitch. What was he thinking? He didn't bother telling me as he walked out with the rest of them. One by one, they left until it was only Ryker and I.

"You really agreed to not worm?"

He was still clinging to the hope that Ruck was making it up. I could tell by the way his eyes went deeper and the fact that it was an actual question. The rhetorical ones had a different tone altogether.

There was a slight chance he wouldn't be a stubborn ass about this. The odds were slim, but I was going to be optimistic for one time in my life.

"Marra was afraid I might get bad information that would hurt someone else." I was extrapolating a lot from what she'd gestured, but I was sure I was correct. I knew her. She was only worried about others.

Ryker turned and paced the room for a second, before stopping by the door. He still had his arms crossed. He glanced at me, shook his head, and looked outside.

This was why I wasn't optimistic. Shit never worked out. Of course he couldn't understand. He used people. I didn't. "I owe her. She was one of my—she *is* one of my people."

His jaw shifted. "You owe her nothing. If it weren't for you, she'd be dead with her sister from starvation."

"I asked the worm if we should cross the river. Sinsy died. It wasn't an absurd request." That I had to defend it was even worse. Did he really think I wanted to not worm? My fingers twitched to dig for a worm almost hourly.

"She might've died anyway. She could've died when we got back, or if she'd never come here, but no one forced her to do anything. They were all her decisions. You need to forget Marra. Something's snapped inside her. I've seen it enough to know."

"She hasn't snapped. She lost her sister. She's in mourning like anybody would be, and she'll get better."

"You're wrong."

"Why are you letting her stay, then? Well? If that's what you really think?" Ryker thought out every angle to the minutiae. Then every consequence beyond that. I respected it, even if I didn't have the patience for it myself. If he truly believed what he said, he could've booted Marra out of here.

He shrugged.

Sure, my life was supposed to be an open book, and yet I couldn't get a straight answer to a simple question.

He turned and walked toward me. "If you want to survive, you use whatever you have. You used to know that."

The inference to when I used to raid chuggers was painfully obvious and also a much different scenario. "We would've starved."

"What about the lives at stake right now? Don't they matter?"

I paced toward the door. So much for being reasonable. We weren't going to come to terms on this one, and the more I talked to him, the worse I felt and the more I feared he was right. "I promised."

"A promise to someone who doesn't deserve it, turns her back on you, and wants you to walk away from one of your gifts."

"Marra didn't turn her back on me," I shot back, but the words still hit me like a one-two punch.

I walked out the door, not wanting a reply. All I needed now were a few minutes away from him.

Everyone was meandering outside of Ryker's, probably having heard a good chunk of the conversation, not that I cared. They could've stayed inside with us if they'd wanted.

Knife stepped in front of me before I got more than a few steps. "I need you to know I meant everything I said in there. They only had orders to make offers to any Wyrd Blood they found, and I don't mess around with the Boom."

"Don't worry, you're still in the running," I told him, words laced with acid. I would've said anything to get away from him at that moment.

I walked around him, and Ruck straightened off the building he'd been leaning against.

"We need to talk," he said as he caught up to me.

I was done talking to everyone at the moment. It wouldn't be easy to lose Ruck, so I dug in instead. "Let's talk about how you gave me up in there."

He didn't shoot back at me the way I expected. The long exhale of breath didn't bode well. "There's some things you need to know."

His steps slowed and mine did as well, even as I knew

this wasn't going to be a talk I wanted to hear. He nodded toward his room, which was closest to us, and started in that direction.

He didn't speak as we walked, marinating his words. Ruck was a shoot-from-the-hip type. Nothing stewed with him.

He opened the door and gestured to a table and chairs he'd set up in the corner. "Maybe we should sit."

I was going to need to sit? I settled in, knowing this day was about to get even worse. "Is this about what just happened with Ryker and me not wanting to worm? Do you disagree too? Is that why you gave me up?

"Ryker can't understand the bond we all have. I didn't make a random promise to a stranger. This is Marra. She hasn't turned her back on us. She's *grieving*. She'll communicate when she's ready. Everyone needs to cut her some slack." And if I had to remind them of that every day of the week, I would.

He slumped into the chair across from me and his fingers drummed a morose tune, full of nerves. "That's the thing: you don't really know everything either."

"What are you talking about?"

His eyebrows lifted as he stared at the table. "Marra didn't really turn her back on *us*. Just *you*."

My brain froze. That was the only way to describe it. When it kicked into gear a few seconds later, Ruck still hadn't explained.

"Why would you say that?"

Ruck rolled his lips inward, biting them as his head bowed. He took a couple of huffing breaths. "Because it's true. She'll communicate with me. Or, at least, she would. I'm the one not talking to her."

If Ryker had kicked me in the gut, this was like taking a

boulder and smashing me upside the head. I couldn't compute what Ruck was saying. "What?"

He nodded, meeting my eyes and then keeping them there.

He rubbed his palms on his pants. "You're actually the only one she won't communicate with."

"Burn and Sneak? Ryker? None of them talk to her."

He nodded. "By their choice. You're the only one *she* won't communicate with." He bit his lip as his chest rose.

By the time he was done preparing himself to let go of the words he feared would hurt me, his silence had already slayed me to the bone. I straightened my spine and prepared for what I knew he'd say.

He drummed his fingers once more before he said, "She blames you, and only you, for Sinsy."

I stayed quiet, stoic even on the surface as I felt brittle, on the verge of cracking, inside. I'd told myself over and over that she didn't really blame me. She needed time. It made sense. Right? Except it was all bullshit.

I kept my shell together even as my insides were shattering.

Ruck leaned forward. "I told Marra it was everyone's choice to go with the worm's decision, but she didn't care. I told her how many times you'd tried to get us to leave, but she didn't want to hear that either. She'd decided you were to blame and wouldn't hear anything else."

At least I knew why he'd given me up to Ryker. He'd agreed with him that Marra didn't deserve my loyalty.

"Are you sure she's blaming me?" Marra didn't talk. Miscommunications were easy when only one party was speaking. He could've seen her look a certain way and assumed she blamed me. Maybe she wasn't talking to me because I was like another sister to her, and the only close female, so she was pulling back?

"Please believe me when I say I'm sure."

I raked a hand through my hair. "Okay." Whatever proof he had, I wasn't sure I needed to hear it. "Why aren't her and Burn speaking?"

Burn and I were friendly, but nowhere near close enough for him to turn his back on Marra for me. I'd gotten the impression more than once he'd favored her, and the stares I'd seen him give her recently had only confirmed it.

"Ryker noticed that Marra wasn't talking to you. He stopped acknowledging her after that, and I think Burn did the same out of loyalty to Ryker, and I think you. There might've been guilt as well, since him and Sneak feel partly to blame for Sinsy's death. They didn't agree with you taking the brunt."

I rested my elbows on my knees and dropped my head in my hands, buying myself a couple of seconds to keep the burning I was feeling in my eyes from materializing into proof on my cheeks.

"Should I have not told you?" he asked.

"There was a time that we were all like family. I'd kill and rob for you guys. When Tiger left, that wasn't the biggest deal. He was more like a distant cousin no one liked much."

Ruck laughed, and so did I for a second.

"Fetch hurt a little more, but I respected his decision," I said. "But then Sinsy died and Marra won't speak to me and you won't speak to her. I just didn't see this coming. I thought we were all tighter than that. I thought we'd die for each other."

"It's still you and me, you know that." Ruck gave me a

light punch in the arm. If we hugged, it would be too much. Neither of us wanted to make this worse than it was.

He leaned back in his chair. "You never see change coming. It just plucks you up and drops you somewhere else. Sometimes the ride is fast and invigorating. Sometimes so slow and painful all you want to do is get off by any means necessary. If you hang on, sooner or later, the ride brings you somewhere else. You just have to ride the sucker out."

I stood, shaking off the sting and refusing to drag this out any longer. She blamed me. I blamed me. Was there a big difference?

"I gotta get going," I said.

He stood too. "I need to relieve Ben. Ryker pulled me off duty too, and he probably needs the break."

We walked out of his place, and I hit him in the arm this time. "Thanks for still talking to me. My numbers are getting a little iffy."

"I kind of have to, or who would you have left?"

We both laughed, even if it was forced, before heading our own way. Ruck and I had been together the longest, since we were both kids, not even teens yet, surviving however we had to. He was my rock and would always be.

19

I walked the largest and busiest road of the Valley, taking the temperature of the place. More dead. That would scare even the firmest of snowflakes if they had a lick of sense.

Apparently some of their snow must be melting off. For a nice evening, there should've been more people about, but most were tucked inside. The few that were out moved briskly and left a buffer between them and anyone who passed.

I kept walking and didn't stop until I got to the place where the latest had died. The entire area was cordoned off. There was a sign hanging from bright red ribbons with a word on it that even I knew. *Out.*

I slipped closer and waited until no one was looking before I slipped under the tape. I'd taken note of which units held the dead when I'd come here earlier today, and headed inside before anyone caught sight of me.

The place looked normal enough. Neat bed tucked into the corner, a table with some writing elements lined up, and some hooks on the wall where the person's clothing hung.

There was no blood to be found and no body to look at. I went to the next units, all unlocked, and found similar scenes. I didn't touch anything as my fingers twitched and I imagined the feel of a worm in my hand. I left with as many questions as I'd arrived with.

I walked for a while until I found myself in front of Marra's door. I wasn't optimistic, but then, I never really was. A glass half-empty could be rationed. A glass half-full would be gulped, and then you'd be really thirsty the next day. And as I'd mentioned before, optimism hadn't worked out so well in the past.

But maybe I could talk to her and she'd agree. I'd explain how it was important. She'd want to do everything she could to help the situation. She was mourning. Not psychotic.

I dropped my head and closed my eyes, running the words through my mind a few more times before I got up the nerve to knock. The door swung open too quickly for her not to have seen me standing there. Her eyes were hard, and my pulse ratcheted up. She was my friend. This shouldn't be so hard.

"Have you heard about the people dying?"

She gave me a stingy single nod. I'd known her for years. We'd grown up together. I'd considered her my crew, my family. Now she stared at me as if I were a stain on her clothes.

This was not going well, but I was here now. I had to try.

"I need you to release me from my promise—"

The door slammed in my face, hitting my toes. The shock hit a lot harder.

She hadn't heard me out. If she'd heard me out, she'd understand. I needed to try harder.

I leaned close to the door with my palm flat on it.

"Marra, I know why you don't want me to worm, but we need to use every tool available that might help shed light on things."

She didn't respond, and I pressed an ear to the wood and heard her moving around inside.

"Marra, this isn't about us."

She still didn't come to the door. I caught a flash of movement by her window and rushed over there. She was standing in front of it, in front of me, but not acknowledging that. A cloth dropped over the window, blocking me.

I wanted to throw a stone through it, but I didn't. I walked away and headed back to my place, fingers playing with the edge of my shirt instead of a worm.

There was a strange little man with a mostly bald head, except for green tufts of hair sticking out above his ears, lingering in the shadows of my building. He looked fearful someone would see him. It didn't seem to matter to him that people were noticing him and yet no one appeared to care he was there. He looked about as dangerous as the clipboard in his hand.

He stepped forward as I approached my door.

"Bugs?" His glasses slid down a long nose, stopping on the bulbous end.

I nodded.

"I'm so happy to meet you!"

"Who are you?" It wasn't the nicest reaction, but polite society was about to go to hell anyway if people kept dying. I was definitely not the person who would keep it afloat. I was too tired to care, and my day had gone too badly.

"I'm Bertie, the burier."

"You're the burier? You collect the dead?"

He smiled, showing off a mouthful of very white, pointy teeth. "You've never met a miner before?"

"No."

"We're an obscure lot of folk; stay to ourselves mostly."

I nodded.

"I'm sure you're wondering why I'm here."

"A little." My hand was on my door, and all I wanted to do was crash on my bed.

"I need to get your information, like your tree and such."

"My tree?"

The sky that had been threatening to rain all day decided to open up and dump it all at once. I opened my door and waved a hand for Bertie the burier to follow me. I didn't want company, but I wanted to be soaked less.

"I'm sorry, but I don't have anything to drink or eat," I said, not really sorry at all. I walked to my table, struck a match, and lit the lamp. Then I collapsed on my bed as if I were alone.

"That's quite all right. I just need to get this paperwork filled out. Considering what's been going on, I thought it pertinent to update all the records and make sure the new inhabitants were listed." He looked at his clipboard, pencil in hand. "Do you have a surname?"

"No. It's just Bugs." I hadn't uttered my last name in a long time.

He hummed, his pencil hovering. "Well, we don't have any other Bugs, so I guess that's not a huge problem. If we get any more, I might have to number you."

I threw my arm over my eyes. "Number away."

He heard him scribble a mark on his paper. "And what shall your tree be?"

"What tree are you talking about?"

"When people die here, they're laid to rest in the Grove of Souls, with a tree marking their grave. I need to know what tree you'd like. Obviously we can't always accommodate every wish, but we try our best."

He flipped through some sheets, and I squinted in his direction. He was shoving a piece of paper at me.

"Would you like to see a list of trees that do well here?"

I waved it off. "You can put me down for whatever you want."

He scratched a green shadow on his chin. "I don't know about that. They're supposed to be chosen by the deceased."

"Okay, fine, let me see the list."

He held out the sheet. Instead of taking it, I pointed to words that meant nothing to me.

He looked it over. "The Whimsy Willow. Nice choice. That tree lives to be seven or eight hundred years old and is said to have been created by fairies. Of course, since it's a new tree, we haven't established if the fairies' boast is accurate about its life span. Either way, they'll be happy to have another planted, and they're already so happy with you to begin with. I think they're running a little short on space in the grove right now."

"Fairies? You're saying fairies made a tree and they're living in the grove? I thought fairies didn't come this far north?" I'd always known fairies existed, but I'd never seen one. Then again, they were rare in these parts of the world.

"Normally they don't. I think they like Ryker. You should come to the grove in summer. The Whimsy Willow nearly glows with the nests of fairies then.

"Well, thanks for your time. I've got to go find some person named Ruck now."

He winked, dropped his clipboard to his side, and headed toward the door.

"He'll be on the third watchtower."

He nodded. "Thank you and have a magical evening!"

"Sure."

I grabbed the book on my table, knowing I wouldn't find sleep for a while. I flipped it open.

Magic, big word, gibberish, gibberish, gibberish, pulls tight together. Two of a soul are marked...

This book from Burn was near torture. Reading when you only understood ever other word was rough. They needed to make these books with more pictures.

Didn't they know how many people couldn't read? Not like I was the only one. You couldn't throw a stone in the Ruins without hitting someone who was worse off than I was now. At least it would solve the sleeping problem. I could barely keep my eyes open.

20

B reakfast wasn't going well. Even though there hadn't been any more dead found since last night, the place was half-empty. The snowflakes were officially melting, and that was only the start of the problems.

Ryker wasn't speaking, but he was doing plenty of staring, of an accusatory variety, while sending out magic in waves. Burn was sweating. Sneak was pulling at the front of his shirt, trying to ventilate.

The rate of chewing was accelerating by the bite. Burn was going to start swallowing chunks whole soon. I scanned the room, since it was either that or watch Ryker watching me. I wasn't sure if he was angry that I hadn't committed to merging magic with him or that I wouldn't worm. Most likely both.

Ruck was in the showers, running late. Of all the mornings he didn't rush in here for food like a starving man, it had to be today.

I found myself staring at the door, since there weren't too many other places left to look. No one at the table was safe. Marra sat with Bugs and Ruck 2.0 in the far corner, and after last night, I really didn't want to see her. That left the area by the door, so I spotted Knife the second he walked in.

He looked at our table and met eyes with me. I gave him a nod, hoping he'd take it for the invitation it was. He wasn't my favorite person at the moment, but I'd take my chances on anyone who might be able to break up the tension at the table. He nodded back, leaving me clueless as to whether he'd come over.

I made the mistake of looking Ryker's way, my eyes getting stuck on him as if his stare had glue.

What? Was I not allowed to invite people to sit at the table now either? Would that be added to my list of transgressions and general fuck-ups? I crossed my arms and forced myself to pull my gaze from his. I'd tear my eyes out and throw them out the door if I had to.

Knife smiled and headed toward our table. Without asking, he placed his dish down beside mine, took the seat to my left, and reclined, using the back of my chair as an armrest. He picked up a piece of bacon.

"What's on the agenda for everyone today?" he asked between bites.

The heat from the magic spiked to boiling. So much for cutting the tension. Ryker shouldn't have bothered inviting Knife here if he hated him this much. Although he was more calculating than he was emotional. If he had emotions at all.

"Probably rolling around in the mud," I said.

Sneak fanned his shirt a couple more times.

"Violet, why don't you come sit with us?"

At Ryker's invitation, my head jerked to see Violet swing around so fast that her enormous breasts almost didn't make it along with the rest of her. I hadn't realized she was in the food building, let alone nearby. I wasn't sure how I'd missed the drumbeat of her hips. She stopped suddenly but didn't move or say something for a few seconds.

She glanced around her, as if unsure Ryker had been speaking to her. "You sure?"

Really? She'd pretty much offered to sleep with him at first sight and she didn't think she could sit at his table? If it wasn't the last chair available, I might've pulled it out for her myself. Someone needed to have a talk with this girl, possibly me.

But none of that was going to happen today, because it was the last chair and Ruck would be here any minute. That made it Ruck's. That's the way it always was, and Ryker knew it. He might've been annoyed Knife was sitting here, but he wasn't making a point with my boy's chair.

I leaned across the back of the last chair.

"Sorry. This is Ruck's seat. It's nothing personal, but he sits with me for breakfast every morning and he's due any second."

Her smile drooped like five-pound weights had been added to both corners of her mouth.

I gave her one of my awkward smiles, trying to soothe the sting. Violet, other than offering herself to Ryker, didn't seem like a bad chick.

"Why don't you find a free chair and pull it up," I said, trying to be diplomatic.

Violet took a step back and looked around.

"Stay right there, Violet. The princess is going to give you the free chair," Ryker said.

Violet took a half step forward, but was chewing on her lower lip and glancing at all the tables with open seats as if she'd prefer to not sit with either of us anymore. Bright girl. She should run while she could.

My jaw locked, and I turned to address the big, arrogant

problem. "First off, where do you get off calling me a princess? I'm not. Second, give her yours if she needs a seat, loverboy." Loverboy? If I wasn't so annoyed with him, I might've been embarrassed for myself. "Princess" demanded retaliation, but that was the lamest comeback ever uttered.

Sneak had stopped fanning himself for a second to look at me cross-eyed. Knife groaned, as if I'd be getting life tips later on.

"You are a princess. You think everything should go your way."

He was so delusional that he didn't see reality anymore. "And it doesn't because you call all the shots. Everything is *your* decision."

"I'm glad you're realizing that."

Knife shifted in his chair. "Ryker—"

"Stay out of it, Knife," Ryker said. "If I want Violet to have the chair, she'll have the chair. It's *mine* and I say who gets it."

Even the chair was his? Seriously? And it better be the chair. If that was a hint at something else, it was going to be even worse.

"Is that supposed to mean something? Why don't you just spit it out?" Knife asked.

I turned my attention to Knife. "Thank you, but this isn't your fight."

Knife threw a hand up and leaned back. "Not so sure about that, but fine."

I turned all my attention back to Ryker. Our magic was churning against each other's. The candles in the room flared and you could smell electricity in the air, as if a bolt of lightning was about to shoot down from the ceiling and char us both, leaving our ashes behind. I didn't give a fuck, and from the feel of the buzz, neither did he.

I leaned closer to Ryker. "You're right: you have perfect control of your magic and you own everything. You're always right and the world should fall at your feet the way all the girls in this place do." I glanced at Violet and said, "Nothing personal."

She shrugged. I kind of liked this girl.

"Yes, the girls do. Bother you much?" He arched a brow as if he already knew the answer.

"Not even a little." I stood, my chair falling back. "You know what? You're right. It's all yours and you make all the calls. But not for me. I don't need your shit. I don't need your food. I don't need your room."

"Really? Where do you plan on going?" he asked, leaning back and crossing his arms.

"Wherever I want," I said as I walked past him.

I didn't look back as I left. I didn't look to the sides to see anyone's reaction to the massive public fight. I kept walking, eyes forward, hoping he wasn't going to tackle me to the ground before I made it out the door.

He didn't, and I kept walking, right until I got to the border. Then I stopped, looked up, and let out a scream, because I knew I was far enough away that hopefully no one would hear.

I couldn't leave. Leaving was death. I wouldn't leave without Ruck anyway. Plus, I didn't know what would happen if I did. I'd lost the challenge to Ryker and I was stuck. Plus, he'd know the second I crossed his ward, so how far would I get if he didn't want to let me go? And most of all, I needed as many stones as I could get.

I dropped to the ground and planted myself. I grabbed a handful of dirt as I sat there, knowing I couldn't ask the worm what to do. I'd made a promise. Plus the worm had already told me what to do many times before. Leave here.

Truth be told, even if I could worm it, and it told me to leave, I probably wouldn't. This place had become my home. I'd rather stage a rebellion and get rid of Ryker than leave.

21

I made my way back to my room and piled up all the books I'd collected since I'd been here, along with my change of clothes and a few other things I'd accumulated. I grabbed the corners of the blanket, slung it over my back, and headed out. I didn't look back. After all, this room wasn't mine. I couldn't afford to miss it.

Ruck hadn't shown for breakfast while I'd been there, but I knew he'd be back at his room afterward to crash. Since he'd been doing the night shift, he'd become nocturnal.

He found me first, halfway to his place. His furrowed brow meant word of the big blow-up had already echoed out fast enough that he'd heard.

"What's with the stuff?" He raised his voice as I weaved in between people and continued to his place.

"I need you to keep my stuff safe for me." I walked into his room and dumped every possession I had on his bed.

Ruck followed in and stopped in front of his bed beside me, his head tilted downward. "What happened to your room? I heard you guys were fighting, but I didn't know he kicked you out."

"He didn't kick me out, but everything is Ryker's, haven't you heard? Every. Single. Thing." I moved closer, my shoulder brushing his. "I don't know where to put my stuff."

"I'm guessing you aren't going to sleep there either?"

I shrugged. "Not my room. It's his, like this entire universe, probably."

And then Ruck did Ruck. He leaned down and picked up the books and brought them to his shelf on the other side of the room. He lined them up on the empty half, opposite his things.

After he finished with that, he took my sleep shirt and my spare set of clothes and brought them over to his hooks. He took his clothes, doubled them up on one hook, and then hung mine on the other.

He turned back to me. "You can sleep here. It'll be like old times, except better, because this roof doesn't have a hole and we don't have to fend off other crews. Plus, even though the food has taken a nosedive lately, it's still better than hollyhoney."

"I can't crash here. This place is his too."

"He said it was mine. *His* words. If it's my room, I get to say who stays in it."

It seemed like a technicality. But it was a valid one.

"Thanks." I dropped my head onto his shoulder. "If I weren't so emotionally scarred and could still love, you'd be the man for me."

He swung an arm around my shoulders. "I know you're a scorned woman and all, but to be clear, I can't be your rebound. Little Ruck won't perform on command, and he's been pretty adamant about not liking vaginas."

My shoulders shook a little. "That's okay. I've seen *Little Ruck*. I'm not sure he'll be missed."

"If I didn't find your girl parts revolting, you'd be the one." He squeezed my shoulders a little too hard. "By the way, don't even think of leaving here without me."

The levity of the moment crashed and burned. "I can't. You know I can't." I had Bones waiting in the wings ready to snatch me up, and I didn't have a plan.

"At least you aren't being totally stubborn and stupid."

"I have my moments of wisdom, but there's always tomorrow."

I PEEKED AROUND THE CORNER OF THE BUILDING, MAKING SURE Ryker wasn't lingering outside his place, before making a quick path to Sneak's. Banging on the door, I hoped he answered soon.

He did.

"What's up?" He looked beyond me as if he expected someone else to be with me.

"You have all the magic books, right?" I tried to see into his place. It was messy with stacks of the books piled up all around. "There," I said, pointing past him. "Those are them, aren't they?"

"Why?"

I faked left, knowing he'd tried to block me, and then shot right. He grabbed for me, and I sent him a shock.

He immediately released me, waving his hand. "Damn. I forgot you could do that."

That was what I'd counted on. I made my way to the stacks as he stood back and watched. I squatted down, trying to read spines the best I could. "Why are you trying to keep these from me? I'm the one who needs them."

"Because you can't read that well, and we need them read," he said, coming closer.

"I'm better. I've been practicing a lot."

History? Was that what that word was? There were a lot of books with that one. Would that have what I needed? It might lead to the history of those stones, but I doubted that was in most. I'd never heard of them until Ryker told me about them, and I knew I wasn't the only one.

"Here," Sneak said, walking to another stack of books on the other side of his living room. "These were the first ones we went through, since they held the best chance of finding out about the Debt Collector. No one found anything, but give them a try."

I wasn't sure how I felt about getting the seconds. On one hand, they'd already been read. On the other, I knew people and how they slacked. "Give me the best ones."

He looked over the pile and methodically plucked out four from the three-foot stack. "Here."

"Thanks."

There was something else Sneak was in charge of gathering intelligence on, and I glanced around his place. There was nothing obvious lying about the living area, but maybe it was somewhere else. If his place was laid out like Ryker's, the bathroom would be off the bedroom. "Could I use your—"

"No. You've gotten all you are going to get." He walked to the door. "You try it, I'll tackle you to the ground, and I don't care how badly you zap me."

"Fine. Fair enough." I took my books, only pausing to make sure Ryker wasn't lingering outside, before hightailing it out of there.

I CLIMBED UP TO THE TOP OF THE TOWER A FEW HOURS LATER. Magical Theory was tucked into the front of my pants, and there was an hour of sunset left.

Ruck looked over. "Is that a book, or are you just happy to see me?"

I stopped short. "That might've been the stupidest joke I've ever heard."

He shrugged. "They can't all be winners."

I dropped beside Ruck. "Your good joke average is dropping."

He ignored my jab and looked at what was in my hand. "Ugh. Not the boring book again. I told you I was done with that when you tried to shove it at me this morning."

"I know. You also told me that same thing before you left for work tonight. Do you remember what I said to you?" I gave him my best teacher look. Whenever I was eaves-dropping on the school and the teacher gave them this look, they all went silent and did whatever the teacher wanted.

His shoulders dropped as he said, "That I'm basically your brother."

"And?" I asked, laying the teacher tone on thick.

"That means I have to do what you tell me." He held out his hand for the book. I knew he would've anyway, even without the spiel, but I liked the practice.

I flipped to the page I'd left off at and then placed it in his hand, stabbing the spot I wanted him to read. "I can't figure out what that second chunk means."

"You watch, I'll read."

I scanned the perimeter as he scanned the page. Ruck understood more than me. He'd had a few more years with a family before things had turned bad for him. Still, neither of us had led an academic life.

"Magic of well suit pulls tight?" Ruck asked, reading the first line, his words stilted.

"What does that mean?"

"I don't know. Let me read the rest. Sometimes it's the stuff around the important words that makes it understandable," he explained as if he were an old hand at this sort of thing.

I kept looking out while he read some more.

"This section is on magical mating," he said.

"Okay. Just tell me what it's trying to say."

"I think the person who wrote this believed that sometimes magic that produces a good line pulls two people together. He's comparing it to a known phenomenon with dulls. He says dulls are attracted to other dulls because they can smell a good genetic match, whether they realize it or not. Looks like with Wyrd Blood, he thinks the magic does it instead, and it's a stronger pull."

He handed the book to me and went back to watching the border. Was that what was happening with Ryker and I? Did our magic want us to get together to pop out little magical babies?

I flopped back on the platform and rested an arm under my head to watch the sunset. "That doesn't make any sense. Ryker told me that most of the time Wyrd Blood magic seems to thin out through the generations until it pops up, like with me. Most Wyrd Blood give birth to dulls, and dulls are the ones who have the strongest Wyrd Bloods. Everything I've seen says he's right."

"Why don't you ask him what he thinks once you start talking to him again, because you know you're going to have to."

I shot up. "Why do you like him so much?"

"I don't know. I get a good read from him. He's got all this magic and for the most part doesn't give a shit what anyone does. He didn't raid the Ruins when he could've of. He—"

"I gotta go." I grabbed my book and stood, ready to leap from the tower if I had to hear how good Ryker was.

I tucked the book back into my pants, freeing my hands up as I turned to descend the ladder.

"Hey, one more thing: have you noticed anyone staring at you weird?"

I paused, one foot on a rung. "No more than usual. Why do you ask?"

He shrugged as if he couldn't quite explain it either. "I don't know. Sometimes when I'm up here, I'll catch sight of you, and then I see people looking at you from afar. It happens a lot."

"They probably think I'm not only Wyrd, but weird. See yah later."

"See you."

22

This was the second dinner being served, and I was one of the last to show up in the food building, by design. There wouldn't be much food left—or many people. I swung the door open to see the delay had worked. I'd get in, get some grub, and get out.

I grabbed a plate and made my way down a mostly empty line. There were only a handful of people eating at the tables and only a few guys in front of me, none of whom I recognized.

I grabbed the last slice of meat left in the tray and a wilted piece of lettuce. I glanced ahead. Two guys that had come with Knife's crew were left, but there were four biscuits to be had. I'd make myself a nice sandwich.

I inched forward, as the slowpoke in front of me didn't seem to like to use his legs much. I wondered when the last time he'd broken past a slow stroll. Plate in hand, I stared at empty dishes while I waited.

He finally moved, and I reached over to grab a biscuit. The basket was empty. I went up on tiptoes, to see if my biscuit had rolled out of sight into the corner. It hadn't. I turned and saw Sluggo turning, three biscuits on his plate.

"Hey!" I said loud enough that Sluggo turned.

I stepped forward, making sure he knew I was addressing him. "You just took the last three biscuits when you saw me standing behind you. You *stole* my biscuit."

He looked down at his plate, then at me. "I was in line first. They're my biscuits."

Pick your fights wisely. I'd lived by that motto my entire life, and it had kept me alive. But damn, Sluggo had chosen the wrong day to steal my piece of dough. I'd been pushed around too much in the last few weeks and I was ready to hit back.

"If you don't give me a biscuit, I'll be giving you an ass kicking. Your choice."

The two guys that had been in line with him were giving me the side-eye. I was a small package, but I was making pretty big threats against a man twice my size. I'd deliver on them, too, magic or not. I had some skills that went beyond Wyrd Blood and plenty of years to size up my competition. I'd run miles around Sluggo before he'd know I was hitting him.

He handed his plate to one of his buddies, with my biscuit still held hostage, and stepped closer, as if I hadn't noticed his superior size that was as doughy as my missing bread.

"I'm not giving you my biscuits."

Sluggo's pudgy fingers approached me; all the time I prayed to the gods of everything magical that he'd do it, he'd give me the excuse I wanted. The offending digits gave me a nudge backward.

And it was on.

I grabbed his wrist with both hands, giving him a nice

sting as I did. I spun, using his momentum shock to help me pull him forward. He landed on his belly, and I fell forward with him, digging a knee into his spine and giving him another zap. My back was to his buddies, but a glance over my shoulder showed they were still too surprised to move.

"You going to hand over that biscuit now?" I asked.

"What the fuck—"

His words turned into a yelp as I gave him another series of zaps. "That doesn't sound like it's going to be the correct answer. Want to try again?" I centered my weight into one spot and twisted. Every time he tried to push up, I zapped him again. Damn, I could do this all night.

I felt the magic as soon as it preceded the man into the room. The air sizzled around me, and I knew my fun was over before he spoke a word.

Ryker's boots came into view. "What's going on?"

"Nothing," I said, knee still in Sluggo's back clear for all to see. The way I figured it, "nothing" didn't sound any worse than fighting over a biscuit.

Ryker squatted beside us, his attention on Sluggo. "Why does Bugs feel the need to keep you pinned to the ground?"

Sluggo coughed. "I don't know."

Yeah, he wouldn't want to admit he was getting his ass kicked for a biscuit.

"So you did nothing?" Ryker asked. Sluggo nodded as much as he could with his cheek pressed to the floor.

Ryker stood. "Let him up."

I hesitated for a split second but let Sluggo up. Not because Ryker wanted me to, though. I did it because this was the easiest out. I wasn't really looking to kill someone over a biscuit, even if I was having a bad day.

Sluggo jumped to his feet, all smiles, as if he'd won. I

wanted to jab him right in the mouth and see how cute he thought he was with bloodstained teeth.

Then he doubled over, like he'd taken a fist to the gut. Except I hadn't punched him, and I hadn't seen anyone else do it either. That left only one person.

There wasn't a trace of a smile left as Ryker stepped forward. "I don't know what Knife has told you about me, or what rumors you've heard, but you should believe them. All of them, even the darkest ones whispered when you think no one is listening."

Sluggo's eyes flickered from his friends back to Ryker, and his skin lost its color.

Ryker looked to Sluggo's friends as well, making sure they understood this included them, before he continued. "After you get done coming to terms with that, remember that Bugs is off-limits. I don't tolerate people fucking with what's mine."

Ryker walked out, leaving a frozen Sluggo and friends—and a stunned me. I was about as slow as Sluggo was to get moving, but once I did, I picked up speed fast. I caught up to him not far from the food building.

"Why did you do that? I had the situation under control. I'd handled it. Now they think I *need* you." If my voice was huffy, it was because I'd ran.

He continued walking. "You hurt his ego. He would've come at you when you weren't expecting it, and more prepared. I made it my fight."

"But that's my point. It's not your fight. What's with the 'Bugs is mine' bullshit?" I asked.

He turned off the main path, cutting into the shadows of the buildings. "Simplest way to handle it."

"Except it's not, because I'm not." This wasn't the first time he'd pulled this, either. He'd done it with Knife. He thought he could tell me what to do and when to do it. Now he was even stealing my hard-earned fights.

"You're one of my people. Same thing."

"No, it's not, and you know that. What will people think?"

He stopped abruptly. "What's wrong? Are you worried Knife might hear and retract his offer?"

If I hadn't stopped, I would've fallen over. "Is that why you did that? Are you trying to back me into a corner?" He would, too. He was the type that would get his way by any method. I had no idea why Ruck had such a high opinion of him.

"You aren't going to go with Knife. Tell him. He thinks he's got a shot."

"Because he does." Yeah, I liked it here, but I liked my magic more. I wasn't handing it over to anyone willingly.

He walked toward me, and damned if I'd stay still and let him get to me. If this was a normal fight, it would be different. I didn't know what this was. It felt off. Ryker looked different. If he hadn't already turned me down, I would've thought he wanted to fuck me or something.

"Why are you running from me?" he asked as he kept moving forward.

"I'm not running. I don't run." I was walking backward. It was an entirely different thing.

"Are you suddenly scared of me?" he asked, continuing forward.

"Never." I couldn't have scoffed more if I tried. My scoff runneth over.

I did add another step back, though.

He kept coming. I hit the wall. I could run to the side or stand my ground. It was a little late for a stand, but it was better than an all-out trot to the side.

He took another step forward until my outstretched hand halted his progress.

"You know as well as I do you don't want to leave."

I could feel his words seep into my hand where it rested on his chest. His magic was winding its way up my arm, wrapping it in delicious warmth inch by inch.

"That doesn't matter. I have to do what's best for me." And the warm, fuzzy feelings I was having right now didn't count either. It was like that book had said: our magic was trying to get together to make magical babies or something. It was a trick. Maybe that was why he was acting the way he was? He was falling under the same spell.

"Staying here"—his voice was rough, and the pressure against my hand increased—"that's what's best for you."

He was going to kiss me. Holy magic. He was succumbing. Did I fight him?

I closed my eyes while I debated. If magic wanted us to be together, maybe we should try it out? I wouldn't commit to babies, but what was a few kisses to see if there was something to it?

I felt his heat in front of me, and he touched my face, smoothing the hair away. Then he was gone.

23

I showed up at the field where we practiced the next morning for two reasons only: I needed answers and I needed things. I was going to get them all. It had nothing to do with him almost kissing me or making me think he would. If anything, that had made me more determined to do what I had to, without any crazy magic messing with me.

Ryker was already there waiting, arms crossed, feet shoulder width apart. I *knew* I was on time, but he looked as if I'd shown up an hour late. I walked across the field, stopping out of range of the magic I could feel spiraling around him. Now that I knew what was going on, I'd have to be much more careful.

Ignoring his mood, I got right to the point. "We need to talk. We've tried it your way, and it's not working. What you call practice is doing nothing. We still don't know why those people died, and I'm rolling around in the mud every day with no more control than I had. And more than that, we need more stones, and we needed them yesterday. We're wasting time." I stopped. That was enough of a mouthful.

The cords in his neck were ready for strumming. "Where'd you sleep last night?"

Had I missed something? I glanced around the field, confirming he'd been talking to me. No one else was here. Did he not hear what I'd said? All he cared about was that I hadn't slept at my place, or the place that *had* been mine.

After another second of shock, I finally replied, "What does that matter? Are you not listening to me?"

He split the difference between us. "Where. Did. You. Sleep? It's a simple question."

"Am I being watched? *Again*." It wouldn't be the first time he'd had me tailed.

"I was at your door this morning. Where were you?"

I squinted, and my hands went to my hips as a toe began tapping. I'd opened my mouth to tell him what I thought of his attitude when one of the messenger kids darted into the field and over to hand Ryker a slip of paper. Even I wasn't barbaric enough to rip into Ryker until the kid left. I was going to be one scary person when I let loose. Might scar the kid forever.

Ryker read it and then put it in his back pocket. When he looked up, some of the fire that was burning seemed to have been smothered.

The kid had taken off. I was free to rip into Ryker, go absolutely bonkers. Except why wasn't he mad now? What was in that note? Whatever it was, it was something interesting for sure.

I had a choice. Lose my mind or figure out what he knew. "What was that you got?"

The gleam in his eye was back. "You want to talk about more stones?"

"Did you get information?"

He smiled and walked off the field, knowing I'd follow.

One day, I was going to know everything and then feed it out to him in drips and dribbles. Slow torture by curiosity.

BURN AND SNEAK WERE STANDING OUTSIDE RYKER'S PLACE, both looking past Ryker, to me.

"I see you found her," Burn said.

How long had Ryker been looking for me? Ryker didn't respond other than a slight tip of his head as he entered his place. Sneak went in after.

Burn followed me. "Been waiting for you. We found some interesting stuff."

If Burn and Sneak had been waiting, and Ryker knew that, what was the note about? It hadn't been about the stone. He'd already had that information.

I got settled on the couch, a few feet from Ryker, while I stared at his pocket. I was well within range of his magic, but I was more concerned about whether I could pluck that note from his pocket. The very tip of the paper was peeking out. A quick graze of our sides and I'd have it.

"Ever heard of Cacoy?" Burn asked.

"Yeah, some island country that's scary as hell because of all the Wyrd Blood running around it." I pulled a knee up to my chest and dragged my attention away from my current preoccupation.

Everyone had heard of Cacoy. I'd seen more than a handful of people make a circling motion over their chests when it was mentioned, as if a silent prayer to magic would grant them protection. I used to tell them to get a big knife instead. They'd have at least a one percent chance of making it if a strong Wyrd Blood got their hands on them.

No one ever listened, so I'd stopped talking. I'd always found it odd when dulls thought magic would protect them.

If it hadn't liked them enough to give them anything in the first place, why would it come and save them from the ones it had favored?

Sneak took a seat on the table. "We're pretty sure we've gotten a location of a stone there. Word is a person called Mushroom Man has one."

A stone? Would two be enough to kill the Debt Collector? I swung my attention back to Ryker, not certain how many he even had. "Would one more be enough?"

"I don't know for sure, but it might." He tilted his head slightly. "Either way, the more the better."

"That's not all we found." Burn grabbed a chair and swung it around, leaning his arms on the backrest as he sat. "There's a book from there with some interesting info on their native plants. It says that they have something called Elibell that only grows there. The seeds from that plant, harvested on a double full moon, purges magic from a person. Conveniently for us, this Mushroom Man also trades in these beans." He dropped that little bomb and then leaned back to see how big the blast would be.

Purge? Would I be a dull after this? What did that mean? Magic had sometimes been a nuisance, but it was me. Would my markings go away? Would I still be me?

I leaned forward. "Purges *everything*?"

"That's not the way it read," Burn said. "My understanding was that it purges intrusive magic, not native to the taker. It could purge whatever magic the Debt Collector has on you. It could set you free of his hold." He waved a hand, letting me know there was a *but* coming. "Of course, there's always a risk."

I glanced at Ryker. He'd understand more than anyone else what the loss of magic meant. Burn and Sneak had magic, but not like Ryker and me. Yes, they'd miss it, but it wasn't the same. Losing my magic was like someone telling me they were going to hack away a piece of my soul. If my magic was intrinsically linked to my life, maybe it would.

"What if it takes everything I've got?" I asked, knowing Ryker had as much of a vested interest in me retaining my magic as I did. Knowing him, he'd probably say he had more.

How many times had I envied dulls, and yet, right now, I wondered if death was the better risk. How did you chance losing something that made you *you*? I'd never break another ward, or push Ryker, or feel his magic churning against mine. I didn't know why that was on the top of my list right now, but it had just climbed up a few tiers.

Ryker leaned a shoulder on the wall and crossed his arms. "It's your magic. Your risk. Your decision."

Now he was diplomatic? The one time I wanted him to be his arrogant and determined self and tell me he knew exactly what should be done, he deferred to me. Yeah, it was my risk, but when had that mattered in the past? Did that mean he would take the risk or not?

All three of them were staring at me, waiting to see if I was game to try.

I stood, feeling the need to stretch my legs.

"You don't need to do it this way. There's always merging," Ryker said.

I nodded, barely avoiding a snort. Maybe he wasn't so diplomatic. He simply preferred a different outcome, one that would give him more control than he had now.

"Knife might've heard something about this," Sneak said. "He's got at least one man from Cacoy."

I spun toward him. "That would make a big difference. If we can up the odds, I'll take the bean."

Ryker's jaw clenched as his chest expanded with a deep

breath. "Fine. Let's get Knife here. Either way, I'm going to need his man Switch to get to Cacoy."

If his body language hadn't told me he didn't want to see Knife right now, his magic did. It was getting to the point that I couldn't *not* feel it when I was around him. I'd moved closer to the door, trying to get some distance and catch a breeze.

Ryker glanced at me, his magic following, swelling and building in the room. It was getting worse. It seemed as if when I moved away, his magic chased me down.

I saw Burn stick a few fingers in his collar and Sneak wipe an arm across his forehead.

"Who's Switch?" I asked Burn.

"He's a Wyrd Blood who can pop in and out of places. He could be standing here one minute and on the other side of the planet the next. He lives right beyond Dorley's walls but comes in when he needs protection for whatever reason. Knife tolerates his pop-ins because of his unique talents."

"I can't get to Cacoy without him," Ryker added. "It'll take too long to cross by boat, not to mention they'll see me as soon as I hit the shore."

"Wait, why do you keep saying 'I'? What if there's a ward in place where you need to get the stone? You can't go alone." I needed those stones more than he did. I still didn't know why he wanted them exactly, but I had a crushing problem only they could fix.

Ryker began shaking his head before I was finished. "That place is crawling with so many Wyrd Blood, you'll be a liability. They might sense you as soon as you hit the beach."

"What about you? Your magic's all over the place these days." I noticed neither Burn nor Sneak disagreed, but looked the other way, as if a bird flying by the door had become enrapturing.

Ryker kept shaking his head. "I might've had a slip-up or two, but I can control it. You can't."

"Then help me get control. There has to be a quicker way than what I've been doing, and you can't go without me. I *need* this stone."

Burn shrugged. "You could always—"

"No. I don't want to do that," Ryker said, shutting him down.

"No what? Are you saying there's another way?" I stepped closer to Burn, trying to block his view of Ryker. "Burn, tell me what you're talking about."

Burn looked over my shoulder at Ryker. That was the problem with being the shortest person in the room. Even sitting, he could still see over me. I needed to start standing on chairs when I spoke.

Burn remained silent, so I turned my wrath on Ryker. "This is my decision, my risks, remember?" He should. He'd said something along those lines a minute ago.

"Fine. Tell her." He shrugged. It wasn't a *yeah, you made a good point* type of shrug. It was a *fine, you asked for it* variety.

It was the epitome of a fuck-you shrug. The middle finger would've been less infuriating. At least that would've shown some effort.

I narrowed my eyes and whistled a breath in through a jaw that didn't want to unclench. I managed to squeak out, "Tell me," to Burn, without turning from Ryker.

Burn cleared his throat. "You take something to free up your magic. Then you and another Wyrd Blood who's stronger than you lock yourselves into a small space for an hour, a day, however long it takes. It forces the other person's magic to sort of condense and get into shape. It might not do anything other than control your range, but that's all you need right now. It's a sped-up process of what you've been trying to do.

"No one suggested it for a reason. From what I know, it's not comfortable. People used to do this as a punishment of sorts to Wyrd Bloods who had no control."

"I'll do it. It can't be that bad, and I'm going to Cacoy."

Sneak hopped down off the table. "He could slip and his magic could accidentally kill you. No one is mentioning that."

For some reason, I found that hard to believe. Ryker's magic wanted to mate with mine and create little Wyrd Blood prodigies. I was pretty sure I was safe. Of course, I wasn't going to say that out loud. From the silence, Burn wasn't going to either, although I was pretty sure he suspected. It was probably the reason he'd given me the book. Why wasn't Ryker worried about it, though? Unless he knew too.

"No one is concerned about this?" Sneak asked, looking around the room.

If Burn looked at me, I wouldn't know, as there were suddenly some very interesting birds flying outside the door. Must be a lot of them today. I didn't hear Burn say anything, and I was pretty sure he was thinking the same as me.

"I won't kill her," Ryker said, shutting that conversation down.

There wasn't the teeniest drop of doubt in his words. He knew, too. That jerk had known this whole time probably. Man, was he frustrating. At some point, he could've said, *Hey, you know how I kind of light your pants on fire? It's just the magic. Don't sweat it.* No. He let me think I had a thing for him when it was all smoke and mirrors.

"Let's get started." If I could control my range, maybe I could stop my magic from wanting to play with his *magic*. That would be a big start in regaining control of my life.

"Tomorrow," Ryker said, as if he'd etched the words on stone.

"Why not now?"

"Because I can't."

He probably wanted more control, even if it were for one more day. Either way, I wasn't going to get an answer out of him because he walked out of the room.

Sneak headed out behind him, and it was only Burn and I left.

"Funny how we both know Ryker isn't going to kill me tomorrow," I said.

"Yes, funny how that is," he said, a smirk forming.

"Did you find anything else about what's going on between Ryker and I? Does it get worse? Stabilize?"

He looked to the side as if he were thinking hard. "Who knows? The guy that wrote the book didn't include anything about that. He could be completely wrong. Maybe you're both having flare-ups?" He threw his hands up. "You never know."

"Would you take a bet on it being flare-ups?" I raised my eyebrows. I'd smelled pig pens with less shit than what I was picking up from him. He hadn't made sure to get that book into my hands because he didn't believe it. He was sold hook, line, and sinker.

"Hell no. I'd never take that bet." He laughed.

"Wouldn't it have been easier to tell me?" I asked, not done with him yet.

"Not a possibility," he said.

Ryker told him not to. Why the hell would he do that? I'd asked, but I knew I wasn't getting that answer either.

I shook my head and headed out, but paused for one last question. "How bad is it going to be tomorrow?"

"You'll get through it."

I walked out, knowing he hadn't answered that question either. What was it with these guys?

24

I could feel the magic pouring off the guy before he came close. I looked around, searching for the source. It was a big guy, markings visible on his neck, walking straight toward me. Didn't he sense me? Hadn't he been warned of this by Knife? Did Knife have any control of his people at all?

I didn't need this today. It was getting so I'd be afraid to stretch my legs. I picked up my pace, hanging a right and trying to get out of his path. The guy hung a right as well, and I realized *I* was his path. He was doing it on purpose. Maybe the guy had a death wish.

He wasn't alone, either. There was a small entourage of dulls following him, two guys and a woman, every one of them Knife's people. I recognized a couple of them from the wave of newcomers, plus they wore their boots weird. All of Knife's people did this weird thing, not lacing their boots up all the way so the tips slouched over.

Now what? I could run, but he'd follow. I knew it. He looked determined to get near me.

I let him get a few feet closer. There were markings on his neck in the form of coils that appeared to dip a little bit below his collar. I had a hunch he liked to claim that he was marked on his torso because of that tiny little drift.

I could scream for help, but I wasn't sure if a dull *could* help, and I'd never been much on asking for help anyway. Another Wyrd Blood might end up dying if they tried to step in. Even if I yelled for Ryker, I feared this wouldn't last long enough for someone to find him.

I quickly got sick of running, so I stopped and turned. He was about twenty feet away.

"Don't come any closer." If I could already feel his magic from here, it meant he was letting it loose, and there was a good chance ours wasn't going to react well to each other. There was already an abrading quality as mine began interacting with his.

"I'm not afraid of you," Coils said. Why did people always say that when they were? Was it to convince me or them?

You idiot. Of course I couldn't say that. He was a walking ego, his head inflated three times the size it should be. If I warned him off, he might run toward me to prove his superiority.

"I know, but why take the chance on one of us getting hurt?" I said. *Fuck, that hurt.* I wasn't built for backing down from a challenge. Even hinting that he might be the one doing the hurting sucked. His friends laughed, and it was a like a one-two punch.

He swaggered another step but then stopped. "See? I told you she wasn't all that," he said, eyeing me up while his friends laughed some more.

"I think you should test it," the lanky guy on his right said, a smirk forming.

"No one needs to die today." I took a step back with my palms up, facing him. This backing down was chafing every nerve ending I had and some I'd just grown. But being stupid shouldn't be a lethal offense. Although he was playing free and loose with my life, too. That *was* definitely a lethal offense in my book. Or it used to be. Maybe all this soft living was starting to turn me to mush.

Coils didn't move.

Lanky took a few steps closer until he was brushing shoulders with Coils. I knew before he opened his mouth that the guy was bad news. Coils was dumb, but Lanky had mean eyes.

Lanky leaned toward Coil's ear. "Just a little nudge, for fun. How much damage could it do?"

Even mean people didn't usually want to kill their friends, but not this Lanky guy. I'd seen people murdered before. It wasn't pleasant, but it was a fact of life. No one had ever tried to use me as the murder weapon, though. I had a greasy feeling in my gut that that was exactly what Lanky was doing. The question was why.

Coil smiled for show. The white shading his knuckles told a different story, but still he edged forward. The second I felt his magic get too close, I took another step back. Shit. I was going to have to run for it again. He was big, bulky, and slow. I was small and fast. I didn't want to run, but I wasn't in the mood to be a murder weapon on a Wyrd Blood too stupid to realize what was happening. When I killed, it was because I chose to.

There was a small possibility I could try explaining what I suspected his friend of, but what were the chances he'd believe me over his buddy? Either I swallowed my pride or the big dumb-dumb died.

I spun, knowing this was what it had come to. I took off, and he followed, but I could feel the distance growing fast.

It would've all been okay if I didn't keep looking back to gauge the distance between us and tripped. But I did. It might've still been okay if he wasn't pushing so hard behind me, but he was, and his big bulk had too much momentum to put on the brakes.

Our magic crashed into each other. I felt his incinerate. I didn't need to turn around to know he was dead, but I did. I pushed up from the ground, small stones still stuck to my palms and dirt all over my legs. No magic pushed at mine; I turned and there he was, no pulse, no nothing.

"You killed him," the girl shouted, sounding less horrified than she did satisfied. She pointed at me, repeatedly screaming, "She killed him! She's a killer!"

THIS WAS RIDICULOUS. I'D DONE EVERYTHING TO AVOID THE fight. I went as far as running away from Coils. The guy's friend got him killed, and now I got grief?

The screeching chick was leading the way as I allowed her two friends to drag me along. They'd left their good friend Coils facedown in mud because they'd been so torn up. Yeah, right. They didn't realize I could've zapped them off me in a second, or that there were other Wyrd Blood off in the distance that looked ready to help. I'd never seen them before, which meant they were probably Ryker's people. The one girl had a mark on her wrist I wasn't able to make out, as she'd pointed to the group giving me trouble.

I waved them off. I had problems, but this crew wasn't my biggest.

They marched me up to where Knife was staying. The woman banged on his door repeatedly and no one answered. The only thing they'd accomplished was more eyes on us.

"We should go to Ryker's," Lanky said.

"Is that smart?" the girl asked, pushing a few stringy hairs away from her face. She'd worked up a sweat with that pounding.

Lanky smiled. "He doesn't like her. I've heard they fight all the time."

Her face lit up. "Everyone thinks you're so special, but you're going to get it now." She stepped in the direction of Ryker's. "Come on, boys."

Special? I didn't know whom she'd been listening to.

By the time we got close to Ryker's, he was already stepping out of his place. A man with harshly drawn features walked out behind him. Ryker took a glance in the direction of me and my entourage before he said something to the guy who'd followed him out. The guy left, and Ryker headed toward us.

Great. He looked all sorts of pissed off. He'd probably heard about the dead guy.

Ryker stepped forward, meeting us, his eyes going to where my escorts were holding my arms.

Stringy instantly stepped forward. "She killed our friend. He was walking down the street, doing nothing to nobody, and she killed him."

Maybe it wasn't just Lanky who was setting me up for murder. Looked like Stringy had no problems standing there lying about how their *friend* ended up dead. This whole setup smelled worse than hollyhoney. I just didn't have anything to back up my gut with. Using me to kill their friend made no sense.

Ryker looked at her for a second before returning to stare at where her cohorts' fingers dug into my skin. The silence drew out until Lanky and his friend finally let go, picking up on the hint that this wasn't going to work out the way they wanted. They weren't the only ones sporting a huge case of shock.

Ryker flicked his wrist, motioning for Stringy to move out of the way. It took her a second, but she did.

"Come on. We have things to handle," Ryker said, taking a step to the side and indicating I should walk in front of him. I did.

Well, that was uneventful. I wasn't sure what things we needed to handle, but I'd expected a bit more of a show after they'd dragged me here. From the ugly scowl on Stringy's face, she had too.

"What about our dead friend?" Stringy demanded. The woman didn't know when to give up.

Ryker turned back to them. "Every Wyrd Blood was warned to stay away from her. If your friend didn't, he was stupid. Stupid isn't my problem."

I didn't know what they did after that, because Ryker steered me toward his place.

"Why did you let them drag you here? We both know you went willingly," he said as we walked to his place.

"I don't know. Long day? Too tired to bother fighting?" I could have added that I was trying to figure out their end game, but I wasn't feeling too cooperative. Something was up, but that didn't mean I was sharing my questions about the incident with Ryker. He wasn't real good at telling me everything he knew.

"By the way, they left him dead in the street." It wasn't my fault he'd died, but that didn't mean I was okay letting vultures pick at his body. Someone should at least get the burier.

"Someone will collect him," Ryker said. He walked

across the room, heading toward his bedroom. "Sit," he yelled back.

I sat, not fighting this time. I wanted to sit. I was too tired not to.

I leaned my head over the couch arm and called, "Hey, who was that guy leaving here when we were walking up? I didn't recognize him."

"That was the guy from Cacoy. From what he says, he's seen the bean work."

The bean worked. Now I needed to get it, or the stone. Either way, Cacoy had two things that might save me.

Ryker walked back in with a bottle in hand. "Knife said Switch won't be back for a few days. We meet him then."

He tried to pull out a cork that was sunk too deep before using his teeth to uncork it. He handed it to me.

I remembered the last time I'd drunk in front of him, and it had led to a strip show with no encore. I took the bottle anyway and threw back a gulp.

"So why did you go with them willingly? Since when do you try and keep the peace?"

That was worse than the stuff Burn drank. I handed Ryker his bottle back.

"I don't know," I said. "Figured I'd try and go the calm route for once." For all the good it did Coils.

"Fuck peace. These people are getting on my nerves. They don't like it here, they can leave."

Ah, now it made sense. He was using me to get rid of some of them. This piece fit.

I stood, feeling a little worse for wear but wanting to go lick my wounds in private. I'd made my way to the door before he stopped me.

"Where are you going?" he asked. "We're doing it now."

"I thought you couldn't?"

He walked to the door and closed it. "I don't give a shit about who you kill, but if it's going to bother you enough to let a bunch of assholes drag you around, better off getting it done."

"What do I have to do?"

"You already did it," he said, holding up the bottle.

25

I walked a few paces away from the couch and banged into the hardest, strongest ward I'd ever felt. The wards I'd struggled to get through in the past always had some give, whether it had been mossy and springy or more like a sheet of wood. They'd never been like the side of a cliff, all stone.

Add to it that the drink he'd given me wasn't booze. I'd always thought I had no control of my magic. Turned out, I'd definitely had some, as evidenced by how miserable it was right now. Whatever control I'd had was long gone.

I slammed a hand on the ward. "Did it need to be this tight?"

I glanced at Ryker where he sat on the couch. Every muscle was tensed. Arms crossed in front of him, every cord of muscle was delineated.

"I didn't set the parameters. I merely set it in motion." His words were forced and the tension was pouring off him.

I believed him. He'd taken a sip of the same thing he'd given me, said a couple of words I'd never heard before, and wham, we'd been in an instant inferno of boiling magic ever since. If I couldn't see the clock on the other side of the room, I would've said it had been hours. In reality, it hadn't been fifteen minutes yet. I'd been in this bubble of hell with him for less than an hour and I was already on the brink of losing it.

"Don't forget, *you're* the one who wanted this," he said.

I sat on the other side of the couch. It was the only spot *to* sit. It wasn't only excruciatingly uncomfortable, it was other things as well. It was making those other feelings burn up too. The ones I resented most. The weird stuff that made me want to crawl all over him and lick his skin and bite his lower lip.

Burn had known what was going to happen. He'd known it and wanted it. I was beginning to realize he was trying to make us get stuck together. Why? So Ryker could have all my magic, probably. I'd forgotten one of the most important things: Burn was Ryker's crew, his family. His loyalty was to Ryker, and I'd been foolish to think that all motives didn't somehow lead to Ryker's benefit. If I lived through this, Ryker was no longer number one on my kill list. It was Burn. I was going to flay him alive, that sneaky bastard.

I dropped my head back on the couch, my skin feeling like it had a blowtorch aimed at every piece of me. Standing didn't help; sitting didn't help. Curling into a ball didn't help. "Why is it *this* bad? Is this normal?"

He ran a hand over his head, looking like he was going to scalp himself. "No. This was why I didn't want to do it." His voice was clipped. The fact that he looked and sounded as miserable as I was made the situation a smidge more tolerable.

"Why is it so bad?" I pulled my legs up to my chest, dropping my head on my knees, trying to find a position that didn't make it feel like my guts were being scrambled.

I glanced between us at the empty spot. If the magic was making us miserable right now, maybe all we had to do was make the magic happy?

"Have you ever heard the term Full Blood?" he asked.

"No. What is that?" I shifted, inching over toward him. Did I feel better? Maybe.

"That's not really surprising. You lived in the Ruined City, which doesn't have a reputation of educated people. Plus, it's not a common term."

I ignored the commentary on my previous neighbors and got to the only question I cared about. "What does it mean?"

"Wyrd Bloods are rare. Having very potent magic is even rarer. Then there's Full Blood. It's used to describe a Wyrd Blood who has so much magic that it's nearly bursting from their veins. They're Full-Blooded, or Full Blood. That's why this is so bad. We're both Full Blood."

"Did you know I was Full Blood?"

"You never know for sure until something like this proves it, but I suspected."

I tilted my legs in his direction, then shifted until I was halfway through the space in between us. The agony eased slightly more.

Is this what you want? If that's it, you can have it, I silently said to the gods of magic. Gods that I'd refused to believe existed but was now talking to. Amazing what a little desperation could do for your faith.

Ryker bent forward, resting his forearms on his knees. "One thing is for sure: your magic does not like to be contained."

"Tell me about it. I don't know how you can reel yours in

and shape it. Mine feels like a wild animal that doesn't come on command. Occasionally it'll happen to do what I want, but it's more luck than anything else." I inched over a little farther, finding every move made it a bit more bearable.

"How many have you killed?"

I shot him a look that was only a warmup for the words getting loaded and ready to fly. When he turned to look at me, I pulled them back. His expression was soft, his eyes not the usual cold burn. That was when I knew for certain it had happened to him. He was commiserating, not accusing.

I pulled a knee up to give me something to hug, only a few inches separating us at this point. "More than I'd like to remember. I didn't realize what I was doing at first. Didn't know it was me, that *I* was the reason they died. By the time I figured out that I needed to avoid others when I got that feeling, I had a trail of blood that felt a mile wide."

He nodded. "You come to terms with it after a while."

"No one told you either?" I asked, remembering his theory about Wyrd Blood being stronger when it didn't show in a bloodline for a long time. Some reason, even with the stories I'd heard of the Cursed King, I'd imagined him always being in complete control of everything around him.

"It happened before my markings showed. I'd killed more than I could count before they did."

I could hear a branch creak outside, it was so quiet. Another few very long seconds passed before I looked at him. His expression had chilled again, back to something I was much more familiar with and a lot less happy to see.

We'd gotten somewhere, to a different place than what we normally had for a moment, and now it was gone and all I wanted to do was chase after it, wrangle it to the ground and hold on.

There might've been some of that desperation leaking

through into my next words, or I could've been using that as an excuse to tell him what I was about to say. Either way, it was coming out. I couldn't seem to hold anything back at the moment. My magic, emotions, or words.

"Whenever anyone found out that I was caught by the slavers and heard I'd escaped, it always made them think I was so tough, especially because of how young I was. The less I wanted to talk about it, the more they built it up in their heads.

"In truth, my escape was a complete accident. There was a Wyrd Blood in the slaver crew. Everyone called him Ice because he could freeze anything he touched. His markings were on his hands, low-level stuff, and he couldn't do much permanent damage.

"The main slave master told him to steer clear of me, but the guy never listened. Every night, he'd come by to visit."

"You mean torment."

My gaze jerked back to him. I guessed it had been pretty obvious. I gave a slight nod but that was all. Sharing didn't mean every tiny detail had to be dragged out.

He leaned back, resting his arm along the back of the couch behind me. I didn't complain.

"He'd been warned to stay away, so he started visiting after everyone went to sleep. The place they kept me, though, in order to get close, he had to unlock the door and come in. One night, he dropped dead. I didn't think. I only reacted. I climbed over his body and ran."

Ryker didn't need to know the joy it brought me. There hadn't been a hair of sadness when I saw Ice drop to the ground suddenly. I hadn't called for help or done anything but watch him for a few seconds, smiling.

"I lucked out because the guards on duty that night had

been drinking. I wasn't some fearless kid. It was fear that made me run, fear of what would come next."

Ryker wasn't judging. He was listening. That was when I realized why I was really telling him everything. He never judged. He might criticize and tell me to do something better, but he wasn't going to turn away from me. If I did something he didn't like, he tried to bully me into being better, but there wasn't a part of me that believed he'd ever walk away from me—at least until he got the stones.

When did I start caring if people left me? Had I always been like this? Had it happened after Fetch and Tiger left and then Sinsy's death? Had it been losing Marra that had made me this pathetic creature?

Ryker shifted, and I realized his side was right against mine. This time, he'd closed the distance.

"I might know how to make this go quicker." His voice was gravelly. Our eyes met, and I knew exactly what he was thinking.

I turned into him—the slightest move, but the loudest yes I could've yelled. That was all he needed.

He gripped my hips and swung me around, until I was facing him, straddling his lap.

I swallowed as I settled into him, our hips—and other parts—pressed firmly together. The oppressive heat pushing in seemed to relinquish its hold almost completely, shifting into a feeling I'd chase.

"Do you feel that?" he asked.

I nodded, pretty sure he was talking about the relief we were getting and not his swollen cock pressing against me.

"I think we should try some more," I said, wetting my lips because it was hot in our little bubble. I was doing this for us as a team, to accomplish our mission. That was it. It wasn't because it felt good or I'd wondered about it for weeks.

His arm wrapped around my hips as the other looped up around my shoulder, pressing me into him as he ground against me.

If I pressed downward, it was only to help the cause. It wasn't to increase the delicious feeling growing lower.

"It's definitely working," he said.

I arched into him, as he shifted his hips up. My head dropped back and his lips found my neck, lighting my skin on fire before trailing their way upward, tasting me as he trailed a path toward my ear.

Moans broke from my lips as I dug my hands into his hair, then his shoulders, gripping the fabric of his shirt.

He flipped us, and I found myself on my back, his upper body hovering over mine as his hips settled between my legs.

My legs were wrapped around his hips when the door swung open.

Burn turned around immediately. "Sorry! Didn't see anything," he yelled, walking out.

"Burn, it's fine. Stop." Ryker jerked up.

I pulled myself into the opposite corner of the couch. Ryker didn't look as startled as I was, but then again, he'd had a lot of sexual encounters in his life. A spontaneous dry-humping session was probably nothing to him.

Ryker sat forward but didn't stand right away. I did, and immediately realized the magical ward that had enclosed us was gone.

I walked forward, testing it, then looked back to Ryker. "It's gone."

Ryker finally stood and walked over to Burn, who had been hovering right inside the door, not saying anything.

"It broke the ward, but I can still feel her magic. Do you feel her?" Ryker asked him.

Burn looked my way, and I let my eyes skim his but had trouble keeping them there.

Burn walked in, getting closer, although he appeared to want to run back out. He looked around as if my magic were something you could see, before he said, "It feels better. She's usually all over the place."

I took a deep breath and realized he was right. I could feel my magic more condensed around me. I gave it a mental stretch and could feel it inflate and deflate around me, but it was calm somehow.

No one was speaking to me as I sorted out this new feeling, walking from place to place, as if that might change it. I took advantage of the moments to gather up all the other things I was feeling. What had just happened between me and Ryker? Had that all been for the cause? Had it been the magic goading us on or the drink that had set everything free?

It hadn't felt like that, but he wasn't exactly showing me any signs it meant more. Although Burn was standing here talking to him. What was he supposed to do?

"Is Sneak next door?" Ryker asked.

"Yeah, I'll grab him," Burn said, giving me an awkward wave as he walked out.

Ryker closed the door behind him. "You need to tell Knife you can't merge magic with him. Don't string him along and let him think you're going to Dorley with him if Cacoy doesn't work out."

Ryker wanted me. Against my better judgment, I felt like I was floating. It didn't matter that he'd turned me down before. It just wasn't meant to happen then. We weren't meant to have a one-night stand. We were meant for something longer and more lasting.

I nodded, crossed an arm over my chest, and put a fist over my mouth so I could hide the smile that wanted to creep up. Just because I felt goofy and lightheaded didn't mean I was an idiot. We'd need to date for a while to see if we were really meant to be together.

Maybe we'd go find some more stones, have some adventures, and then he'd fall in love with me.

He turned, walking toward the door and opening it back up, as if he were wondering what was taking Sneak so long.

He was looking outside as he said, "It's obvious we're stuck with each other, so the sooner he knows, the better."

And then gravity hit. My head cleared and my feet smashed back onto the ground. "Stuck?"

He shut the door again, as if he'd decided we were going to need a little more privacy. "You know this is going to happen. The magic is making it unavoidable. You're a realist, Bugs. Surely you see that."

"I see a lot of things, and we're not stuck. I'm not *stuck* with anyone." He wasn't saying he loved me, or even liked me. He was saying he was "stuck," like stuck in the mud, or stuck in between a rock and a hard place. There was nothing good about being stuck with somebody.

Damn, I was an idiot. That swig of stuff that unleashed my magic must've done some other crazy things to me, because thinking I wanted to be with this man was insanity. I didn't need anyone anyway. I had Ruck: he was my crew, my family. Ryker could go to hell.

"If we merge magic, I won't use yours unless you tell me it's okay, if that's what you're worried about," he said, staring at me as if I were a book in a foreign language.

"No, that's not a concern, because we won't be merging, even if Cacoy is a total bust."

"What is wrong with you? Why are you acting so erratic?"

We were standing on opposite sides of the room, and it might as well be opposite sides of the world, when Sneak opened the door and walked in.

I didn't say anything else as I walked out.

I WALKED AWAY FROM RYKER'S CURSING SILENTLY. THAT potion had done something crazy to me, or I never would've messed around with him. I should've sat there in pain. There was one thing I wasn't ever going to be, and it was someone's albatross.

I stopped and pounded on the door in front of me, belatedly thinking of the time. What if he was sleeping? I'd killed his man and now I was waking him up too?

Knife swung open the door, shirtless and, I had to admit, pretty damn sexy. None of that meant he wouldn't kill me after he found out, but I wasn't going to let Ryker tell him first. He'd really think I was his dead weight.

I launched into an apology before he could whip out the razors.

"Hey, I wanted to tell you what happened earlier today before—"

"I heard. We're good." He stepped back and waved a hand inside. "Want a glass of wine? I was just having one."

That was it? Did nobody care that I'd killed another Wyrd Blood?

I'd done enough drinking for the day, but how did you turn someone down when they'd waved off an unintentional murder? There had to be some sort of obligation there.

"Sure." I stepped inside. The place was comfortable enough, with a large bed and a couch and table set up in the corner, but probably not what he was used to. I'd seen his Dorley castle from afar. This was a mouse hole in comparison. I made my way to the couch, having no other place to go.

He was still standing right inside the door. He raised his finger as if to point at something but paused. "Your magic? It's not..."

"Yeah, it's fixed." It was hard to believe myself, because all in all, I didn't feel that much different.

"How did that happen so quickly?"

"I don't know. Something clicked, I guess." I was short, hoping he'd take the hint. The last thing I wanted to discuss was how that had gone down. "So you're really not upset about the guy?" I asked, more prepared to talk about death than what had happened with Ryker.

He shut the door and walked to the couch. "I only brought him with me because I was hoping he'd like it and stay here. Seemed a good way to get rid of him."

Thinking about some of the other people he'd brought with him, there were definitely similarities. How many people did he want to dump? I was going to have to talk to Ryker tomorrow, even if it killed me to do so. We weren't getting stuck with all of Knife's cast-offs.

Knife picked up the bottle from the table, topped off the half-empty glass, and handed it to me. "Sorry. I don't have a spare. It's pretty basic here."

I took a sip, and he took a swig from the bottle. We sat there for a few minutes in silence, which Knife seemed to be very comfortable with. He stared at me most of that time, while I tried to come up with small talk and wondered how long I had to sit and play civilized because I'd killed someone. Ryker never made me sit and act normal.

"You're very attractive. Even if you didn't have magic, I'd still be interested," Knife said, still staring. He reached forward and started twirling a piece of my hair. Ryker would've grabbed a hank of it and pulled me to him.

"Thank you." I needed to get control of this conversation before things went south. "So you and Ryker have been— friends for a long time?" Amazing what you could do when really pushed.

He smiled and laughed softly. "I guess you can call us that. I know, it's curious. It's a relationship born of convenience, but there's been a certain bond that's been built over the years. He doesn't want what I have, and I don't want what he has, or I haven't in the past." The look he shot me made it obvious what he was referring to. "It works. I wouldn't trust him with my belongings, but I trust him with my life. We know we're better off in an alliance."

I took a small sip of wine, wondering how much longer I'd have to sit there. Was ten minutes enough when you killed someone, or was fifteen the minimum? I should've waited until tomorrow, when he was busy doing something. But no, I had to come now and get it over with. I took another sip of wine.

"Have you given any more thought to merging magic with me?"

"Yes, and I still can't answer." I put the glass down on the table, having had about enough of this shiny, pretty show. "Can we cut the bull for a second? Is this is about getting my magic, getting in my pants, or aggravating Ryker?"

He dropped the suave act instantly and said, with a shrug, "I'd say equal parts."

There might be something I could use here after all. "I'm not agreeing to merge magic with you, and I'm not jumping in bed with you. But I might be able to help with the Ryker part. Can you erect a ward?"

He let out a huff of air. "Of course I can. That's basic."

"A strong one?"

"You saw my torso. What do you think?"

I smiled.

26

"Ryker thinks he can do whatever he wants and dictate to me, but it's not going to happen." I sat on Ruck's bed, tugging on my boots. I took a bite of the biscuit he'd brought me because I'd slept through breakfast.

"Are you getting crumbs on my bed? I don't like sleeping on crumbs."

"No." I waited until he turned his head and wiped off a couple of specks. "And when did you get so picky? We used to sleep on dirt."

He wasn't the only one, not that I'd admit it. I missed my bed badly. It was amazing how fast you could get used to having it better. Not that sharing was a big deal, since Ruck worked the night shift.

"Look, I know men. He didn't get close because of the magic or because he had to, so don't be insulted. He wants you."

Ruck didn't understand magic, though, or the way mine and Ryker's reacted, the way it ignited when we got close, and I wasn't going to keep explaining it either.

"I don't care if he wants me. He's an asshole. It's better

that he keeps making that as painfully obvious as possible."
I wouldn't bother explaining. It was impossible unless you
felt it.

I stood up, grabbing the last of my biscuit, and heard
Ruck huff. "Why did you do that?"

"What?" he asked, all innocent and naive.

"You huffed at me."

He looked like he was going to feign ignorance but then
he huffed again. "You're full of shit. For someone you hate,
you track that man's movements like you're dying of thirst
and he's a cool glass of water."

I sucked in a breath. "No. I don't."

He rolled his eyes.

"If I watch him, it's because he's a python about to strike
at any moment."

He put his hands on his hips. "And you're hoping to get
bit, unless you already were?"

My cheeks felt warm and tingly. Were there marks on
my neck? Hoped not. "No, I'm not, and no, I didn't."

"I think if the man wants to do you, you do him and get
it out of—"

"Agree to disagree," I said before he could continue. I
didn't know when we'd started the tradition, but that phrase
was our "crying uncle." We'd both only used it a handful of
times. It did the trick because he fell silent.

Ruck exhaled so hard his hair blew up. "Fine. Agreed."
He kicked off his boots and took the spot I'd vacated on
the bed.

I made my way to the door.

Right before I left, he said, "I was only trying to help."

I stopped. "I know. I'll stop by the tower later."

"Bring snacks with you," he said, settling in.

I walked away, hearing him yell, "I feel crumbs," when I was only a few feet away.

I HEADED TOWARD THE PATH, KNOWING RYKER WOULD BE waiting for me. After what had happened last night, he wouldn't seek me out, just as I wouldn't seek him out. But he'd be there, and he knew I was going to show. I couldn't give an explanation for either.

As expected, Ryker was waiting in the field.

"Did you talk to Knife?"

"I didn't tell him what you suggested, if that's what you're asking."

"You know as well as I do you aren't ever going to merge with him."

"I might not have to merge with anyone, and if I do, why would I want to make you get stuck? He *wants* to merge." *Stuck*. That word was still jammed in my head. It was as if it was glued in there with old, sticky hollyhoney and I wasn't sure if I'd ever be able to pry it out.

"It's not a matter of want. The magic isn't going to let up until it happens. It's getting worse, and I don't share."

"Really? I thought you shared quite nicely."

"It's different. They aren't mine. I…" Ryker looked to the side and seemed at a loss for words.

"What? Do you borrow them for a night?" I huffed into the air loudly, stealing Ruck's move. "Yet you wonder why I'm not jumping all over the opportunity."

Yeah, he didn't want to share, but what about me? Was I supposed to watch him have women coming and going constantly? Not that I'd bring that up, because then it would sound like I cared. I didn't. And it wasn't happening anyway.

I'd merge on my deathbed. I hadn't made it this many years on my own to hand over control now.

"If I collapsed onto my knees and declared undying love, you'd know I was full of it. I didn't think you were the type to prefer lies."

"I'm not asking you to pretend to love me. I'm just not overjoyed to get stuck either, especially with someone who thinks I'm a necessary evil."

"Would you feel better if I called it the best possible outcome of a bad situation? What about rock and a hard place? Is that more palatable to you?" He looked calm even as his magic was starting to shoot zigzags around me, and mine flared right back. For as much control as I might've gotten, when it came to him, I still had zilch.

"Wait, I got it. Why don't we call it saving your ass? How do you stomach that?"

"I'm done."

"Oh, you didn't like that one either? I'll keep thinking on it, then. Want to make sure you're happy," he said to my back.

I ignored him. Total ass. Why had I come this morning? I walked away and slammed right into an invisible wall.

Fucker! When had he done that? I'd been standing here, staring at him the entire time, and I hadn't seen so much as a flick of his wrist.

I turned. "You put that down, right now."

"I'm sorry, princess, but no. We're practicing."

"Put it down. I'm not doing anything with you right now."

He settled onto the rock and crossed his arms.

I turned around, raised my hands, and focused on making him put it down. Screw him. I was beyond this. If I could break the ward around Bedlam, I could break his.

Or maybe not. This one was bad, almost as bad as the one from the other night around his couch. I slammed a fist into it.

"What did you do to this thing?"

He reached into his pocket and tossed a stone up into the air. The sun glinted off it, shining like a gem. He tossed it again. I narrowed my eyes.

No wonder I couldn't get through the ward this time. He had an advantage. "That's..."

"Yep."

"I knew I felt something weird." I'd written it off to our magic again, but I'd been wrong.

He stopped throwing. "Why didn't you tell me you felt it?"

"Because I thought I imagined it."

He stopped tossing. "Next time you think you imagine something, tell me anyway."

"Sure." *Hell no.* Last time I'd acted on something I thought I'd imagined, I'd stripped in front of him. I'd be keeping all feelings to myself.

He leaned back, watching me. "I'd get to it. It's probably going to take you a while."

"Sometimes I hate you. I don't know why I thought there was even a shred of decency in you."

"The dead don't get the luxury of hate. Keep going, because when we get to Cacoy, you're going to have to be ready to break a ward like this. He's not as stupid as Bedlam. His stone will be better protected."

"How do you know?"

"Because it's what I'd do."

I started working. "I still hate you."

"And you're still alive."

Knife walked into the field a few hours later. I was coated in sweat and using the last of what I had in me to break the ward that didn't want to budge.

He was looking from my sweating form to Ryker where he sat comfortably on the stone. Knife stopped just shy of the ward, as if he felt it. "You were looking for me?"

"I want to leave early tomorrow to meet up with your man Switch," Ryker said.

"Sure. He should be back." Knife lifted his head, bouncing his stare back and forth. "What are you doing?"

"Practicing. Did you need something else?"

It was as clear an invite to leave as I'd ever heard.

"Isn't there an easier way to do this?" Knife asked, probably noticing my hands fisted at my sides and the look of blood rage in my eyes.

"No, and she's not your business," Ryker replied.

"That hasn't been established yet."

"Are you saying you want to help? Because I don't think that's what you're offering at all. And before you say anything else, we both know which one of us will walk away from this fight."

"Ryker, I'm not trying to interfere. I'm just wondering if there's an easier way to help her than the way you handle things."

Knife *knew* Ryker could kill him, and he was still pushing. Had to give him credit that he still stuck to it, even if a bit more politely.

"She's got to get stronger. You *saw* the mark on her back."

"Obviously."

"It's growing, and fast. It's more intricate and pronounced than even a few weeks ago. She's Full Blood and she's too stubborn to do the one thing that would most likely keep her alive. Do you think you're the only one who is going to want to use her?"

"Not wanting to merge my magic is far from being stubborn," I interjected.

Ryker paused long enough to give me a look that expressed exactly what he thought of that statement before turning back to Knife.

"You've been around a long time. You know what's coming. You know what happens the stronger you get. They'll come out of the woodwork. First it will be nice overtures, probably similar to yours, until she turns them down. Next, they'll decide they need to band together to take her out before she gets stronger, because she's too big of a risk. Are you going to stand in front of her when they come? Or are you going to head back to the nice, tall walls of Dorley?"

"Maybe she'll come with me behind those nice tall walls?" Knife asked.

"Sure. Dorley will make a great cage and an even better mausoleum. I'm her only shot."

I stepped closer to Ryker, just shy of blocking Knife from his line of sight. "If I don't broadcast it, they might never know."

The anger flaring in his eyes dimmed. He knew something.

"Word's gotten out already, hasn't it?" I asked. He should've just punched me in the gut. It would've felt better.

I had to give him credit: I didn't know if it was an act or not, but he looked genuinely remorseful. His nod even appeared strained.

This was what had been bothering him today. This was the thing that had been driving him as if he had a demon on his back. It wasn't what had happened with us last night. He probably hadn't given that another thought.

"How?" I asked. "Where did you hear it from?"

"I don't know, but word is spreading. They're even describing your markings. It's too late to hide."

My head dropped, and I shook it as I stared at the ground and then off at the distance, anywhere but at him. Ryker was right. They'd come for me. Even if I got past the Debt Collector, I was doomed by my magic.

I'd never have the calm life I'd hoped for. I'd hidden for so long because I knew what happened to Wyrd Blood. I'd gotten here and some strange sense of safety had clouded my mind and nipped away at the walls I'd built. At some point I'd pushed that fate to the back of my mind and gotten lax.

I dragged in a deep breath, trying to reset myself.

"Bugs, you okay?" Knife asked from right beyond the ward.

"I'm good." I let out a short laugh that sounded slightly hysterical even to me. "But I better get practicing."

Knife gave me a last look. I ignored it. I turned my attention to the ward.

"If this was because of Bedlam, I'm sorry."

I nodded but kept my back to him. I wasn't ready for this conversation or the I-told-you-sos he deserved. He'd known what he was getting me into. Now he could help me get out of it, if that was even possible.

27

"How many more fire stones do you have left? You've been running a lot of chuggers lately," Knife said from the right-hand side of the chugger cabin.

"A few. What about you?" Ryker shifted the chugger into a lower gear as we hit a muddy incline.

"A few," Knife answered, and I felt his shoulder shrug against mine.

Bunch of liars. I could tell from their tone they were both hoarding. It had started an hour ago with food supplies, specifically apples. They'd switched to livestock after that and then moseyed on over to beeswax. At least these little bluffing games were a distraction from being crammed in from both sides in the small space. It was also better than holding on for dear life, like Burn and Sneak were probably doing as they rode in the back.

"How much longer until we get to Switch?" I could've guessed in walking time, but this was only my third drive ever.

"Not long," they both answered. They glanced over me and at each other, both feeling some squashed toes.

I reached down to the bag at my feet and pulled my stash of berries out. I was going to need more nourishment to withstand the rest of this ride.

Ryker glanced at the bag in front of me, and then the purple berry in my hand. "Where did you get those?"

"I picked them from a bush." There was a whole cluster of Bamber bushes that grew right outside the border of his land, right beyond where his ward was. I hadn't thought of it at the time I'd picked them. I'd been too excited to find them because the Bamberberries had the sweetest flavor you'd ever tasted.

Ryker didn't need to tell me why he was so fixated on the berries. It was because I'd crossed his ward and he hadn't known. Turned out a friendship with Knife was beneficial for me as well. I popped another berry in my mouth, waiting to see if Ryker would pop a vein. I couldn't very well let them go to waste.

"How long did it take for you to walk through Burn's ward without him sensing it?" he asked, guessing at whom I might've practiced with first.

He'd find out, too, even if he had to drag this out. Fuck me. I'd just wanted a snack.

"It wasn't Burn," I answered, hoping he'd put down the saw and get to the ax. The slow go was more torture. I guessed I could've picked up the ax myself and told him, but I'd never been into self-mutilation.

"Sneak?" Ryker's jaw clicked to the side.

I felt Knife shifting, the heat building in the cab.

"Nope," I said, leaving only the man to my right.

"Are you going to be too tired to make the trip, or is Ruck's floor more comfortable than it looks?" Ryker asked. I wasn't sure if Knife picked up on the jab, but I certainly did.

I'd known Ryker would figure out I'd been sleeping at

Ruck's. It wasn't a big deal. I'd wanted him to know initially, but the way he'd just laid it out there? As if that was the only place I would be sleeping? Like I wouldn't really sleep with Knife because I wanted him or something? The gloves were coming off.

"I'll be fine. How you feeling, Knife? Did you get a nap in after we finished? I know we went at it last night for a *really long time*." We had, too. I'd practiced getting through Knife's ward until the morning sun had come up, and gotten Bamberberries to boot.

"I'll be fine," Knife said, but he was tugging on his collar and looked like he was about to gasp for air. Another few seconds passed, and I knew he wasn't going to make it.

Knife pulled on his shirt again. "I didn't sleep with her. Can you cut that shit out?"

Ryker's magic reeled back, and he stopped the chugger with a smile. "Sorry about that. Hadn't realized. Sometimes it gets away from me."

I popped a couple more berries in my mouth so that I wouldn't curse aloud.

We hopped out of the cab, and I made a point of jumping down on Knife's side. It was petty, but all I had at the moment.

Burn and Sneak jumped out of the back. Burn opened his mouth, and I would've sworn it was to bitch, and then he set eyes on a sweaty Knife. His mouth shut as he tapped Sneak, and then pointed to an unknowing Knife. They both turned their backs to take in the landscape, with only a few muffled laughs making it over to us. I slung my bag over my shoulder and followed the direction Knife was walking.

IF I HADN'T BEEN LOOKING FOR IT, I NEVER WOULD'VE SEEN

the lean-to covered in branches surrounded by Icky Itchy bushes. One brush against the blue leaves and you'd not only itch for a month solid, but you could pass on that itch to anyone who touched you. Then there was the smell that came with the sores, a mixture of vomit and decomposing animals left in the sun. We all kept our distance, afraid of a stray leaf blowing near.

"He lives there?" I took a swig of my water.

"If you're the only Wyrd Blood around that can pop in and out without brushing against a blue ball bush—I mean an Icky Itchy, it makes sense," Knife explained.

I smirked. I might be limited in sexual experience, but my best friend was a guy. Those sores would seriously crimp anyone's sex life for a while.

Knife stepped closer but still a few feet short. "It's perfect for him. Not even a horde of Chewers would go in there."

The last time I'd heard or uttered that word had been when I'd retold the story of how Sinsy had died to Marra. I felt eyes graze over me from several different directions. I took another swig of water, pretending that they weren't.

"You sure he's coming back?" Ryker asked, moving the conversation along. If I were the suspicious type, I might've thought he'd done it for me. But I knew him better.

Knife looked around. "He's around somewhere. He's been here for fifty years and will probably be here two hundred more."

Everyone was looking for the guy except me. Hundreds of years? Knife couldn't mean that literally, could he? "That's an exaggeration, right? I know Wyrd Blood live longer, but hundreds?"

"That might be a drop in the bucket. The stronger you are, the longer you last." Knife pointed to Burn. "Hell, Burn's eighty and he doesn't look older than thirty."

"Eighty?" I nearly screeched.

"Hey? Nice outing me, douchebag," Burn said. "And I'm only seventy-five."

Knife laughed, oblivious to the insult before turning to Ryker. "Do you tell her anything, or do you like to keep them young and stupid?"

"Hey!" I said, whacking Knife's arm. "He's not keeping me anything."

"Sorry. That was meant for him," Knife said.

"I thought you liked stupid, Knife? How would you ever get laid otherwise?" Ryker asked.

I put some distance between the two of them and me. I could see this might continue for a while, and I had a bigger picture to think on. I'd known I'd live longer. I'd seen Ryker barter away years like he was tossing popcorn. But if Burn was seventy-five and he wasn't nearly as strong as Ryker, Knife, or I, how long would I live?

"That him?" Ryker asked, pointing.

We all swung in that direction as a dot appeared on the horizon.

Knife took a few steps closer and squinted. "Yeah, that's him. Let me approach him alone. If you guys spook him, we might not find him for a year."

We hung back as Knife took a few steps forward. The dot stopped walking.

"Switch, it's me," Knife yelled. "If you take off, I swear, I'll kill you right now."

Even without knowing the guy, I thought there might've been a better approach. The dot shrank, agreeing with me.

"Switch, get over here," Knife yelled. "How long have I been saving your ass?"

The dot grew slightly larger until I could make out the man. Switch looked like he hadn't run a comb through his hair in five years. Tangles of burnished gold curls hung around his shoulders, with an occasional twig adorning the locks. He had the kind of eyes that sloped down instead of up and wasn't a person you'd forget seeing, or smelling, since we were unfortunate enough to be downwind. But he could get me to Cacoy, so he was my favorite man right now.

Switch stopped fifteen feet from us, out of reach of a solid lunge. "What's going on?" he asked.

"We need a lift to Cacoy," Knife said.

"Who needs to go?" Switch asked, looking at our group.

"Her and—him." Knife jerked his head toward Ryker. His tone would've made a lemon taste smooth.

"Two? I can only do one at a time. It's a long jump." Switch crossed his arms and took another step back, as if expecting someone to hurt him for giving the wrong answer.

"I'll go alone," Ryker and I said at the same time.

I edged closer to Switch. "This is my thing. I need it more."

Ryker matched my steps. "You don't know where to go or who to deal with."

"How well do you know Cacoy?" I put my hands to my hips. It certainly hadn't sounded like a lot, unless he was holding back—again. Wouldn't that be a surprise. Ryker keeping secrets?

He crossed his arms and angled his head down. "I can get in to the place I need to go."

"I'm getting a bean. How much experience do I need?"

Knife stepped almost in between us. "Not that I don't enjoy the turmoil and all, but maybe you can juice Switch? You do that, right?"

"Would it work on him?" I glanced at Switch, who had taken several more steps away.

"Hang on a second. I'm not getting juiced," Switch said, now jogging backward.

They should've called this guy Twitch with the way he rattled so easy. No wonder he didn't live within the walls of Dorley.

He wouldn't have lasted a day in the Ruins. Nervous wrecks never fared well. If you couldn't at least act calm, people thought you were up to something. Maybe you could get away with it once in a while, but not for long. More often than not, they thought you were going to screw them over and your guilty conscience was making you crack. The last thing you wanted to happen in the Ruins was have someone think you were plotting against them. It was the surest way to end up dead.

And if Switch left, I was going to be dead. Back to square one, trying to cross the Great Ocean on a trip that would take weeks for a bean that might not work and stone that might not be there.

Knife held out his hand. "Switch, it's nothing bad. One of the things she can do is pump magic into other people. That's all juicing means."

So much for Knife's rapport with his people. Switch took another step back, and we were getting very close to losing him. I knew the look in his eyes. The guys wouldn't understand, but I did. I'd *had* that look. At some point, somehow, Switch had been thoroughly caught, used, and abused.

Knife was about to take another step forward when I put my arm out in front of him. "Stop. Give him room."

Switch shot his attention from the guys to me, as if I were the threat.

"I can show you what juicing means on someone else. I won't hurt you."

He tilted his chin up and surveyed the group. "On who?"

I wasn't going to pick Ryker, that was for sure. I didn't want to use Knife, either. Sneak might be a hard demonstration.

"Burn." I reached, dragging him forward. I'd juiced Burn before and knew what we'd get. "Give me your best flame."

He rolled back his sleeve, held his hand upward, and produced a moderate-sized torch. It was impressive enough, but nothing compared to what we could do together.

I grabbed his arm and pretended I was cupping a worm. Flames shot out at least fifty feet up, so strong I could feel the burning heat on my face.

I let go and turned back to Switch. "That's all juicing is. I lend you some of my magic."

He didn't say anything as the information sank in. It was another nail-biting minute before he said, "Okay. I think I can do that. What do you pay?"

"You get to keep running behind my walls at the sign of trouble," Knife said.

Ryker reached into his pocket and tossed something at Switch.

He caught it midair and held it up. The stone glinted brighter than a thousand diamonds in the sun. I'd heard of these, but I'd never seen one. It couldn't be, though. You didn't toss those away so easily.

Switch was squinting as he stared, his mouth open. "Is this..."

"Dragonstone. It's yours," Ryker said.

Holy magic, it was one. Dragonstone was mined from the caves where dragons nested. They would heat caverns with their fire, over and over again. They weren't that rare; they were that hard to get. You didn't go near a dragon lair. The life expectancy of a Dragonstone miner was twenty.

Knife cleared his throat, leaning toward Ryker. "How many of those you got lying around?"

"A few," Ryker said.

Switch pocketed the stone, smiling. "When you want to leave?"

Ryker unfolded a piece of paper and pointed to a spot. "We need to be here."

Switch looked it over and nodded, patting the outside of his pocket, making sure his stone was safe. "I'll try. If she's not strong enough, we might end up in the ocean. If that happens, I'm leaving you there."

Ryker glanced at me. I was expecting him to ask me how I felt. He didn't. "Don't worry about that. She'll give you enough. We'll be ready in five minutes. We've got to change."

I looked down at my leathers and ran a hand over my cotton shirt. It wasn't fancy, but it was clean. Clean-ish? It wasn't like I had all day to scrub my clothes.

I glanced up, and Ryker was already on his way back to the chugger. "What's wrong with what I'm wearing?"

"We need to blend." Ryker climbed into the back, grabbed a bag, and began digging through it. "Mushroom Man's having a party."

"How do you know?"

"Word is he has a party every night." He pulled out a piece of silver fabric and gave it to me.

"I thought we were going to sneak in?"

"A lot easier to walk in the front door. Plus, I think he'll hand over the bean willingly. It's the stone that will be the problem."

"What's this?" I asked. The fabric shimmied in front of me and sort of slinked, draping around my hand.

"A dress Dezz lent you."

I watched as he pulled out more items from his bag that looked like a white shirt for him.

I looked down again. "You don't think I could go with what I'm wearing?"

"If you want to broadcast that you're a killer, then sure, that's a great look." He stood at the edge of the chugger and let his eyes hammer home his point.

"What about my hair, then? My hair isn't going to blend." I held up a hand to the locks that were somewhere in between curls and a wave. If he thought my outfit wasn't good, he'd certainly have an issue with the mop on my head.

"What about it?"

I leaned forward an inch, wondering if he had bad vision. "It's a mess?" I ruffled it with my fingers in case he still didn't get it.

He shook his head. "It looks good like that." He pointed to the part I'd mussed. "I like what you're doing there."

I looked like I'd rolled around on the ground for an hour, but somehow that wasn't an issue.

Wait. Maybe I did have an out. I held the dress back to him. "I can't wear it. I only have boots. I'll really stick out with that thing on with boots."

"No, you have sandals." He dug into the bag and handed them to me. "She thought you should wear some sort of heel with that dress, but I wanted to make sure you had something more practical in case we need to run."

Because the silver slinky dress was going to work out really well in a chase?

He tossed the sandals down to me and then another small bag. "She said you might need some of this girlie stuff to get ready."

I looked at the scrap of fabric dangling from my fingers

before trudging behind the chugger. The more I looked, the worse I felt.

"If we're going to walk in and ask him to give us the bean, why do I have to wear this? Why do we need to blend?" I yelled loud enough that he could hear me on the other side.

"*Because* we'll be able to move around the place after-ward without drawing more attention."

Magic, fuck, bugger, dammit. He was right. It made good sense, but I hated it. I stalled for another second before I pulled my clothes off in haste. I needed to get this over as fast as I could and then forget what I had on.

"You almost done?" he called.

My shirt was off and the dress was over my head. I didn't have to worry about Dezz being taller, as the dress barely covered my thighs. That didn't bother me as much as the way it exposed my back with the way the fabric draped to nearly my waist.

"There's no back on this thing?"

"Won't your hair cover it?" he asked.

It would, but then what would I do about the front? I tried splitting my hair, half hanging in the front and half in the back. It wasn't reliable that way. It was going to come down to either my chest hanging out or my markings. My markings won.

"Bugs," Ryker said, his patience running thin.

That man was getting as bad as me.

"I'm coming." I slid on the sandals with long strings attached and tied them around my ankles. They might as well have given me heels for as combat-ready as I'd be.

"Bugs!" he yelled.

"I said I'm *coming!*" I took a step and stopped. I took another step but stalled out again right at the corner of the chugger. This was stupid. It was a dress. It was flesh. So what?

I marched out, keeping my head high and pretending I didn't look like a fool.

"Don't you dare say anything," I told Ryker as I walked around the chugger.

He didn't say a word, but he looked as if he'd never seen me naked before.

I crossed my arms and walked back toward the rest of the guys, hoping they'd act normal. They didn't.

"Stop staring."

They all jerked their gazes away.

I stopped in front of Switch, who was the only one not acting weird.

"You look very pretty," he said, his eyes glued to my face. It was most unnatural, as if he were afraid to unglue them and look at the rest of me again.

"Thank you," I replied softly, hoping no one else was paying attention.

Ryker joined us. At least he wasn't acting weird anymore. He'd only seen thousands of naked bodies, though. I'd ask him how many, but he probably couldn't count that high. No one could.

Switch shook out his hands and rolled his shoulders. He leaned his head back, cracking it from side to side. This went on for long enough to make me nervous but shy of calling it quits.

There would be no quitting. I needed that bean. A bumpy ride wouldn't be the end of the world, and Ryker could swim. Hopefully I'd juice Switch enough to get us close to dry land and Ryker could haul us to shore.

Switch shook out his fingers and then extended a hand to Ryker and I. "Normally I'd hold both hands of the one person traveling to create a loop. You two will have to hold and we'll see if we can do this."

I took Switch's hand and then grabbed Ryker's to complete the loop, hoping no one noticed my sweating palms. "You want to do a little hop first? Maybe just ten feet away to see if it'll work?"

"Can't, not unless you want to go tomorrow. Distance isn't the problem so much as taking off." Switch glanced at Ryker and then turned to me, his eyes rounder than they'd just been. "This is a lot of extra weight for me."

"So, if you get us out of here, we'll have a good chance of making it the whole way?" I asked.

"Oh yeah, it doesn't work the way you're thinking. Everyone imagines it's like flying or something. It's not. We're here. Then we're there. Or we're not there, depending on how it goes." He wiggled his shoulders again. "But then we'll still be there, wherever there is."

"We've got it," Ryker said. "Let's go.

Switch raised the hand that was holding mine. "Juice me up," he said, as if it were an everyday thing.

witch was right. There was no flying or swishing. No floating, either. We were in one place and then we were in another without any clue how it happened.

We'd gone from early afternoon light to night. Two moons waning in the sky, but one a little further along than the other and surrounded by trees. The forest was dense and muggy, and the leaves were fat and big. Bugs were everywhere, buzzing around and trying to get a bite. I'd heard of places like this—the tropics, they'd called them. Recently I'd seen pictures in some of the books I'd been going through.

"How long do you need?" Switch asked. "As long as she can keep juicing me, I can do it whenever you need."

"Two hours, exactly. Do you have the watch Burn gave you?" Ryker pulled one out of his pocket and looked at the dial.

Switch nodded, pulling his out and comparing it to Ryker's.

"Will you be waiting here?" I asked.

He swatted a hand over a bug that landed on his arm. "No, but I'll be on time."

Switch ducked as a bug took aim for his face and disappeared before it could make another flyby.

Ryker pointed in the distance. "You see that light? That's where we're going. Once we get to the mushrooms, he'll know we're here. Don't say anything you wouldn't want him to overhear. They'll relay that information back to him."

"Mushrooms?"

He tilted his chin down. "Asks the girl who talks to worms."

I shrugged but kept my mouth shut. He had a point.

"So we're going to walk in and ask him for the bean?"

"Yes. Then we blend in and rob the stone."

"He's going to let us waltz up and take it?"

"He's not going to think anyone can."

"Why?"

"Because before you, no one could."

"How were you going to come on your own?"

"I was going to get the bean. I wouldn't have been able to get the stone."

He kept walking as I faltered. He was going to get the bean? Only the bean? He was going to come here and leave the stone, the thing he wanted the most?

He looked over his shoulder. "What are you doing?"

"I'm in sandals, remember?" I asked as I caught up to him.

WE WALKED FOR A GOOD TEN MINUTES BEFORE WE CAME TO A road with a large path leading off it. There was a building at the end of the path that rivaled any castle I'd seen in its sprawl. That wasn't the thing that caught my eye. Everywhere in view, there were mushrooms growing. Some seemed to tower as large as the house, and others were small and clustered.

As we walked down the path, a light dusting flowed from the undersides. Scents floated in the air, some musky, some floral. I grabbed Ryker's hand, and he looked down. I made an exaggerated inflation of my chest. He breathed deeply in response, signaling that the air was fine. I kept breathing, but only because I had to.

Torches of gold lit the path and set the stone of the building to shimmering. Nothing about this place looked like it would exist in the world I'd known. I'd never seen a place with such obvious wealth.

There were people standing around in small clusters with fine glasses filled with sparkling liquids on the front patio, and the buzz of magic was in the air. Markings were on full display, from legs to arms. Still, my hand went to my hair, making sure it hung down my back.

No one stopped us as we strolled among them, as if they accepted us as their kind. They continued to laugh and converse, no idea we were the enemy.

There were more people inside, all dressed decadently and drinking from their glasses. Ryker's arm moved to circle my waist as we navigated through the rooms. Servants dressed in scraps of fabric held together by strings walked around with trays of food and yet more drinks, ready to replenish.

"Where is this Mushroom Man?" I asked softly.

"He's here somewhere."

He steered me into a different room, and I knew immediately who Mushroom Man was. He was sitting on a throne made of wood at the end of the room, holding court. He wore white from head to toe, and jewels blazed on his fingers. Dark hair was pulled into a ponytail, and I could see markings climbing up his throat, hinting that he'd have marks on his torso as well.

He stood as he saw us approaching. "I send you an invitation every single year and yet you've never come. But now here you are, and with the loveliest companion."

The crowd parted, paying a little more attention to us as Mushroom Man approached.

"Marlin," Ryker greeted him, as if they'd met before.

One of these days, I was going to walk into a situation and know all the details ahead of time. But for now, I could only control what I was going to do tomorrow, and that was kill Ryker.

"Who is your lovely?" Marlin asked.

I forced my arms to stay at my sides as his eyes roved over the length of me. "I'm Bugs."

"Unusual name." He waved a hand over his shoulder, and a servant appeared, offering us drinks from his tray. Ryker took one and handed me the other.

"What brings you here? Did you want to meet the queen? I'm sure I could get you an audience tomorrow."

"Thank you, but we can't stay that long," Ryker said. "I'm here because I need a seed of the Elibell plant."

"And you think I have one?"

Ryker lifted his brows.

Mushroom Man laughed. "Yes, well, of course I do. Why do you need it?"

"You can give it to us or not. I can owe you a favor. Or not."

It was clear Ryker wasn't much of a socializer, which was fine. But when I had to step in to save the day, it was bad. And I needed this seed.

We'd done it his way, but my life was on the line, and

Marlin definitely favored a feminine touch, from what he was showing so far. "*I* need it. I've got a little issue with a spell I can't seem to dislodge."

Ryker turned to me and stared. He wasn't the eye-rolling type, but his glare had the same effect.

"What kind of spell?" Marlin asked, getting even closer, breathing deeply.

"Just a silly little thing of a personal nature that's been plaguing me." I added a giddy little laugh at the end, hoping he'd take me to be a flake.

He leaned forward, breathing deeply, as if he liked something about my scent. "Your magic is strong."

Ryker inched nearer, placing a hand at my back, his hand directly on flesh. Skin-to-skin contact that would keep me alive.

"Which is why you want *me* to owe you a favor." Although after we took his stone, Marlin wouldn't want a favor. He'd want us dead.

His chest rose and fell several times as he looked over my exposed flesh. "How strong are you?" he asked.

I could see the confusion. He could sense my magic, but he couldn't find my markings.

"Does it matter?" I asked.

"I like having strong friends."

If he was saying that all I had to do was prove my strength to get the bean, I had this in the bag. Now I needed to swallow back years of the instinct to hide, which had kept me alive.

Every person here would be another person who would know what I was. What was growing inside me. Then again, word was spreading anyway. Did it matter? It was do or die, and I needed that bean.

"Let me show you." I turned to give him my back, and

heard the intake of breath from the crowd watching on before I lifted my hair.

I pulled it out of the way and I heard murmurs shoot through the crowd, some oohs and ahs and a few whispers of "Full Blood."

Ryker's fingers had relocated so that they curled in and grazed my side.

"They're magnificent. May I touch?" Marlin said, close behind me.

I didn't know why I looked to Ryker before I answered, but I did. He stood unflinching. He'd have my back either way. I felt as sure of that as if it were Ruck, which was the oddest feeling, since I hated Ryker most days.

There was a slight shift of his head that I read to mean it wouldn't hurt me even if neither of us liked it.

"Sure," I said.

I stood, letting Marlin trace my markings for as long as I could take it, which was about three seconds. Then I turned, dropping my hair back over them.

"I'll give it to you"—he broke into a sly smile—"if you take it from my lips. A kiss isn't too much to ask. Is it?" He flicked his hand, and one of his men ran off to do his bidding.

I felt Ryker's magic flicking at my back, a special kind of heat brushing at my skin that could only be created by one person. It didn't flare or dissipate, a slow, steady burn.

"I'd be honored." The heat spiked but pulled back immediately.

A servant brought forward a box that Marlin took. He opened it; inside was a single seed, solid black. And large. He took it, lifted it to his mouth, and placed it between his teeth. He then cupped my cheeks, pulling me closer.

Our lips met. He released the seed immediately, and then his lips grazed mine.

He pulled back and then paused, our lips nearly feathering. "You need to swallow it whole for it to work," he said softly.

All in all, not as horrific as I'd prepared myself for. I swallowed it but needed a large gulp of the drink I'd been handed to get it down. "Thank you."

"I couldn't let a magic as beautiful as yours be marred." He turned and waved his hand toward the crowd. "I hope you'll stay and enjoy yourselves for a while?" he asked me.

"Of course."

Sensing he was done with us, women walked over and draped themselves across Marlin, moving their hips to the beat of the music. He was quickly distracted, and we faded into the crowd.

The mood was changing from conversation to more intimate scenes of women and men kissing and grinding against each other.

The farther we weaved into the crowd, the tighter Ryker's arm wrapped around my waist.

He continued to weave us through groups of people, and I knew where he was going. It was where I would've gone as well. We were heading toward the master bedroom.

There were people wandering the halls as we moved deeper into the house. Most of them were coupled up and paying more attention to each other than us as we went.

We made it up the stairs, and there were double doors at the end of the hall. He pulled me to the wall, leaning into me as people left one room and then passed us.

As soon as they were out of sight, we moved in unison and shot down the hall.

The room only had one piece of furniture, and it was a

large bed in the center that would hold five people easy. Every single wall and ceiling was mirrored.

"Where would it be?" I asked, walking farther in the room.

Ryker was scanning the mirrors, as if they were hiding something. "The intel said he keeps it close. It's got to be here somewhere."

I heard steps outside the doors and froze. Then someone said, "Because something was triggered."

I heard the door open, and before I could think, I was on the bed with Ryker on top of me.

Ryker's lips were on mine, a hand in my hair. Another was at my side, slowly learning the curve of my hip, the softness of my stomach as it glided upward over my ribs, stopping right beneath my breast. His hand took some of its weight, molding it to the shape of his palm.

My nipples pebbled and ached. That was when his hips shifted into me. I could feel the length of his cock through my dress, pressing, pushing my hips higher, my back arching.

All thoughts of company disappeared. We could've had an audience of a thousand and I wouldn't have noticed. Soft groans escaped my lips as I pressed into him.

It was a show, charade for all, an act so we could get what we needed. It was what I was supposed to do, even if it felt so good I'd die if we never touched again.

His arm slipped back around my waist, moving us both to the center of the bed. He gripped under my knee, pulling it up so he could settle in closer, and I arched, adjusting to help him.

My fingers dug into his shoulders; my leg wrapped around him and pulled him in.

It was bittersweet.

He didn't *really* want me. He was aroused because he was a man and because of the magic. He was doing this because we *did* have an audience. So was I.

He paused, but didn't move away. "They left," he said, his lips hovering above mine.

"Yeah." They had?

He didn't move, and I didn't ask him to.

"We should get back to work," he said, still not moving.

I'd thought that's what we've been doing. I nodded. "Yeah, we should."

He stood, grabbing my hand and pulling me up with him.

29

I searched the room, laying my hands everywhere, trying to sense magic with everything I had. "Should we be doing this? Maybe you can make friends like you did with Knife?"

Ryker was walking the perimeter of the room doing the same. "There's a reason I've ignored every offer to come here, and he'd never hand over the stone."

"He didn't seem that bad. Maybe we could work with him?" We'd been walking around this room for ten minutes, and there wasn't that much in it. "We might have to work with him."

"He doesn't work with anyone. He didn't get all this by being nice."

I turned toward him, stopping my search for a second. "How bad?"

"The worst. And now that he knows what you have, you can bet he'll be in line with the rest coming for you."

I went back to searching. I climbed up on the bed to run my hands over the walls above it. Once, twice, and then I paused as I zeroed in on a spot. "I think I've got something."

Ryker walked over. "There?"

"Yes. It feels exactly like the one you made with the stone."

I placed both hands on the spot and felt power buzzing through my fingertips. "It's here. I can feel it. This wall is an illusion."

"You sure?"

"Positive." I continued to run my hands along the area, trying to figure out how large it was and if there were any weaknesses.

"Can you get past it without him sensing?"

"I don't know, but I've got to try."

"Agreed. Do it."

He stood between the bed and the door, but close enough to touch me if things went bad.

Both hands in place, with desperation driving me forward, I went to work. I didn't know if the bean would work, but I'd felt the power the stones could generate, could feel it now in this ward. If all else failed, the stones would be my salvation.

I moved my hands along the ward, trying to coerce the pattern that I knew was there out of it. Over and over again, I ran my fingers over the same spots.

"You've got to hurry. We don't have all night," Ryker said from behind me after about fifteen minutes had passed.

"I know." Sweat coated my brow as I continued trying to find a weakness to get a foothold in. "I think I've got something."

Magic tingled across my spine. It wasn't like any of the wards I'd felt. It slithered forward as I worked farther in, choking out some of my own. I tried to focus past the foul magic, knowing something was different here. Then I realized it wasn't the ward but something behind the ward I was feeling. I was nearly through it, but the worst might lie ahead.

"Ryker, move away from me."

"Why?"

"If you want the stone, do it. If things go bad, I don't want someone connected to me. I want someone who can move in quick and get me."

"You sure you know what you're doing?"

"I'm positive."

He moved a foot away from me, and I knew that was all I was going to get. It was enough. This thing was contained within the ward. If I could get the stone and pull it out, without completely breaking it, we'd be okay.

I pushed forward. The thing, or whatever it was, churned against every part of me that was beyond the ward. I couldn't see what it was doing as the illusion of the wall stayed intact, but my skin felt as if it were being shredded.

I shoved deeper, until my shoulders were within it as I felt around, grinding my teeth from the pain.

"What the fuck are you doing?" Ryker asked.

"Watch the door," I said.

He froze halfway back to me, torn between doing what I'd asked and what his instinct told him to do, which was help.

If he touched me, if he made my magic flare, the ward might come down. I was balancing on a razor's edge of control.

"Please, Ryker, stay away. I can do this, but I can't worry about it coming for you too."

"What coming for me?"

It was there again, burning, shredding skin. Writhing around my body. The pain wanted to force me to my knees, but I needed this stone, so I stayed standing, blindly groping around, knowing the stone was there.

A soft cry escaped my lips.

"What's going on?" Ryker asked, and I knew he wasn't going to stand idly by for too much longer. "Pull out of there."

"One more minute." I dragged in a breath, afraid I wasn't going to be able to keep going.

My fingers grazed something, and I knew immediately it was the stone. Pure power surged through my fingers. I wrapped my hand around it and I pulled it out.

"I've got it," I said, turning and dropping to my knees on the bed.

Ryker wasn't looking at the stone. I looked down at myself and then wavered slightly. It wasn't from seeing the blood, though. I'd seen plenty of that. It was from the loss of it. My arms were shredded as if something had rubbed the flesh from them, all the way up to my shoulders and part of my chest. Every part of me that had reached into the ward had been lashed. My dress was quickly becoming soaked in blood.

Ryker sprang into action. He grabbed the blanket from the bed, wrapping me in it and then scooping me up, my hands still gripping the stone.

"I've got you."

I curled into him.

"You're going to be okay. I'll get you out of here and to the witch. You're going to be fine."

I didn't know if he was talking to me or himself. I swallowed through the pain, forcing air into my lungs. "I know. You need me too much. You'd never let me die."

He walked out into the hallway. Whenever someone looked at us, he laughed and joked that I'd drunk too much.

It was a blur as I let my head drop to his shoulder, hoping he could get us out peacefully. I knew what would happen if he couldn't.

I heard a commotion growing and knew someone had gone into the room and seen the blood on the bed. I heard yelling.

We'd made it all the way to the front patio when I heard Marlin's voice.

"You came here and stole from me?" he asked.

Ryker turned to face him. I feared for how many lives might be lost. I moved my hand to rest on the bare part of Ryker's chest. He glanced down, and I could see he didn't want to do it, but he would.

He looked to Marlin. "I know where you got this stone, and I know what happened to the person who had it before you."

There was silence. "I thought we could be allies," Marlin said.

I heard other people walking outside to watch the exchange, but I couldn't seem to lift my head at the moment. I didn't want to, either. I'd rather not watch them die.

Ryker's words vibrated through me as he answered Marlin. "That could never happen. Now you're going to let me leave here, because you know what will happen if you try and stop me."

"I will come for you," Marlin said.

"If you do, it won't end well."

Ryker turned and left, and the second we cleared the mushrooms, he broke into a run. It didn't have anything to do with Marlin and everything to do with the blood soaking the front of Ryker's shirt.

"Holy fuck," Switch said in the distance.

"You're lucky you're here, or I was going to kill you. Get us out of here."

"How? She looks half dead. How's she going to juice me?"

"She can do it."

I reached out with one bloody arm and latched on to Switch, giving him everything I had left.

"Bugs. You have to wake up." Ryker gently shook me in his arms.

I lifted my lids slightly to see familiar faces gathered around me.

"Bugs, I need you to juice Switch one more time. You can do this," Ryker said.

My eyes drifted closed again. Right now, I couldn't do anything but sleep.

"How do you not have a healer close by?" Burn shouted at someone.

"Because they *died*," Knife shot back.

Ryker shook me again. "Bugs, listen to me. We need to get back to the Valley, and we don't have time for a chugger. You have to do this."

There was pretty much nothing I wouldn't do to get him to stop shaking me back awake at that point. Someone grabbed my arm and pulled it out from where I'd tucked it in between my body and Ryker's. I jerked with the pain as it jarred me fully awake.

"Be careful," Ryker said.

"There's nowhere to grab her that isn't shredded," Burn replied.

"You sure she can do this again? She doesn't look—"

"Switch, shut up and take her hand," Ryker said. His

voice softened as he looked down at my face. "One more time, okay?"

I felt his magic surrounding me like a warm cloak, trying to soothe me. It did nothing for the pain, but I doubted anything would at this point. The pain wasn't even the issue. It was keeping my eyes open.

"I can do it." I stretched out my fingers and felt Switch's hand gently wrap around them. I didn't wait for him to say he was ready. I gave him what little I had left.

30

The sound of the door opening woke me, and I had to orient myself to my surroundings. The last time I'd been awake, I was outside the walls of Dorley, my skin had been shredded from my body, and my blood was pouring out.

Now I was lying in Ryker's bed. The skin on my arms looked fresh and pink, like a newborn baby's. I wore a white shirt without a drop of blood marring the soft fabric.

Ruck walked over and perched on the side of the bed. He wouldn't look me in the face. His back was stiff and his fingers were tapping on his legs. "How you feeling? Burn and Sneak filled me in last night. You were a bloody mess when you got back here."

"Considering? Pretty good." I flexed sore arms but was feeling whole. "What happened after we got back here?"

Ruck waved a hand. "It was crazy. Out of nowhere, Ryker popped into the middle of the street with you in his arms dripping blood. He stood there and screamed for the healer, baring his teeth at anyone who tried to get a closer look at you. Between you and me, he was scary as *fuck*. I've never seen people scramble so fast to do what he said.

"By the time I climbed down the tower, the healer was already running over to him. He locked the three of you away in his place. Thankfully, Burn and Switch showed up and filled me in before I had to bust the door down. Course, I wouldn't have had to wait to find out what the hell happened if you'd told me the truth about what you were going to do and taken me with you."

He paused, waiting to see if I'd respond. His hurt ripped through me as badly as that creature behind the ward had.

"I'm sorry," I said, not for leaving him behind but because I'd hurt him.

"Ryker didn't come out again until this morning, and they finally let me in." His eyes ran my length for the first time since he'd walked in the room. His face paled, as if what he'd seen last night was burned into his memory. "You didn't look like you had any blood left."

My fingers went to my arms, the horror of my skin being shredded fresh in my mind.

"Have you seen Ryker?" I asked, not ready to talk about what happened.

"He went to the border. Said something about shoring up the wards."

His eyes went to my hand, where it was still running over the new flesh. I was thankful he didn't push me for more details. Ruck might be mad, but he was my family. He knew me. He knew when to push and when to leave things be. And I knew he'd always be there for me, no matter how mad he got.

"Are you hungry? Want me to grab you some breakfast and bring it back here?" Ruck asked.

"Nah, I can get up." I sat up slowly, the muscles in my

arms and chest feeling like they'd gotten a hell of a workout. Ruck clasped my hand, helping me ease the rest of the way up.

"I have to know one thing. Did you not take me with you because I'm a dull?" he asked.

"I left you behind because your life matters too much to me. It mattered more than my own. I had to go. You didn't. And if we went there together and I came back alone, I couldn't have handled losing you. I did it because I was selfish."

"And how do you think I would've managed if you didn't make it back and I knew I might've been able to save you?" He leveled a hard stare at me.

Of course he'd have to turn this around on me. "Fine. I'll keep you in the loop more, if I can. It's not always my choice." Ryker didn't know it yet, but he was going to start getting blamed for a lot more crap.

Ruck nodded.

"I'm glad we cleared that up," I said.

His smile only made me feel slightly guilty.

"Give me a second." I ducked into Ryker's bathroom and pulled the shirt down, afraid of what I'd see. The skin looked similar to my arms, tinged pink and raw, as if it were brand new. It was. I hadn't had much left after last night.

I finished up in the bathroom and made my way back, wobbling on my feet until I got to the bed. "You still want to bring me breakfast?" I asked, dropping back on to the messy covers and knowing I couldn't have made it a few feet further.

Ruck stood, looking me over. "Yeah, rest. I'll grab you something. Even with all the crap you pulled, you're okay now, and it was worth it for the bean."

Yep, we were going to be okay. Until I left him behind

again and he hated me. Ryker had said to me once that the dead didn't have the luxury of hate. I hadn't truly understood it until now. If I had to choose between Ruck hating me but staying alive, there was no choice.

It shed some light on what Ryker might've been thinking when he'd said it. Except that didn't make any sense. Me and Ryker didn't have that kind of bond.

And speak of the devil, I could feel him close by. He appeared in the doorway. His arms were crossed and he looked like if he could kill someone, he would. "The bean didn't work. The healer said we can't see the mark, but it's still there."

I sank down into the bed. If I was the type to cry, I might've been shedding tears right now out of frustration. It wasn't all lost, though. That stone had been the real deal. It felt like it, anyway.

"Maybe it needs more time to work?" Ruck asked.

Ryker took a few steps into the room. "Or maybe that weasel never gave you the right bean in the first place. The healer has seen them before, and what she described didn't resemble what he gave you."

"At least we have another stone," I said, shoving my hair from my face. As long as I could kill Bones first, he couldn't kill me.

"There's other options as well," Ryker said, staring at me. "How many more chances do you want to take? How long do you want to let this go on?"

"I'll get you some breakfast and be back," Ruck said quietly as he slipped from the room.

Ryker stepped to the edge of the bed, looking as if he were about to go to war.

"The bean didn't almost kill me last night. The stone did."

"The only reason we went for that stone was because of the bean. I would've found a softer target otherwise."

"I know what you think I should do, but I can't do it, not yet. And you can't tell me you'd hand over all your magic to a stronger Wyrd either."

He still looked as angry as before, but he stopped arguing. That was how I knew I was right. He wouldn't have been able to do it either.

"Thanks for keeping me alive."

He nodded.

"How many years did it cost you?"

"Don't worry about it. I'll catch up with you later." His clipped reply left me sorry I'd tried to be nice and thanked him.

He walked out still mad at me. You would've thought he'd been the one to almost die. Didn't change anything, though.

31

I walked to the watchtower and could feel eyes on me. I looked around but couldn't match any bodies to them. It could've been paranoia, but I didn't subscribe to that emotion anymore. If I got a weird feeling in my gut these days, I was probably going to be fighting for my life soon.

"You going to make it?" Ruck yelled down as I got to the ladder.

"Don't worry. I've got this," I shouted back, in case the eyes watching me also had ears pointed in the same direction. Didn't want them to think I was an easy target.

There were beads of sweat on my forehead by the time I got to the top. I took a seat beside Ruck, letting my feet dangle over the ledge.

"How you feeling?"

I shook out my arms. "I'm good."

He laughed. "When did you start lying so well?"

"I've always lied well. You're the one who needs practice." I scanned the streets below me, using the bird's-eye view to see if I could spot anyone suspicious. "By the way, someone, maybe a few, are definitely watching me. I felt their eyeballs on me even as I walked here. I'm starting to think every time I survive something, it makes somebody else want to kill me."

"I told you I thought people were watching. Do you think they want you gone from here?"

"I don't know, but I'm not going anywhere, whether they want me to or not." I looked around the platform. "You don't have any snacks?"

"No. I was hoping you'd bring some."

Damn. Maybe I should go get something.

Ruck leaned forward, the line of his back tensing. I'd spent so much time knee deep in shit with him that I knew when his hackles were up.

"What?" I leaned closer, trying to pick up his line of sight.

"There's someone heading this way that I don't know, and he's not giving the signal. I think I need to set the alarm."

I stood, getting up to do it for him, when I spotted Burn and Sneak walking over.

"Hey," I yelled down to them.

They both stopped and looked up.

"We've got a stranger heading in." I pointed in the direction he was coming from.

"Ryker already picked up on him. We're heading there now," Burn said.

I looked back to where the guy was and realized Ryker must've extended the territory with his last ward.

Ruck and I watched as the guy made his way closer. Burn and Sneak greeted him, and I saw nodding on both sides, but that was the extent of the good vibes. They turned and walked toward us, Burn and Sneak on either side of the newcomer, and a chill shot down my spine.

Maybe I *was* paranoid. Every sign of danger wasn't directed at me.

They walked past the tower, and the man looked up, his eyes landing on me, as if he'd been scanning people for someone who fit my description. They continued to Ryker's, and the door opened before they got there. Ryker moved to the side, and Burn, Sneak, and the man walked in.

The stranger was out of sight, but the feeling stayed. Ryker glanced up at me before he followed them in. In that second, every tingle of warning felt like it had been stamped and approved. Ryker thought this was going to be about me too.

"You seeing all this?" I asked Ruck.

"Yeah." Ruck leaned over the rail and called to Ben, who was also watching the happenings from down below.

"What are you doing?" I asked.

"Ben will cover for me. We need to hear what's happening," Ruck said.

I didn't want to get anywhere near that man, but I'd still go. Better to know what was coming at you than to sit ignorant.

By the time Ben climbed up and I climbed down, Sneak was there waiting for me before my feet hit the ground.

"Ryker asked me to come and get you." He waved a finger at Ruck. "Only you."

"Why?" I asked.

"The guy's here to give you a message."

I paused, then looked at Ruck. "Hang here. I'll be back."

"I'll be watching." Ruck pointed to the top of the tower, where he'd have the best view of trouble.

I nodded and then walked toward Ryker's with Sneak.

As soon as we were out of Ruck's earshot, Sneak said, "Ryker said it's your call. Either way, he'll back you."

What was I walking into? I nodded, keeping my face blank and my breathing as even as the water in the lake on a balmy day. I pulled my magic tight to me, as best I could. From my quick read, the guy had been a dull, but that didn't mean I wanted to walk in magic ablaze. If Ryker was on edge, or if Burn or Sneak were, I didn't want to push their buttons, because I was bouncing all over the place.

I opened the door, Sneak behind me. The man was standing in the middle of the room. Ryker was a few feet from him, glaring. That was the only good word for it.

Burn had a sneer on that said, *I don't fucking like you.* How could we all get the same feelings and be wrong? This guy was bad news.

"What's going on?" I asked, keeping it light—for now.

Ryker nodded toward the guy. "He's got a message for you from the Queen of Cacoy."

I turned my attention to the man but said nothing. Why would the Queen of Cacoy have something to say to me? Did the Mushroom Man rat us out and get her involved? But wouldn't he want Ryker? Why me?

The man assessed me silently for a minute. He definitely wasn't Wyrd Blood, but he was looking for markings as if he'd been trained. "I'm from the queen. She said she can provide you with real seeds from the Elibell plant if you provide her with a lock of your hair in exchange."

I immediately put another foot of distance between us. "Why does she want a lock of my hair?"

"Because it travels easier than blood but provides the same proof. She wants to know if you're from her lineage." His words were without emotion. He was a messenger. Paid to do a job. That was all.

The seed I needed for a lock. It seemed simple enough,

but I'd already been tricked once. What if this queen decided that I was from her lineage? What then? Would she want a piece of me too? Did she kill off anyone from her bloodline?

No. We had the stones, and that would have to be enough. Hopefully, I'd turn down his offer and that would be the end of it, but I didn't think it would.

"I had very humble beginnings. I'm not related to any queen, so you can go back and tell her that."

"Word has reached her about your markings. She believes you might be."

"And I'm telling you I'm not. You can keep your seeds." I felt Burn and Sneak step behind me.

The man reached into his pocket and held out a case. He opened it, and there was a single shiny black seed. "It'll be easier if you give me a lock of hair."

I saw the bean and wanted to snatch it from his hands. I also heard the threat.

Ryker stepped forward. "Is that the bean the queen sent you with?"

The messenger looked at it as if making sure himself. "Yes."

"The only reason I'm letting you live right now is so that you can take whatever that thing is back to your queen and tell her that the next time she tries something like this, I'll view it as an invitation to war."

The messenger looked at the bean again and nodded. "I'll forward that message."

"You do that," Ryker said, holding the door open for him.

The man walked out, and Ryker nodded toward the door while looking at Sneak to follow him.

Ryker shut the door, and I could hear a fly buzzing about

the room. It wasn't a metaphor. There really was a fly, and it was pretty loud. But still, no one was talking.

"It was a fake?" I asked.

"The healer said it would be a deep purple. It was closer than what you got from Marlin, but not the real thing." Ryker walked over, each step sounding like a countdown until he stepped in front of me. His eyes traced every angle of my face. "Is there any reason you are aware of that the Queen of Cacoy would believe you are a relation?"

Burn leaned in, making sure he heard the answer.

I shrugged. "No."

Ryker turned and walked a few paces, scratching at the stubble on his jaw. "I've never pressed you on your history, but could it be a possibility?"

Ryker was so calm that I had to look a little bit closer. Had we found this mysterious middle ground I'd always heard of? We didn't often tread there, but I'd heard lots of people met in the middle all the time. Had he come to the conclusion that, just like him, I had secrets and things I didn't want to discuss?

"I don't remember much of my family, but none of my memories lead me to believe we were royalty in any way. We were too poor. If we were related to a queen, someone kicked us out of the castle decades before I was born."

Ryker nodded, looking as conflicted as I felt. The queen of a place riddled with Wyrd Blood was not someone you wanted to notice you.

"How bad is this?"

"I don't know," Ryker said.

"I do," Burn said. "it's pretty fucking bad."

32

I left Ryker's, my head already bursting with new questions, and saw the commotion near the third watchtower. I picked up my pace. It was probably nothing. Everyone's nerves were on edge. There'd probably been a fight and people had stepped in to break it up.

I got closer and saw some people were squatting around something; others were backing away. I broke into a run and saw Ruck's legs sticking out of the group.

It was a haze after that. For some reason I didn't understand, I might've screamed Ryker's name. It was the only thing that would explain how he got to my side so quickly as I shoved through the crowd.

Ruck had no visible signs of injury, but he was barely breathing. I felt like my lungs had stopped altogether. Or maybe I wished I would. He couldn't leave me here alone. Not now. I'd lost too many and I couldn't lose him. I'd break.

I grabbed his hand. I knew he was a dull, but I gave him everything I had, trying to throw all my magic at him and juice some life into him if it were possible.

"Ruck, don't you dare die. You hear me?" I was nearly

screaming it at him as Ryker kneeled down and lifted him in his arms.

"Get the healer now," he yelled into the crowd.

Ryker carried Ruck to his place, and I followed, never letting go of Ruck's hand, even as Ryker was laying him on his bed.

"Keep talking to him and holding him. I think it might be working enough to keep him breathing," he said.

Ryker left me alone for a few minutes before he walked back in with the healer.

She stopped as soon as she saw Ruck. "He's a dull. I can't fix him."

"You're going to try," Ryker said, rolling up his sleeves.

The healer was huffing all over the place but pulled out her instruments, carrying on and saying we were more work than we were worth.

Ryker's voice chilled the air as he warned her to shut up and get to work.

She pointed to me. "You need to leave. I can't have you affecting him. It's going to be tricky as is, and I don't need you pulling at his magic while I'm working and needing it all."

Ryker moved to my side and took Ruck's hand from mine. "I've got him. I won't let him die."

I nodded, but Ryker still had to pry my fingers from Ruck's. Burn grabbed my shoulders and pulled me the rest of the way out of the room.

I walked from Ryker's alone and then kept walking. I didn't pay attention to where I was going. I needed to get out of there, away from everyone.

I knew what Ryker was doing, and considering the shape Ruck was in, it would be a while if it worked. I had hours to kill and lots of dwelling on the worst-case scenario with which to occupy myself.

I was a pro at worst-case scenarios. In a way, it was a blessing. I'd always been prepared for the worst. In times like these? It was a curse that could drive me to my knees.

Ruck couldn't die yet. I'd always counted down how many birthdays someone had left. By my estimation, Ruck should have at least fifty more. That number had always given me comfort.

It was an illusion. It had led me down a stray path. I'd never told him how funny he was. How I'd relied on him and been thankful for him every single day. I'd taken for granted that he knew. I'd never said any of this because I'd thought I had fifty more years of moments to tell him. Turned out, I hadn't had anywhere near that long.

I walked past the crowds that were whispering, afraid if I stopped and heard them, I might kill one of them. I kept going until I hit the forest.

I wandered for hours, might've shed tears that I'd never admit to, before Sneak caught up to me, branches cracking underneath his feet.

I dragged an arm across my face quickly, making sure I'd gotten rid of the evidence before I turned to face him. "How long have you been following?" I asked, words full of a bravado fueled by the idea he might have seen me at my worst. I knew he could move silently when he wanted. The guy's nickname wasn't Sneak for no reason.

"I'd like to say a few minutes, but long enough." He cleared his throat, as uncomfortable as I was about sharing the moment.

I let out a breath that wobbled in my chest. Figured: the one time I cried in a decade and I'd ended up with company. If he told anyone, I'd kill him.

"Did you want something?"

"I know you're in rough shape, but we're getting pretty far out. You've got a ton of enemies, and I can't leave you out here alone."

Ryker hadn't had a chance to send Sneak out after me. This had been all him. It soothed the hurt of being spied on, mostly.

"Why didn't you tell me you were here?" I asked as I turned to go back.

"I knew you wanted to be alone. I didn't want to leave you alone, so I faked it."

I dropped my head, feeling even worse about being mad at him. "Thanks."

"I do what I can."

I walked back toward him, hoping by the time we got back, Ruck would still be alive.

"Just so you know, I'm hoping he pulls through. I like the kid," Sneak said.

I stopped walking and took a few deep breaths, afraid his words were going to trigger another crying jag.

"You okay?" he asked.

I nodded. "Yeah, but go back to your silent thing."

"Got it."

We walked back together. I dragged my feet more the closer I got. Right now, Ruck was still alive in my mind. Once we got to Ryker's, and I went in, he might be truly dead.

Ryker walked out of his place, nearly staggering as he did, and that was all I needed. I ran forward. "Is Ruck okay?"

"The healer says he's going to make it." Ryker was walking stiffly, and the color was drained from his skin.

"What's wrong with you?" I asked, looking him over. I'd never seen Ryker look under the weather, let alone as bad as he did right now. He couldn't get sick or hurt. He was the one that was always okay. Nothing could happen to him. He was too strong. Right?

"Nothing. I'll be fine tomorrow."

Sneak walked up to him. "Crash in my place. Burn and I will keep an eye on everything," he said to Ryker.

"Are you sure you're okay?" I took a few steps following Ryker.

"Ruck needed a lot, and quickly. I'll be better soon," Ryker said, as he made his way into Sneaks.

"Thank you," I said, right before the door closed.

Sneak came up beside me. "He'll be fine. You're lucky he did it, though. No one else would've been able to."

"I hadn't realized he liked Ruck so much," I said, still looking at the door Ryker had disappeared behind.

"He likes him, but not *that* much."

I dragged my eyes away from the door. "Then why'd he do it?"

"Because you needed him to," he said, as if it were the most obvious thing in the world.

33

I woke up on Ryker's couch and tiptoed over to see Ruck asleep in the bed for the twentieth time. With his chest still rising and falling, I felt safe to go out and get him some breakfast for when he woke up.

I walked past Sneak's house, but it was closed up. I banged on the door, but no one answered, and when I peeked through the window, I didn't see anyone about, and the bedroom door was open. I left for breakfast and scanned every face on my way there and back. Then did another couple of laps.

I didn't stop making laps until I spotted Ryker by the tower. He was talking to a guy with marks on his hand, but I wasn't focusing on that. Ryker looked healthy again. He glanced at me and nodded. I nodded back, feeling like I could breathe again.

I walked back to bring Ruck his breakfast. My steps got slower and slower as I realized what I'd just done. I'd tracked Ryker down and hadn't been able to stop until I'd seen he was okay for myself. I'd known he was going to be fine; Sneak and Ryker had both told me so. But it hadn't been good enough. I hadn't felt normal or right inside.

A thought wiggled into my brain. It was a tiny suspicion that felt as if it were on the verge of growing and blowing my head apart. It stole my appetite and made it hard to swallow the biscuit I'd just taken a bite of. I did swallow, because I'd never waste food like that, but it was a struggle.

The idea kept invading until it seemed to move lower and settle in my chest, where it took up so much space that it pressed on my ribcage. My palms got clammy like I had a case of the Heebies and was about to sprout sores.

I was a stumbling mess by the time I got to Ruck with his heaping plate of lukewarm food.

"Hey, you're up," I said, trying to infuse my voice with cheer. I held the plate to him. "Figured it was my turn."

He sat up quickly and took it. "Thanks, I'm starving." He picked up the fork resting on it and began shoveling in food at a pace I hadn't seen since back in our Ruins days.

"You look good," I said, taking in the healthy color and knowing I'd lost some of mine.

"I feel great, thanks to Ryker. Told you he wasn't a bad guy." He shoved some more food in his mouth.

I sat down beside him, putting my biscuit on his plate and biting my lip instead.

Ruck paused between bites. "You okay? I'm good, right? You got a look that's scaring the shit out of me."

I nodded. "You're fine, and I want to tell you I love you and you're very funny." There, at least I'd gotten something good done today.

"Are you dying, like quicker than we thought?" His voice was a whisper, as if he didn't want to ask the question.

"No, that's not it. I just had to get that out."

He whacked me with his free hand. "Duh. I already knew all that."

"Who knew you'd go to the worst place imaginable? I didn't know you were so doom and gloom." I leaned out of the way when it looked like he was going to take another swing.

He went back to eating and spent another minute shaking his head in faux-disgust before he asked, "So what's wrong? You look off, considering you just got your best friend back."

His hand safely back to shoveling food, I slumped, knowing I looked pathetic. It matched how I felt.

"I think I've got feelings and shit. Like, romantic feelings, and for someone that is not a convenient person to have feelings for."

"At least you're finally admitting you like Ryker. It's not a big deal. Every chick in this place has a thing for him, old, young, taken, free. Hell, I've got a thing for him. The man is prime meat." He picked up a piece of sausage and wiggled it.

"It's worse than that. I think I might really be into him." I had too many other problems. I didn't need more complications, and caring this much about anyone was a dangerous thing in this world. Caring about Ryker? It was a monumental disaster.

"What's different than it was a week ago, other than you realizing it?"

"You're not understanding. I think I'm falling in love with him."

Ruck jerked his head back. His eyes did a weird squinty thing, and then he shook his head. "Now you're getting silly. You haven't even slept with him. You can't love someone you haven't fucked. Not possible."

"I don't know, Ruck. Something isn't good." I was willing

to concede that Ruck knew a lot more about fucking and love but had my doubts he had it right this time.

He patted the air in front of him. "No need to get all hysterical and dramatic. I know how to fix this."

"How?" I would've called it more melodramatic and morose, but I wouldn't argue if he could fix it.

"I'm going to ask you a series of questions that will disprove this assumption."

I nodded. It sounded like a decent idea. I'd never been in love. Maybe he was right and I was freaking out over nothing. I rolled my hand, encouraging him to get on with it.

"Do you care if he's happy?"

I leaned back and thought on that. All I could envision was his laugh, even when it was at my expense and I wanted to choke him. It still lit me up inside. Like his happiness, made my day brighter.

"I think so. That's bad. I know that's bad."

"That's not a super-important question. You want a lot of people to be happy because you're not a jackass. Forget that one. What do you think about when you're going to sleep?"

"Dying? Killing? Killing and then dying? Different variations of how I'll kill and die."

He shrugged. "See, you're fine."

I flopped back on the bed. "What if some of the killing I'm imagining is because I saw another woman go in or out of his place?" How many nights had I imagined tackling either the woman or Ryker himself to the ground? Way too many. "What if some of my thoughts were about snuggling into him? Sometimes I think I'd crawl into his skin if it were possible."

Only one side of Ruck's face rose, making an awkward half-squint *what's wrong with you* expression. "Maybe it'll go away. Don't think about it and see if it fades?"

"Yeah, sure." If I had any shot of that, it wasn't going to happen now, not after he'd saved Ruck, and for *me*. I couldn't tell Ruck that. I didn't want him to feel partly responsible for the bad shape I was in.

"What happened with the stranger? I missed the details due to my near death. Do you think that guy did something to me somehow? I didn't even come close to him, though. What was he here for?"

I grabbed the edge of his blanket, trying to curb the need to worm as I told him what had happened with the guy.

"The queen thinks you might be some long-lost relative? Do you think it's possible?"

"No." I rolled the cover in my fingers and then dropped it as Ruck caught sight of me.

"You should ask the worm. You're being stupid," he said, giving me a look that could've been taken from Ryker.

"Ruck, you know I made a—"

"To someone who turned their back on you. You agreed under false pretenses, and I need you to know something." His head dropped. "I didn't want to tell you. I thought it would make it worse, but I think I have to. You know the problem you had with the biscuit guy and the Wyrd Blood? I think some of that weaves its way back to Marra."

He'd stopped eating altogether to watch my face.

"Why would you say that?" I would've given my life to save Marra. If this was a case of her being out of sorts, I wouldn't begrudge her an outlet—to a point. But I needed to know what was going on.

"She's been stirring the pot a lot. I fucked a guy who fucked Marra's Ruck imposter. He was a real pillow talker. The new Ruck and the guy I fucked. She's stirring up shit for you."

"She doesn't even talk."

"Either way, she's been getting the message out how you think you're better than all the other Wyrd Bloods and think you should be getting special treatment. They said Ryker threatened to throw her out if she didn't cut the shit."

I should feel bad, right? I didn't. I felt relieved, like I'd been walking around with shackles and I'd just tossed them off. I'd been the only one trying to fix our relationship, but I felt like I'd been dealt the final blow that would let me walk away from it with a clean conscience.

I didn't owe her anything. I'd kept her alive for years. I'd plotted, stolen, taken the majority of the risks in our crew to feed her. I hadn't even wanted Sinsy to come. I'd begged them to leave, but that hadn't been good enough for Marra. But then, this had never really been about Marra. It had been about my guilt.

I stood, feeling lighter than I had in weeks.

"Are you okay? Where you going?"

"I'm going to worm."

I saw him smile before I walked out.

34

I made my way up the path and to the middle of the field where Ryker and I usually practiced. With a stick in my hand, I picked out a place to start and got to work. It took me about a half an hour to try and think through the questions, but they were all laid out in front of me.

I was still standing there, preparing myself, when Ruck came up, followed by Ryker. They stood behind me silently as I focused on what I was about to do. It shouldn't have been a big deal. I'd wormed more times than I could count, but I'd never done it to this extent, and all at once. It felt like jumping off a cliff and wondering if my wings would flap.

I knelt on the ground, nearly forgetting that Ryker and Ruck were there, and dug my hands into the dirt. I focused all the magic that was around me into my hands, feeling the energy that flowed through the soil. I was going to need a lot of worms for what I was about to accomplish, but if the magic gushing through my veins was any indication, I could pull this off. I needed to pull it off.

I didn't dig for a worm the way I normally would, but spoke as if the ground would carry my message. "You know my questions," I said. I'd spoken every one of them aloud as I'd drawn them out. "I need you to help me see what's coming."

I curled my fingers into the dirt, channeling my magic to my hands. A small hole appeared in the ground above where I knelt. As I watched, it grew longer until there was a clear line as the dirt sank inward, only an inch or so wide and deep but several inches long. The ground continued to sink, the line growing longer and longer, branching out across the ground.

It slowly made its way out, like the roots of a tree. It took about ten minutes or so before it finally stopped. I stood on shaky legs and looked at all my answers. Well, damn, it worked.

No one moved for a few minutes.

Ruck was the first to speak. "You said you were going to worm it, but what's this?"

"These are answers," Ryker said, stepping forward. "But what were the questions?"

My marks wouldn't make sense to anyone else, and I walked through it, trying to make sense of all the answers. "The one thing I could never do while worming was give it too many options to choose from."

"It's binary," Ryker said.

"If that means it's only yes and no, then yes, it's the binary thing." I yawned as I picked up the stick to point. I'd never felt tired after worming it, but this had been a whole other level.

I stepped up to the first question that was the tip of an upside-down triangle. "I started here, asking if the deaths were a sickness."

I followed the groove the Y, which was clear to all. "Obviously, the next question would be: is this a natural sickness?"

We all looked at where the line led to N.

I moved to the next question. "Trying to be very accurate, I asked if it was caused by someone."

Ryker stepped over to the next answer. "Yes." He pointed to the next markings. "What was that one?"

"I asked if it was caused by someone here." I couldn't hold back the yawn that interrupted that.

"It wasn't," Ruck said.

I yawned again. This really had sapped my strength.

"Did you ask if it was the Debt Collector?" Ryker said, pointing to the next. His brow furrowed. He was as confused as I, because the answer had been no.

"I figured it would be the logical progression. It's not him." I moved to the next spot, "So I asked if I knew the person, and I got another no."

Ryker pointed. "What are the last two?"

"I asked if you knew the person." The N was clearly marked.

"And the last?" Ryker asked.

"Was it someone *you* knew of." That was a yes.

Ryker walked up to the last spot and looked at the line. "Do you realize how many people I know *of*?"

I yawned again. "Yeah, I was afraid of that too, but I couldn't think of anything else."

I shook my head, trying to clear the fuzz gathering in between my ears. "But at least we know we're being targeted by someone other than the Debt Collector. Maybe it's the Mushroom Man? But that doesn't make sense. The deaths started before we ever went to the island. Besides, his magic was strong, but nothing compared to us. Maybe his queen put him up to it? But then we're back to why would she do that when we didn't steal from her but from the Mushroom Man.

"Maybe I should ask that?"

"You can't, not right now, or you're going to crash," Ryker said.

I took a seat on the ground. "Why am I so wiped out?"

"Different magic acts differently. When you break a ward, you're busting through something. When you put your hands into the soil to do this, you are feeding it magic, and probably more than you were prepared to give."

Ruck sat beside me as Ryker looked about the diagram of questions. "At least we know we've got more than one enemy coming for us."

Ryker lifted his head, his magic changing.

"What's happening?"

He turned to me. "Something strong just crossed our first ward."

35

W e made our way down the path to chaos. People gathered up things while others herded them away from the boundary of the Valley. Several people were calling to go wait in the Grove of Souls until the danger passed.

Ruck helped me keep up when I knew Ryker would've rather left me behind.

Burn was running toward us. "He's here. Bones is here."

Ryker turned toward his place, and I knew exactly what he was doing. He was getting the stones.

While Burn waited for Ryker, I detached myself from Ruck to wait with him.

"You need to stay here," I said.

"No way. Last time I stayed behind, you nearly died." Ruck moved closer to me, and I knew I wasn't going to be able to lose him.

Ryker came out of the house and rejoined Burn. Sneak was waiting up ahead as others ran past him.

Ryker turned to me. "Go to the Grove of Souls with everyone else. I'll tell you as soon as he's gone."

"Absolutely not. This is my life on the line."

"Me neither," Ruck said from beside me.

Ryker looked over at Sneak.

"He's out there waiting now," Sneak said, making it clear there wasn't any time for this fight.

Ryker turned back to me. "You stay close enough you can touch me." He turned to Ruck. "You, follow Burn and Sneak's lead and keep an eye out for an ambush. If I have to try and take him out now, I don't know if we have enough stones that he's going to stay dead. If things don't go the way we hope, I need you to take off."

"Leave?" I asked. I'd never run from a battle in my life, and now he wanted me to leave him?

"Yes."

I glanced at Ruck, who was giving me a look I knew well. *Placate him,* his eyes said.

I turned back to Ryker. "Sure. We'll both run." If Ryker believed me, that was his fault for not knowing me well enough.

He shook his head. Maybe he knew me better than I thought. Still, he turned. As a group, we marched out to meet the Debt Collector.

THE DEBT COLLECTOR STOOD IN THE FIELD, ALONE AND CALM. The better he appeared, the worse I felt. What did he know that we didn't? I ran fingers over my chest, feeling for an ache that wasn't there.

Ryker and I stopped ten feet away from him, affecting the same calm even if I wasn't feeling it. I glanced over my shoulder to see Burn, Sneak, and Ruck were fifteen feet away from us.

"Why are you here? You said three months," Ryker asked.

Bones glanced at Ryker's pockets. "I know what you carry, but you won't need them today. I'm here to say good-bye." He turned his full attention on me. "I no longer own your life. It's been purchased by someone else."

"Why would you do that?" I was having a hard time believing he would sell my soul. What about all the magical power he would gain with my soul?

"Let's just say I was offered a large number of Wyrd Blood souls in exchange for your one, without the tedious task of fighting for it."

Maybe he was telling the truth and the two stones wouldn't kill him, but I had a feeling it was close. Maybe three was the number?

"By who?" I demanded, afraid the purchaser was going to be a lot harder than him to eradicate.

"That I cannot answer." He held a hand up to his chest, and I saw a flare of magic spark from between his fingers. "I'm bound by an oath."

"Why bother telling us anything, then?" I asked.

"I know what you're collecting. While you don't have enough to harm me now, I thought it prudent to let you to know that your quarrel is no longer with me. I'd save the fight for what's coming for you. I'm not the only creature you call evil that walks the world. There is worse to fear... even for me."

I wanted to yell and scream that he couldn't walk away from what he'd already done to my parents, but I didn't. Right now, he could, and would, unless we gathered more stones.

I held my tongue. There'd be time to get my vengeance on him when I was stronger, when we had all the stones.

He turned and walked away, giving us his back. Slowly, his form began to break apart until there was nothing but mist, and then that was gone. The creature that walked in here alone, and walked out, was afraid to tell me who held my debt. I had a feeling I already knew.

"I still want him dead," I said, not caring if he was somehow hovering nearby invisible to us.

"We don't know who's coming next, but I think we both have an idea." Ryker stared at the spot where Bones had disappeared. I could feel his magic rolling outward in that direction.

"Why would the Queen of Cacoy want me when she already has an island filled with Wyrd Blood?"

"Not Full Blood, and not with a vulnerability that would let them be controlled." He turned, and his eyes met mine.

"We need more stones," Ryker and I said at the same time.

RYKER HAD GONE TO DO A SWEEP OF THE PERIMETER AS THE people came back from the grove. I walked back to my room, not Ruck's, knowing deep down at this point I'd never leave this place willingly. I settled onto the bed, letting the exhaustion from earlier finally settle in.

Gnawing pain woke me sometime later, like someone had shoved a hand inside my chest and was peeling away layers of my heart, tiny piece by tiny piece. My skin was flushed; a burning heat built inside me as I lay in a growing puddle of sweat. I knew if I looked at my chest, the bruise would be there. The Debt Collector had said he sold my life. The new owner was coming to collect.

I struggled to my feet, knowing that my time was limited. I stumbled down the roads, wondering if I'd make it or if my legs would finally crumble. If I'd have to scream for help first or I'd be able to crawl there.

Ryker's place came in view, and I dug down to the last of my reserves until I crashed through his door.

I fell, a heap of tangled arms and legs, sprawled on his floor. I'd barely crossed the threshold when he was at my side, grabbing my arms and cushioning my head in his palm.

He didn't say anything, but took in my form, the lines of pain carved in my face. The tears in my eyes.

I reached up and pulled down the neckline of my shirt, revealing what I knew would be there. It was dark and mottled, black and red lines spreading out from its center. Viscous in its coloring and deadly in its intent.

"I'm out of time," I said, grabbing the front of his shirt.

Ryker launched into action, lifting me in his arms and running out of his place and directly to Burn's. He shifted me to free a hand and banged on the door.

"Burn's been preparing," Ryker said to me. Burn swung open his door. "It's time," Ryker said, his eyes going to me.

"Go to the grove," Burn said. "The fairies said they'd help. I'll round up everyone else. They've been waiting."

That little manipulative shit. I was going to give him a kiss and hug if I made it through this.

I shuddered as another surge of pain shot into my chest and seemed to swallow the rest of me whole.

Ryker held me close. "Hang on. Don't you fucking die on me now, or I swear I'll beat your dead body and then go and kill Ruck."

A huff escaped my lips that had started as a laugh. Ryker had just traded unknown years to keep Ruck alive for me, so the threat didn't hit home. We were going to have to work on his motivational speeches. He could've saved them anyway. I hadn't made it this far to quit now.

He ran toward the grove, with me in his arms. I could feel the eyes on us as we went.

The grove was the most beautiful place I'd ever seen. Old trees made a canopy above a mossy ground. I could see twinkling lights in the trees and realized they were fairy nests.

Ryker settled us on the ground, my back resting against his chest, his arms wrapped around me, holding me up. Tiny sparks of light flew toward us, more and more coming as the fairies flew above our heads.

Then Burn was there, a trail of people behind him. I could feel the collective magic heading our way as they started to form circles around us.

I'd had no idea how many Wyrd Blood lived here. It had to be nearly a hundred. How had they all avoided me? The first ring had maybe twenty Wyrd Blood, and then there were two outer rings, each progressively bigger.

They held hands and began to circle. Burn made a motion with his hands and chanting began. I watched through a haze of pain as their combined magic filled the area with a haze of light. Sparks started flaring in the air, born of nothing but magic.

"Hang on," Ryker said, his hand wrapping around mine. "It's going to work."

I believed him. He'd tolerate no other outcome.

Burn came and knelt beside us. "I need to get out of the ring. I can't be inside when it finishes."

"Thank you," I said.

He smiled and then moved to the first circle of Wyrd Blood and joined them. There were more sparks until the entire area around us seemed permanently lit. The circle warmed, and I felt I was sitting with Ryker in a cocoon of warmth.

Golden trails of mist began winding their way around us slowly, and the pain in my chest began to subside. The more trails that appeared, the better I felt, until the pain was gone and exhaustion replaced it.

The light dimmed as I lay, remaining slumped against him, fairies still overhead and Wyrd Blood watching on.

Burn stepped forward cautiously, looking us over for some sign. "Did it work?" he asked.

"It worked," Ryker said.

That was how I knew he felt it too. Where I'd once only felt my magic surrounding me, there was now a link so strong it seemed as if it had always been there. Attached to me was magic so vast it was startling in its immensity, and I knew it was Ryker. It hovered nearby and felt like it could swallow mine whole.

This was what I'd feared.

"Don't betray me," I said softly, fear lacing my words.

"I won't."

I didn't ask Ryker what came next. Neither of us knew.

LOOK FOR THE CONTINUATION OF BUGS' STORY IN **2019.**

SIGN UP HERE TO BE NOTIFIED OF NEW RELEASES BY DONNA.

DONNAAUGUSTINE.COM

https://www.facebook.com/Donnaaugustinebooks/
https://twitter.com/DonnAugustine

ALSO BY DONNA AUGUSTINE

Ollie wit

A Step into the Dark

Walking in the Dark

Kissed by the Dark

The Keepers

The Keepers

Keepers and Killers

Shattered

Redemption

Karma

Karma

Jinxed

Fated

Dead Ink

The Wilds

The Wilds

The Hunt

The Dead

The Magic

Born Wild (Wilds Spinoff)

Wild One

Wyrd Blood
Wyrd Blood

ACKNOWLEDGMENTS

It's kind of hard to believe that this book is number eighteen and I've had mostly the same people by my side this entire journey. Donna Z., Camilla J., Lori H. and Lisa A., you four have been my rock through this bumpy ride. Christine J. And Ashleigh M., I might not have known you as long but I hope you stick around for the long haul. Soobee D., I have no words for how great you are!